Everything She Wants

SARAH ALVA

Everything She Wants

A NOVEL

Covenant Communications, Inc.

To my sister, my first fan

Acknowledgments

I AM BEYOND GRATEFUL FOR the talented and generous women in my writing group: Miranda Renaé, Stacy Codner, Emily Inouye Huey, Apryl Lopez, and Julie Whipple. Their friendship and support mean so much to me. I must thank Ron and Alison Christiansen for introducing me to E. M. Forster. My sister, Emily Daw, was an excellent beta reader and fact checker for all the food-science stuff. A thank-you belongs to Jenny Proctor for her help with my first chapter and to Serena Hinton and Brittany Larsen for their thoughtful feedback on my manuscript. I'm thankful for my editor, Sam Millburn, for her kindness and guidance. And lastly, a big thanks to my wonderful husband, Brandon, who I promise is nothing like Charles.

It isn't possible to love and part. You will wish that it was. You can transmute love, ignore it, muddle it, but you can never pull it out of you. I know by experience that the poets are right: love is eternal.

—E. M. Forster, *A Room with a View*

PART ONE

Mid-March
London

Chapter 1

LUCY WAS *NOT* RUNNING AWAY. She was simply taking a spontaneous vacation. And if that spontaneous vacation happened to put a few thousand miles between her and Charles, then all the better. At 30,000 feet in the air, she felt almost untouchable. The quick phone call she'd made eighteen hours ago to her aunt was all it had taken to arrange her escape.

"Do you still want me to go to London with Charlotte and Ellie?" Lucy had asked Aunt Mary.

Back in December, Lucy had been invited to chaperone her cousin Charlotte and her friend Ellie on their London spring-break trip. Lucy had declined. At the time, visiting London again had seemed like a silly indulgence. But now, getting to London seemed like a necessity.

"But the girls' flight leaves tomorrow!" Aunt Mary had said.

"That is the least of my problems," Lucy had replied, and they'd quickly made arrangements.

In her first-class seat, Lucy reclined and closed her eyes. If she slept, she wouldn't have to think about what she'd done. She tried to focus on the hum of the plane and the blackness behind her eyelids. Instead, she pictured Charles's face. His angular cheeks. His bright-blue eyes. His white hair. The way his mouth moved when he spoke her name. How earnest he had looked when he'd proposed.

Lucy was a terrible person. How could she have left that night without giving him an answer and then boarded a plane headed to London a day later? They hadn't even officially been *together* when he'd asked her to marry him. They'd been on one of their breaks. Why had he thought it was appropriate to kiss her and then pull out a ring? What signal had she unknowingly given him a week before when she had said, "Charles, I think we should take a break"?

Lucy was always putting them in break mode. Mostly because she became terrified whenever she thought about a life with him. For the last year and a half, they'd been doing a complicated dating/not dating dance. Lucy would call time-out, and Charles would wait patiently on the sidelines for her to make up her mind. Eventually, a new terror would creep in about her future—one in which Lucy spent the rest of her life alone, with only her successful career keeping her warm at night. She wanted to be married and have children. She felt ready for those things now, and Charles loved her. So Lucy would resume their relationship. But then Charles would start talking about marriage and how he pictured their future together—all in the hypothetical—and Lucy would panic and put them back in break mode.

Lucy let out a quiet groan and opened her eyes to the dim airplane lights. She needed to figure out this Charles thing once and for all. He deserved a firm answer from her when she got home, if he was still waiting for her.

She switched on her overhead light and pulled her carry-on from beneath the seat in front of her. Inside, she found her journal and the handkerchief her father had given her before he'd died. The handkerchief was her worry stone, and right now, she could use all the small comfort it would provide. She placed the handkerchief on her lap and pushed her bag back under the seat with her foot. She could be mature and logical about this. Feeling quite adult-like, she opened her journal to the next blank page and wrote, "Reasons to Marry Charles Buffington."

Lucy clicked her pen open and closed a few times and stared at his name. *Charles Buffington. Ugh.* She shook her head and silently scolded herself. That was unfair. It wasn't like *he* had chosen his name. Charles— who didn't like to go by Charlie or Chuck—couldn't help that he had the name of some British aristocrat. His stuffy name aside, he had a lot of good qualities.

She started by listing the obvious things: He was an English professor at BYU, so he was clearly intelligent. And he was the elders quorum president, so that meant he was a worthy priesthood holder. He was also ambitious, witty, honest, good-looking (in a skinny way), patient (kind of), and he knew Lucy better than anyone else and still loved her. She continued listing things: returned missionary, has a good relationship with his family, loves children, can cook, keeps his house clean, has never gotten a speeding ticket. She filled up almost a full page, and when she finished, it was clear: on paper, Charles would be a perfect husband. He had all the qualities that were supposed to matter. So what was missing?

On the next page, she wrote, "Reasons Not to Marry Charles." She tapped her pen a few more times while she reviewed her "Reasons to Marry Charles Buffington." Was she being too picky? At thirty, could she afford to be picky? Was there something wrong with *her*?

It felt like a betrayal to write the things she found wrong with Charles. How would she feel if she knew Charles had made a pro/con list about her? She clicked her pen one last time and wrote, *He can be a snob.* She felt both relieved and a little disgusted at having finally admitted there was something wrong with him. But didn't it make her a snob to point out that he was a snob?

Chatter a few rows up at the flight attendant station drew her away from the list. She peered up the aisle and noticed one of the pilots speaking to the flight attendant assigned to first class. The pilot wore a white uniform, complete with epaulets and a cap. Lucy admired his broad shoulders and the clean lines his long legs made in his navy-blue pants. His black shoes shone, even in the dim light. She watched as he smiled at the flight attendant, confident and charming. Good grief, he was handsome—dark hair, strong jaw, a dimple in his left cheek.

"Captain Strong sent me back to get coffee," he said. His voice had the same tenor as a soap-opera star. Despite her best efforts, Lucy swooned a little.

"You want a coffee too?" the flight attendant asked, her voice sounding a little Midwestern. Lucy couldn't remember where the flight crew was from, but she knew they were from somewhere in the U.S.

"No, a Coke's fine," he replied.

The attendant nodded, turned to the coffee station, and began fixing a cup. The pilot leaned against the entryway to the cockpit. Lucy studied him. He seemed so relaxed in his own skin. His mouth went lopsided as he watched the other woman.

"How's your little brother?" he asked.

She handed him the coffee. "He's fine. Having the time of his life, actually." She moved to the beverage cart and scooped ice into a cup, then found an unopened can of Coke in one of the drawers. "Now, don't go spilling this on the controls," she said, handing it over.

The pilot laughed, revealing the dimple again. Lucy leaned forward in her seat, feeling like a sucker for falling for a dimple. Sure, he was handsome, but guys like him usually ended up being jerks, right? At the very least, conceited. Lucy watched as he took the can from the attendant and tucked it under his arm so he could carry the cups of ice and coffee in his hands.

"Thanks, Mindy." He turned to leave but stopped. "Hey, when do you have time off next?"

"When I get Stateside again, I'm off for a few days," Mindy replied.

"Oh, I'll still be in London." He shrugged. "Too bad."

"Yeah?" she asked. "What were you thinking?"

"I wanted to do a long weekend up at the lake."

Lucy scoffed. She was right. How like a cocky pilot to hit on a flight attendant.

"I haven't been there in years," Mindy said.

"Grandma's been bugging me about painting the cabin," he replied.

Grandma? Lucy now sat on the very edge of her seat, her head craning into the aisle. Were they related? Had she been reading this exchange all wrong? Her journal and pen slipped from her lap, but she managed to catch her handkerchief.

"Maybe we can request the same schedule and have our last flight end in Milwaukee," Mindy suggested, but Lucy sensed some doubt in her words.

"Yeah, good idea," the pilot said. "I should probably get back." He motioned toward the cockpit with his head. "I need to make sure the captain's still awake."

Lucy moved to pick up her journal but slid out of her seat and fell on her knees in the aisle. She scrambled back into her chair, her cheeks blazing, and opened the in-flight magazine to cover her face. She counted to five before peeking over the corner of the periodical to see if the handsome pilot had noticed.

Yep. He stared straight at her. Their eyes met briefly, and Lucy felt like lightning had restarted her heart. An amused smile appeared on his lips. He tipped his head in her direction. "I think that passenger needs something," he said to Mindy. Before disappearing into the cockpit, he gave Lucy one last long look. Her cheeks flushed further, and her heart pounded wildly in her chest.

"Is everything all right, ma'am?" Mindy asked.

Lucy shook her head no but said, "Yes, everything's fine." *The plane must be about to crash. Why else would I feel this unbalanced?* she thought.

Lucy knew what to write next under "Reasons Not to Marry Charles:" *He doesn't make my heart pound.*

Chapter 2

As the passengers deplaned, Emerson stood by the exit and thanked them for flying Delta. Mindy stood beside him, smiling big and bright in the way flight attendants are trained to. "How long is your layover?" Emerson asked his cousin.

"I've got about two hours," Mindy said.

"Do you want to grab a quick breakfast?"

"Yeah, that'd be fun," she said, then busied herself at the refreshment cart, gathering trash and taking inventory.

Emerson looked down the plane, and nearly all of the seats were empty. He noticed a blonde woman still sitting in first class. She stood with her back to him and craned her neck as she watched the last two people in coach, who were taking their time gathering their belongings. The blonde sighed, turned around, and sank back into her seat. It was the woman from last night, the one who had been eavesdropping. Her steel-gray eyes looked up and met his for a moment before darting away. He watched as a blush colored her face, and his stomach did a funny little leap. She chewed on the inside of her cheek and seemed very interested in her cell phone. Emerson moved forward. Perhaps she needed help with something. "I hope you have an international plan," he said, putting on his most charming grin.

She tensed before returning his gaze. Her eyes were the same color as storm clouds. "That's what I'm working on right now," she replied, raising an eyebrow before looking back down at her phone.

He studied her features for a moment. She appeared to be in her late twenties. She had a delicate face and a heart-shaped mouth. She wore her wavy hair knotted to the side at the nape of her neck.

She put her phone down and peered out the window. "If that's taken care of, the plane has landed," he said. "You can safely exit now."

"Yes, thank you," she answered, returning her gaze to him. She had an American accent, so she was probably just a tourist. The flight had connected in New York, so she could be from anywhere in the United States. "I'm waiting on my friends," she added, gesturing behind her to the two girls in coach. They were now moving down the aisle toward them. She turned her head. "Oh, look, here they come now." She stood and nodded her head. "Sir."

"Ma'am," Emerson said, tipping his hat. He used to pursue girls like her, women who seemed unfazed by his charms. Getting them interested in him was part of the game. Given the chance, he knew he could warm her up. He'd start by asking her name and if she wanted a tour of the cockpit. That usually got a girl interested.

He stopped himself from thinking anything more. He didn't do that anymore. He couldn't. He was trying to be different. He stepped back to allow the woman room to enter the aisle. Her friends joined her, apologizing for taking so long.

Emerson retreated to the front of the plane. Before entering the cockpit, he glanced back. The woman looked at him, her expression unreadable. She had stunning eyes. A pounding grew in his chest, and he swallowed hard to keep his heart in place. Lately for Emerson, the right thing and the hard thing were exactly the same.

He disappeared into the cockpit.

* * *

Mindy and Emerson sat at a table in a little bistro at the Heathrow airport. They were between breakfast and lunch, so the shop was mostly empty, except for a few customers who were engrossed in their iPads.

"How long are you in London for?" Mindy asked as she sipped hot cocoa.

"Three days," Emerson said, clearing his throat. "My mom requested the last of her ashes be sprinkled in Kensington Gardens."

Mindy's mouth made a silent "Oh," and she set her cup down. She leaned forward and put her hand over his. "How are you doing?"

His mother had passed away almost a year ago, but the loss still felt fresh. He'd put off this trip for months, even using sick days to avoid any haul out to London if he'd had to. The last time he had been here, he'd come with his mother. She had wanted to see the graves and places of all her favorite authors before she died. He'd spent two weeks with her, first touring New England and then London. He hadn't been ready to revisit those memories. He probably wasn't ready now. "I'm okay," Emerson said. "I'm hoping for some closure after this is taken care of."

"I wish I could come with you," Mindy said, frowning. "I can only imagine how hard something like this must be." She gave his hand a little squeeze.

"Thanks," he said. Pressure built in his chest. He exhaled deeply, trying to get the feeling to subside. He didn't want to cry in front of her, let alone in public.

"Have you spoken to your dad recently?" Mindy asked.

Emerson stiffened. He hadn't spoken to his father since the funeral ten months ago. "Did something happen to him?"

Mindy shook her head and pulled her hand away from his. "No, he's fine. I was just wondering if . . ." Her words trailed off. She was probably wondering if, in light of his mother's death, Emerson was trying to repair the relationship with his only living parent.

"Let's talk about something else," Emerson said.

Mindy didn't need any more prompting than that. "Don't you think it's silly that we only see each other when we're on the same flight crew, especially since we live in the same city?"

"You're right. I haven't seen Dan or baby James since the funeral." Emerson winced. He didn't mean to bring his mom up again. But she really was always on his mind.

"Well, James is not a baby anymore," Mindy replied, glazing over the mention of Emerson's mom. "He's now a little terror on two legs."

Emerson laughed. "We should plan something when I get back to Atlanta," he said. "The weather is getting nice. We could do a barbecue."

Mindy looked apprehensive, and Emerson knew why. *He* was the reason they never got together. Before his mom died, he'd been too busy working and chasing women, flaking on family events if "something better" came up. And since his mom's death, he'd almost become a shut-in, consumed with grief and regret.

"I'm trying to be different now," Emerson said quietly.

She raised her eyebrows, rightly skeptical. Over the years, Emerson had tried countless times to be different but always fell back into easy habits.

"If I tell you something, you promise not to overreact?" he asked.

She took a slow sip of her cocoa. "Sure. I'll stay cool as a cucumber."

Emerson doubted it, but if anyone was going to understand, it would be Mindy. "I've started going to church," he said.

Mindy blinked and set her cup down. She did a poor job of not appearing shocked. "Like *the* Church, church?"

He felt his neck growing hot. It had been awhile since he'd felt embarrassed like this. "Yeah, like *the* Church, church."

She slumped back in her chair. "Wow," she said, a look of admiration appearing on her face. "Good for you."

He rubbed the back of his neck. "Yeah?" After Emerson's parents divorced when he fourteen and he lived with his mom full-time, he'd stopped going because she hadn't been a member. He had always liked church, but without a parent at home encouraging him to attend every Sunday, he'd stopped. Since his mother's death, though, he'd felt lost and anxious. He was looking for peace and direction. He hoped the Church could offer that to him.

"Really, it's awesome, Emerson. I thought something was up, but I didn't want to say anything."

"What do you mean you 'thought something was up'?"

"Well . . ." She smiled. "For starters, you're drinking hot chocolate right now, and on the flight, you asked me for a Coke instead of a coffee." Emerson tried to keep his face neutral but had to fight to stop the corners of his mouth from turning up. Mindy continued. "But the real tell was when you were talking to that pretty woman in first class."

"I talk to women all the time," he replied.

"But you didn't invite her to tour the cockpit."

Emerson flushed again. He couldn't tell if he felt embarrassed or ashamed. His cousin was perceptive. She always had been, even when they were kids; she could read him too well.

Mindy grinned. "So, how's it going?"

Emerson shrugged. He had a lot of changes to make, and he was really just starting. He had decided to begin with the big things. He'd given up coffee, tea, and alcohol, which had been rough the first few months, but it was starting to get easier. He was going to church every Sunday that he didn't work. And he was avoiding women altogether for the time being. It was easier to draw the line there. "Good, I guess," he said. "I've been meeting with the bishop since January. He said I'm making progress." Honestly, Emerson wasn't even sure what that meant or how he felt about it. The Church and the culture had become so foreign to him in the fifteen years he'd been gone that most of the time he felt awkward and uncomfortable. It didn't help that he was the only single adult male in his ward. Everyone else his age had a wife and kids. He had checked out the singles ward in his part of Atlanta, and it was full of young twenty-somethings, and he'd felt like a creepy old guy. The family ward was a better fit but not perfect. He was still waiting for being active to feel like the right decision.

"I know coming back can be hard," Mindy said. "So let me know if you want me to come to church with you, or you can come with Dan and me sometime."

Emerson took a drink of his cocoa and missed the taste of coffee. "Yeah, maybe I'll do that," he said. The pressure returned to his chest. He'd never felt this unsure and unconfident in his life, not even when he had been deployed to the Middle East. More than anything, he wanted certainty that he was on the right path and that his life had meaning. His mother had been so afraid when she had died, and he didn't want to feel like that. "Hey, Mindy?"

"Yeah?"

He hesitated and stared down into his drink. "Do you think I can be a good Mormon?"

She laughed. "Absolutely. You'll figure it out."

* * *

After breakfast with Mindy, Emerson took a train into the heart of London. He sat in the back and stared out the window, the green countryside and then the city passing in a blur.

He remembered his first trip to London six years ago. He'd been given a few days' leave from Afghanistan and had met up with some battle buddies. They'd spent their short trip roaming the city, drinking at pubs, and picking up girls. Some of his friends had died in combat, so they hadn't been on vacation with him as planned. He could stomach his friends' deaths, he'd told himself, because their deaths had had meaning. They had died heroes. Plus, the alcohol and girls had helped distract him from the pain.

But his mother's death felt different. It felt so empty. So without a plan. So cold, and so final. She had been only sixty-five years old and had spent most of her life being healthy and active. She'd been smart and cynical in a way most people had found refreshing. It seemed unfair that she had suddenly become so sick and grown so weak and died so quickly.

On his first trip to London, Emerson had felt like he was at the beginning of something. Combat and duty had been turning him into a man. On his second trip to London, with his mother, he'd felt like he was at the end of something. That trip had been a final decree that all that he'd thought was certain was in fact false. Now, in London for a third time, he felt like he was starting again. But this time he didn't have the principles of freedom, liberty, or war with him. Or the end of a life guiding him down these city streets. This time, it was just him, a man on the cusp of change, shaken and grasping for anything steady.

When the train stopped, he gathered his things and departed. He usually stayed at a flight attendant crash pad, but they had coed sleeping arrangements, and he was trying to avoid those types of situations. Instead, he was staying at the same hotel where he and his mom had stayed. He'd even requested her room: a room with a view. She had wanted the sun and the city to wake her. Emerson wanted the same thing too.

Chapter 3

"IT'S TOO BAD WE DIDN'T get a room with a view," Lucy's cousin Charlotte said as she threw open the curtains of their hotel window. Lucy looked up from her suitcase, which she was rummaging through for her toothbrush, and peered out the window. Their second-story room overlooked the roof of the pub next door and down into the alley between the two buildings. It was raining lightly outside and appeared chilly. Typical March weather for London.

Ellie, Charlotte's friend, scoffed. "We don't need a view. We're hardly going to spend any time in here." She joined Charlotte at the window and drew the curtains closed. "The goal is to explore the city, not look at it from a window."

Charlotte nodded, and Lucy returned to her search for toiletries. Traveling always made her feel greasy, and before she did anything else, she wanted a shower. She'd been to London before and wasn't as eager as the two younger women to get out and see the sights.

"Where should we go first?" Charlotte asked Ellie. "We have a few hours before afternoon tea is served."

"We don't need a plan," Ellie said with authority, looping her arm with Charlotte's. "We'll just wander the streets and see where we end up." Ellie eyed Lucy, seeing if she would challenge her. Lucy knew she was unhappy to have a sudden chaperone, but lucky for them, she wasn't totally invested in the idea of following them around. Her main reason for being in London was to get away from Charles. Ellie and Charlotte were both seniors in *college*. They could handle a week in London, with or without Lucy's constant supervision.

Without a reaction from Lucy, Ellie continued her lecture on the importance of really experiencing a city as Charlotte nodded like a bobblehead doll. Charlotte lacked any sort of street smarts. People like Ellie latched on to her all the time, girls with big personalities, who needed someone meek to follow them around. Ellie treated Charlotte like she was a project, a person who needed her help to come up to standard.

Charlotte had a lot going for her, so Lucy wasn't sure what Ellie was trying to fix. Charlotte was cute and fashionable, so it wasn't her appearance. And she was usually the smartest person in the room, even if it wasn't obvious because she always looked like she was seeing everything for the first time. In fact, Charlotte had been accepted to all five medical schools she had applied to. She was definitely smart enough, so Lucy couldn't help but think Ellie was trying to corrupt Charlotte's innocence. But Charlotte was incorruptible. Ellie had to know that by now. Everything was black and white for Charlotte, and she wasn't afraid to speak up or intervene if even the slightest bit of gray edged in. She was a righteousness ranger, and she kept the people around her in line. Maybe Ellie was Charlotte's project.

"Do you want to join us?" Charlotte asked Lucy.

Lucy hadn't really heard what they'd decided. She thought maybe they'd said something about Harrods. "I think I'll take a shower and catch up on some work," she replied. Lucy couldn't help but think what Charles would say about the two girls venturing out alone. He'd disapprove, claiming is wasn't safe, and shame Lucy for slacking on her chaperone responsibilities. But Charles wasn't here. "How about we plan on meeting in the lobby for afternoon tea around 2:30?" Lucy suggested.

Ellie tipped her head as if to say, "Suit yourself," and the two young women left the room arm in arm.

* * *

After a long, hot shower, Lucy dressed in her favorite pair of skinny jeans and a pink sweater. She rinsed with some mouthwash since her toothbrush was still in Salt Lake, she'd discovered, and then settled on the bed with her iPad. She combed her fingers through her wet hair and took a few calming breaths. She had to at least check her email. She didn't have to read any messages Charles may have sent, but she did need to make sure things hadn't fallen apart at work.

She was *the* research and development department at an ice-cream company, and her hasty departure had come at a bad time. They were in the middle of settling a big account and were in the process of bringing two new flavors into production. Lucy had called her boss, Tanya, while she'd stood in line for security at the airport and briefly explained where she was going and why. It was hard to sell that she wasn't running away from Charles. Tanya, while angry, wasn't going to fire her over this. Lucy hadn't taken a day off in almost six months and had never flaked out on work before. But she still felt guilty about leaving last minute and planned to work remotely as best she could.

She tapped open her email icon and held her breath. Of course. Sitting at the top of her inbox was an email from Charles. Her heart started to pound when she saw it but not in the good way. Not the way the pilot had made her heart pound. She grabbed her phone and switched it on. Once the plane had landed, she'd hopped on the airport's free Wi-Fi to update her phone account to allow for international calls, and it looked like her request had gone through. Her phone now showed twenty missed calls from Charles, two from her brother Freddy, and one from her mom.

No! Did Charles call her mother?

She started to sweat, and her face felt hot. She tapped the voice-mail icon and brought the phone to her ear. The first message was from her mom. Lucy relaxed just a little. "Lucy, Freddy said you've left the country? Is everything all right? Call me when you can. Love you." Good. It was Freddy who had sold her out and not Charles.

The next message was Freddy's. "Luce, what did you do to Charles? I know you told me not to tell anyone where you went, but I had to let him know. The guy's wrecked. You should call him."

Lucy swallowed the bile in her throat as guilt rose out of her chest and spewed into other parts of her body.

The next message played. "Lucy," Charles's silky voice said. "Please don't tell me your running off to Europe means the answer is no." There was a long pause, like he was waiting for her answer. "I know we are supposed to be broken up, but I don't want to be. I want to marry you, Lucy. So take whatever time you need to figure out your feelings. I love you and will be here when you get back." The soft sounds of him pulling the phone from his ear followed, then, "The email is . . . well, I was angry when Freddy said you left. But I've calmed down, and I know we can figure this out. Please delete it. What I wrote isn't really how I feel."

As the voice mail asked if she wanted to save the message, her phone slipped from her fingers. She slumped back against the bed's headboard and exhaled deeply. A lump of emotion formed in her throat. She stared up at the white ceiling, conflicting emotions of relief and confusion swimming through her. She thought of the list she had made on the plane, how perfect

Charles was, and how stupidly she had acted. If anything, he deserved better treatment than this. She was being casual with his heart. She covered her face with her hands and wanted to scream.

Charles still wanted her, even though she'd broken up with him for the fifth time two weeks ago. He still wanted her, even after she'd stood speechless, literally, after his proposal. Instead of assuming her inability to answer was a no or a joyful yes, he'd risen from his knee, told her to think about it, and pocketed the ring. And he still wanted her, even after finding out she'd left the country to avoid giving him an answer. His persistence should have solidified *something* in Lucy's mind, a clear picture of her feelings for him, at least. His devotion to her was unmistakable. She couldn't ask for a more qualified husband. What was missing, then? Why wasn't this a no-brainer?

She was thirty years old! She should have a better idea of what she actually wanted in life. Instead, she felt like a teenager, wanting a sizzling romance rather than the friendship that had eventually bloomed into something more. Chemistry didn't have to be the end-all, be-all, right? In fact, it was quite shallow of her, really, to dismiss someone perfectly decent because he didn't ignite some superficial spark. Like that spark she'd felt with the pilot.

The pilot. Where did that thought come from! Her heart even started to pound just thinking about him. She took a deep breath and shook her head. Even though both of her interactions with him had been beyond embarrassing, she had still felt an attraction to him that she'd never felt with Charles. It had probably been one-sided though, and there was a pretty good chance she would never see the pilot again, so why did she even think about him?

Lucy felt like, with the given data set, she had exhausted all possible conclusions. Until there was more data—i.e., she figured out if she really wanted to be with Charles—she would have to return to this inquiry later.

She picked up her iPad and checked her inbox again. She read the preview text from Charles's email. *Lucy, I'm finding it difficult to . . .* Her throat grew dry. One tap and she could open it. He'd never know she'd read it. Her finger hovered over the email, her pulse increasing. One tap. Lucy took a breath and deleted the email. It was the least she could do after what she'd done to him. And so she wouldn't spend another moment thinking about her predicament; she busied herself with things she was sure about, like ice cream and its many variations.

* * *

Emerson stood at the window and took in the city. He could see Big Ben and the London Eye. The Thames river looked black and still from this distance. Gray clouds moved in the sky, and the streets below were puddled and slick.

His mother had believed each city had its own unique petrichor and always asked him what the rain smelled like in the various places he'd traveled. The rain in Afghanistan smelled like dust and burning mortar shells. Atlanta smelled green with gasoline. Madison smelled like fresh lake water and decaying leaves. He cracked the window and breathed deeply. The scent of garbage and wet pavement hit his nose. He could have been in any big city.

Emerson shut the window and looked around the room. It held the echo of his mother's presence. His gaze settled on the bed, the one his mother had slept in a year ago when she'd still breathed and thought and lived. He'd been too afraid to leave her alone at night, so he'd slept on the sofa bed in her room, even though he'd had a room of his own. He had fallen asleep listening to the even rhythm of her breathing, praying for it to continue and for the necessary strength he'd need when it would finally stop.

At the memory, a nausea brewed in his stomach. He wouldn't be able to sleep here. He was wrong in thinking this vigil would make him feel like she was still alive. He skirted around the bed and went to the sink in the bathroom, where he filled one of the glasses on the countertop with water and took a long, slow drink. His stomach rumbled as the nausea subsided, and he read the clock on the nightstand. He hadn't eaten in a few hours, and traveling and time changes always left him ravenous.

He knew the hotel would be serving afternoon tea about now. But he didn't drink tea anymore, and he needed something more filling than just finger sandwiches and pastries. The pub next door served delicious fish and chips, but he didn't think he'd be strong enough to say no to a beer if he was offered one. He didn't want to mess up almost three months of good behavior, but nothing was better than fish and chips with a dark ale. His mouth watered thinking about it. He really missed beer. He swallowed, trying to remember the yeasty taste. Instead, he felt trapped and almost helpless. He wanted to swear, but he'd given that up too.

It would just be one beer.

He wished he had someone to call when this happened. Someone to talk him down. An assuring voice that could convince him that one day, all these sacrifices would be worth it. He knew Mindy was on a flight and couldn't be reached. He didn't feel that close to her husband anymore. Besides, they'd never had the type of friendship where they'd shared feelings. And Emerson wasn't going to bother his bishop with this. He swallowed again as frustration grew in his chest. Every muscle in his body felt tense. He'd heard stories at church about God interfering to protect people, so he stood as still as a pointer, waiting for divine intervention. If he'd ever needed interference, now was the time.

He closed his eyes and waited some more. The room remained silent. Nothing was happening, and Emerson's resolve completely slipped. He popped his eyes open and looked around. No one was watching. Not Mindy or his bishop. He was thousands of miles away from them. They would never have to know what he did.

He moved quickly, knowing if he gave it too much thought, he would change his mind. He left his room and hurried down the hall to the elevator, which was waiting open for him, just like a sign. When he stepped in, he pressed the down button over and over again until the door closed. He felt like a fugitive, like he was being watched and judged. "You did nothing to stop me," he said aloud to the black ceiling of the elevator. Praying had always felt inorganic. He'd much rather yell at God.

The elevator slowed and stopped on the second floor. Emerson held back a frustrated groan. He'd never felt this determined and this stymied in his life. The door slid open. Emerson's chest constricted.

Unbelievable.

There stood the blonde from the plane.

Chapter 4

WITHOUT MAKING EYE CONTACT, LUCY stepped into the elevator, smiled politely at the man inside, and then studied the design of the carpet to avoid any awkward conversation. The door slid shut.

"Hello again," the man said to her, breaching elevator protocol.

Again? Lucy, startled, looked over at him. He offered her a charming, dimpled smile, and it took her a moment to recognize him out of uniform. She couldn't believe her eyes. It was the pilot. "You. Again." She returned her eyes to carpet, her heart pounding wildly in her chest. A red heat moved up her neck and to her cheeks. This was truly strange. She gulped. *Calm down.* Perhaps having a boyfriend who didn't make her heart pound was the way to go since she felt like she could faint at any moment right now.

"This is a nice coincidence," he continued.

Lucy was afraid to look at him. She didn't want to be assaulted by his hotness. Her heart couldn't take much more today.

The elevator came to a stop, and the door dinged open. Lucy glanced at him quickly. "Yes, this is . . . interesting." She stepped off the elevator with no intention of looking back and hoped her aloofness would deter him rather than interest him. She heard his steps following behind as she headed for the dining room.

"Hey, wait," he said.

She stopped walking—why did she stop walking?—and turned around. That was a mistake. She almost bumped into his chest. *Oh boy.* He was tall and broad shouldered. He made her feel tiny, which was hard to do since she was 5'8". She took a step back, steeled her gaze, and met his eyes. Another mistake. His eyes weren't just brown; they were as warm and rich as caramel. She felt melty.

He spoke, and she watched his mouth. "Don't you think we should do something about this coincidence?"

"Like what?" she asked.

He raised his eyebrows, the corner of his mouth ticking up.

She blinked. Was he serious? Did he really think she was that kind of woman? "Like have a week-long fling?" she asked, her mouth growing a little dry.

His lips curved into a full grin, and she felt a spark move between them. "That won't work," he said, leaning toward her. "I'm only here three days."

Lucy gulped and resisted the urge to fan herself. While it was wonderful to feel desired . . . "No thanks," she said and turned around, heading for the dining room again. This was proof that Lucy wasn't *really* a teenager when it came to love. She knew better. While in theory guys like him were appealing, in practice, they were impractical. Besides, he probably wasn't LDS.

Lucy entered the ornate dining room lit by chandeliers, their crystal throwing rainbows across the muraled walls, and searched the white-clothed tables for Charlotte and Ellie. She checked behind her once to make sure the pilot wasn't following her, then let out a sigh, though she couldn't tell if it was one of relief or disappointment. He was probably the best-looking man who'd ever spoken to her, let alone hit on her.

Lucy came to a sudden stop. *Oh my gosh!* Was he even hitting on her? Or did she assume he was because he *looked* like the type of guy who was cocky and confident and hit on random women? She replayed their conversation, and while he'd been flirtatious, was he even suggesting they engage in a week-long fling? He had said, "Shouldn't we do something about this coincidence?" which could imply something romantic but didn't absolutely have to. Had she been projecting? Was she really the one who had wanted a week-long fling with him? She felt flushed and stupid. It was his eyes. His interesting, remarkable—much like this coincidence—eyes. They threw her off. If only they had looked like mud, she would have been able to behave rationally.

"Lucy!"

She turned, following the sound of her name to see Charlotte waving her over to the buffet line. Lucy joined her and Ellie as Charlotte jumped into a detailed account of their two-hour adventure at Harrods. Lucy kept her eyes trained on the girls, resisting the temptation to look around the dining room for the man. "Can you believe they charge $2.00 for a pear?" Charlotte exclaimed. "A single pear!"

"It must be a delicious pear," Lucy replied.

They moved forward in line, and each got a plate of pastries and finger sandwiches and a glass of lemonade. Ellie found them an empty table, and the two chattered on about their walk. Lucy kept drifting in and out of the conversation. She was equal parts distracted by her plight with Charles and the odd encounter with the pilot. She didn't know what to do about either or if she should even attempt to do anything.

"Lucy, are you okay?" Charlotte asked, pulling her out of her fog.

"Oh, I'm fine," she said, taking a sip of her lemonade.

Ellie gave her an inquisitive smirk. "I suspect a man problem."

Lucy narrowed her eyes just slightly. Ellie sat back in her chair with a smug expression.

"Is it Charles?" Charlotte asked with rounded eyes.

Lucy took a bite of her eclair and made a noncommittal gesture with her head. She didn't really want to get into this with them. Charlotte wasn't the type of friend Lucy talked to about her problems.

"That's why you've run off to London with us," Ellie said. "Isn't it?"

Charlotte gave Lucy's shoulder an awkward pat. "I'm sure he's sorry, whatever he did."

Lucy snorted. Like Charles had anything to be sorry about. It was she who had reason to apologize. "I really don't want to talk about it," she said.

Charlotte frowned, and Ellie huffed, folded her arms over her chest, then looked around the dining room, clearly put out that Lucy wasn't going to share her life's drama.

They weren't friends. Why did she feel entitled to Lucy's personal life?

Ellie's mouth dropped open, and her eyes grew wide. "No way," she said.

Lucy followed her gaze, expecting to see a celebrity. She didn't see anyone she recognized.

Wait . . . Her stomach bottomed out. Of course.

"Hey, isn't that the cute pilot from our flight?" Charlotte asked.

He reached the end of the buffet and scanned the room. Maybe for her. Maybe for an empty table. Lucy felt something in her chest shrinking.

Ellie adjusted her ample bosom and flipped her dark hair, then stood and waved him over. "Yoohoo," she called.

Seriously? Did "yoohoo" even work?

The pilot saw Ellie, and a slow smile appeared on his face. It was devastatingly handsome. He made his way over to their table. Lucy felt her insides beginning to melt, and she fixed her eyes on her glass of lemonade.

"Sit with us," Ellie said, sticking out her chest. Oh, to be young.

"Hi, ladies," he said, taking the empty chair. He looked right at Lucy, but she wouldn't fully meet his gaze. How had she not seen him earlier?

"We were on your flight," Charlotte said, smiling nervously and fiddling with her napkin. "In case you don't remember us."

"I remember," he said. "How could I forget a group of such beautiful women?"

Charlotte flushed, and Ellie giggled.

"It's quite the coincidence that we would all be at the same hotel," Ellie said, touching the rim of her lemonade glass seductively.

Lucy rolled her eyes.

"Yes, it is," he replied.

"What floor is your room on?" Charlotte asked.

"The seventh," he answered.

"Oh! Do you have a view?"

It was Ellie's turn to roll her eyes. "Not this again."

Charlotte gave her a look. "I'm just saying, it would be nice to have a room with a view. I mean, we could be in any city in the world when we're in the hotel. If we had a view, we at least could see that we're still in London."

The man chuckled. Like most people, he seemed to find Charlotte's apparent naivety amusing. "I have a view," he said.

"Really?" Charlotte asked. "What can you see?"

"I can see Big Ben and the London Eye."

Charlotte's eyes lit up. "It must be wonderful at night."

Lucy watched the pilot carefully. Was he going to take advantage of Charlotte and invite her to come by for a private viewing tonight?

"Why don't we switch rooms," he said. "I think you'll enjoy the view more than I will."

Charlotte looked like she'd won the lottery. Lucy tried to catch her eye and shook her head no.

Charlotte either didn't see or didn't care. "Really?" she asked. "That would be—"

"That would be so nice of you," Lucy interrupted. She met the man's gaze, and the blood rushed to her head. She cleared her throat. "But we're happy with our room."

"No, we're not," Charlotte said, looking at Lucy.

Lucy raised her eyebrows, hoping Charlotte would follow her thinking as she spoke. "We don't want to obligate ourselves to a stranger." She was already imagining a number of lurid scenarios, the most vivid of which involved him keeping an extra room key without their knowledge so he could murder them in their sleep.

"I don't have to be a stranger," he said, his dimple appearing. He extended his hand to Lucy. "I'm Emerson."

She noticed his hand was large and calloused, like he had done years of hard labor. Not the hands she'd imagined belonging to a pretty-boy pilot. She glanced up at his face. His dark hair was a little messy and begged for fingers to smooth it into place.

When Lucy didn't move, Ellie grabbed his hand and introduced herself. "I'm Ellie. And this is Charlotte and Lucy," she said, pointing to them. "Why don't we talk for a while. And when you're not a stranger anymore, we can decide on the room."

Okay, so while Ellie was annoying, she could have social suave when she tried. Lucy steadied her breath and took a sip of her lemonade so she had something to do with her hands and something in her mouth to stop her from talking.

Ellie asked Emerson where he lived, and Lucy examined him for signs of a serial killer. He appeared clean cut and freshly shaven, but wasn't that part of a serial killer's ruse? That they looked like normal, harmless people? He pushed up the sleeves of his navy-blue sweater before picking up a sandwich. Lucy caught a glimpse of a tattoo on the inside of his left forearm. It was a quote written in a small, clean font. Serial killers usually had tattoos, right? She didn't want to be caught staring, so she didn't try to read the words.

"And where are you ladies from?" he asked after talking about Atlanta for a few minutes.

"We're visiting from Utah," Ellie answered for them.

Lucy watched his reaction carefully. She traveled a fair amount for work, and most people reacted one of two ways when they found out she was from Utah: they either apologized on her behalf, like being from Utah was something she should be embarrassed about, or they asked her if she was Mormon.

The pilot did neither. His smile became lopsided. "What part?"

"The Salt Lake area," Charlotte said.

"That's a beautiful city. My dad lives there," he said, looking right at Lucy. "Another coincidence."

Her heart started pounding again. Was she scared? Nervous? Excited? Geez! Why couldn't she tell? She wet her lips. "Where in the valley does he live?"

"The Avenues," Emerson replied. His eyes met hers for a heart-stopping moment, and Lucy grew speechless. Could Emerson be LDS? She noticed he wasn't drinking tea. And his dad lived in Salt Lake. But a lot of non-Mormons lived in Salt Lake. And Emerson had a tattoo. And he'd tried to pick her up in an elevator. Plus, wasn't being LDS the type of information he would volunteer once he found out they were from Utah and were so clearly LDS? Most Mormons loved meeting other members of the Church in unlikely places. But being a member still didn't guarantee that he wasn't a serial killer. After all, Ted Bundy had been a member for a while.

"Lucy lives in Sugar House," Charlotte said when the silence went on too long. "Ellie and I actually live in Logan right now. We're students at Utah State."

Emerson asked Charlotte and Ellie about their majors, and they jabbered on about school. He remained polite and interested, laughing at the silly things Charlotte said and feigning tolerance when Ellie said something snobby. He did an excellent job of keeping the conversation focused on the two younger women and didn't engage Lucy, except to glance at her periodically like he was trying to figure out how he was doing. She kept her face neutral.

When his plate was clean, he excused himself for seconds.

"I like him," Charlotte said with bright eyes once he was out of earshot. "I think we should switch rooms."

Lucy sighed. Charles would say absolutely not, and Lucy would have to agree. Why weren't Charlotte and Ellie being more careful? Shouldn't they be the ones discussing the likelihood of Emerson being a murderer?

Lucy watched him from their table as he perused the buffet line, stacking his plate high with sandwiches. It was almost amusing to watch women react to him when he came near. They simpered and flipped their hair, and some even tried to talk to him. In the two minutes he was gone, Lucy saw two women try to flirt. He offered a friendly glance and maybe a few words but nothing more. He wasn't acting like the player she had judged him to be.

Emerson made his way back to their table, and Lucy looked away before she could get caught staring. "Let me talk to him alone for a minute," she said to the two girls. "I'll meet you in the lobby."

Ellie stood and dropped her napkin on her plate. "I was done anyway," she said.

Charlotte hesitated a moment while Emerson took his seat, but she soon followed after Ellie.

He watched the two girls leave and then turned expectantly to Lucy. She waited for him to say something inappropriate about being alone at last or something equally ridiculous, but he didn't. When Lucy didn't speak, he resumed eating, taking only one bite to eat each tiny sandwich. Interacting with him was so much easier when he played the part Lucy wanted him to. She didn't know what to do with him now.

"We really can't accept your room," she said at last. "But it was nice of you to offer."

"No, really. I want you to have it."

She raised her eyebrows. "You do understand why we won't take it, right? How inappropriate it is?"

"Of course," he replied. "You think I'm some sort of pervert that's hidden cameras in the room so I can watch you undress later."

Lucy's mouth fell open. That hadn't even occurred to her! He *was* a pervert for thinking up something like that, even if it wasn't true. And it wasn't true, right?

A smirk twitched at the corners of his lips. "I'm not a pervert," he continued. "I'm harmless. My room has a view of the city, and Charlotte clearly wants one. I thought I was being nice. I didn't mean to offend you."

"I'm sure your room isn't big enough for the three of us," Lucy said, now hoping to appeal to something logical since he wasn't buying into the idea that he was a threat to their safety.

"I have a grand room with a king-sized bed and a sofa bed," he said.

They had a club room, which was smaller than his. "Oh, in that case, we wouldn't be able to afford the upgrade," she replied.

"I won't ask you to pay the difference," he said.

"You're only here three days, and we're here for the whole week. It won't work."

"When I leave, you can just move back into your old room," he countered.

Lucy sat back in her chair. She hadn't realized she'd slowly been inching closer to him during their conversation.

"Really, I want you to take my room," he said. "Please."

She examined his face, noticing a deep crease had appeared on his forehead. "Why?" she asked. "I don't think you're just being nice."

He dropped the sandwich he was holding back onto his plate. He let out a deep breath. Lucy frowned. She was familiar with broken people. She had met a lot on her mission. She wanted to assure him that whatever it was, it would be okay.

"My mom died about a year ago," he said. "We stayed in that room when we came to London before her death. I thought staying there would make me feel close to her again but—"

"You don't have to explain," Lucy interrupted. His eyes found hers, and their gaze locked. "When my dad died," she said, "I couldn't go into my parents' room for months. It felt like he should have been there, but he wasn't. It was too strange."

He nodded and swallowed. "How old were you?"

"Seventeen." She gnawed on the inside of her cheek, uncomfortable with the turn the conversation had taken. Emerson was still very much a stranger, and she didn't want to share personal things with him. She spoke slowly. "I still don't think we should take your room."

"I understand," he said. "We live in a messed-up world. You can never be too careful."

"I'm sure you can work something out with the front desk." Lucy sighed and stood to leave. "It'll be okay."

He reached out to grab her hand but stopped short. "How did you . . . survive?"

She didn't need to ask if he was talking about her father's death. She sat back down. "I didn't survive," she said. "I'm still *surviving*." She met his eyes again. The light from the chandeliers highlighted their warmth and depth. He seemed to be appraising her eyes with the same fascination. Her heart began to pound again, and she looked away. "You promise you aren't a pervert or a serial killer?" She glanced back at him.

He held up his hand in a three-finger promise. "Scout's honor."

Charles would hate this. "How soon can you clear out of your room?" she asked.

Chapter 5

EMERSON LEFT THE DINING ROOM with Lucy walking by his side. Their hands brushed and then their shoulders, and Emerson took a small step away from her. Some strange feeling grew in his chest, one he liked but wasn't entirely comfortable with. To him, Lucy felt a lot like salvation. The fact that she was clearly LDS and had lost her dad made this encounter seem like divine intervention . . . exactly what he'd asked for. He stopped himself from thinking any further about how remarkable this meeting was. For a reason he couldn't quite pinpoint, he felt uncomfortable with a God who knew him so well and was so willing to interfere in his life. Of course Emerson's salvation would come in the form of a beautiful woman. *Touché, God, touché.*

They found Ellie and Charlotte sitting in large leather chairs by the concierge desk. Ellie observed the lobby with a critical eye, while Charlotte leafed through a travel brochure. Emerson liked the two girls. They were microcosms of youth: Charlotte and her bright naivety and Ellie with her insecure snobbery. They entertained him and created a comfortable buffer between Lucy and him, especially because he didn't know how to behave with Lucy or know what he was supposed to do with this coincidence. In his previous life, he would have pursued a three-day tryst that would have ended with no intent to stay in contact. Thinking of his old self nearly made him sick. Had he really once been that selfish and single-minded? And how much of him had really changed?

Charlotte hopped up from her seat when she saw them approaching. She beamed. "What did you decide?" she asked, dancing on the balls of her feet.

Emerson grinned at her excitement. Lucy looked demure, and he couldn't figure out if she was really always this guarded or if it was because of him.

"We're switching rooms," Lucy said evenly, her tone revealing nothing. She glanced at Emerson and offered a restrained smile.

Ellie stood and elongated her neck and squared her shoulders. She was the type of girl Emerson usually went for: young, with the type of good looks that money and vanity created. But she wasn't appealing to him. His eyes kept returning to Lucy. "Oh, good," Ellie said. "Finally, Charlotte will have her view."

"Emerson!" Charlotte exclaimed. "Thank you so much." She threw her arms around his neck, and he stepped back to keep from falling. He patted her back, laughing but also growing a little heartsick. How rare and far away joy seemed to him, but here was Charlotte bursting with life.

"Thank Lucy," Emerson said as Charlotte moved from his embrace.

She turned to Lucy and grinned, her hands on her hips. "I knew you would make the right decision," Charlotte said.

Lucy shrugged, and one corner of her mouth curved up. Emerson felt something pull in his stomach. How could he get her to smile at him like that?

"If Emerson ends up being a serial killer, this is all on you, Charlotte," Lucy said.

Charlotte laughed, and Ellie rolled her eyes. A sudden feeling of calm rushed through Emerson. He could do this, he realized. He could bear his mother's death.

He took a step toward the elevators, and the calm disappeared.

* * *

Fifteen minutes later, he stood at the door of the room without a view, a suitcase at his feet. He knocked, and Ellie answered. She didn't open the door all the way and wedged her body in the opening so Emerson couldn't see into the room. She stuck out her chest and gave Emerson an obvious once-over, her red lips sliding into a coy smile. He raised his eyebrows, interested to see what she'd say. She cocked her head to one side. "I'm pretty sure I know your secret," she said.

Emerson's heart pounded just a little more than usual, but he knew it didn't show. He had only a handful of secrets, and he could imagine only one of them complicating his interaction with these women. Had Ellie figured out somehow that he was Mormon(ish)? Or did she know something else about him? And how?

"Oh, is that Emerson?" Charlotte asked as she appeared at the doorway. She nudged Ellie out of the way and flung open the door. "Come in! We're almost ready."

Ellie gave Emerson a meaningful look as he picked up his suitcase and stepped across the threshold. Charlotte retreated to the bed and lay down with a flourish. Ellie took a seat at the writing desk.

Emerson set his suitcase to the side and scanned the room. The décor was similar to his room: browns and rust reds. The room was smaller, with just a king-sized bed and a sitting area by the window that had a couch and two chairs. By the bathroom was a kitchenette with a microwave and mini-fridge. But unlike his room, this one had no ghosts. He could sleep here with fewer memories haunting him.

Lucy came out of the bathroom. She stilled when she saw Emerson, then looked to Charlotte. "Oh, you let him in," she said and went to the suitcase on the bed.

"It would have been rude to make him wait in the hall."

Lucy zipped up her suitcase and lifted it off the bed. "I'm ready."

Ellie rose from the desk, and Charlotte sat up. Emerson pulled the two key cards from his pocket, and Charlotte hopped off the bed and took them. "We are forever indebted to you," Charlotte said.

"Emerson did this out of the kindness of his heart. We don't owe him anything," Lucy said, eyeing Emerson. He got it. He wasn't supposed to be a part of their vacation. He sensed this would be one of their final interactions, except for when they'd have to switch keys before he left. But he didn't want this to be it. It wasn't because Lucy was beautiful. It was because he wanted to believe all of this was happening for a reason. He wanted this to be a test of faith.

Ellie grabbed their room keys off the desk and handed them to Emerson.

"Thanks," he said as he took them.

She offered a cool shrug.

Lucy moved to the door and motioned for the other two ladies to follow. Emerson stepped aside to make room for them, and they picked up their bags. Lucy opened the door and stepped into the hall, taking a brief peek at Emerson over her shoulder. Ellie winked as she passed him.

Charlotte glowed. "Thanks again," she said. "I hope you enjoy the rest of your stay."

Emerson nodded, and his smile wavered. "You too," he said. "It was a pleasure to meet you."

Charlotte waved and hurried down the hall to catch up to Ellie and Lucy. He shut the door to his room and kicked his suitcase aside. It fell, and the thump of it hitting the ground seemed impossibly loud. A cold loneliness weaved through his expanding chest. So much for divine intervention. So much for faith.

He moved to the window without a view and opened the curtains to see what Charlotte had seen. He looked down on the roof of the pub next door. Something broke inside him. He curled his hands into fists. He felt absolutely forgotten. So, so quickly had it happened, it almost knocked the breath out of him. He didn't bother with bargaining or berating God this time.

God wasn't there. And Emerson needed a drink.

Chapter 6

LUCY WATCHED WITH OPEN AMUSEMENT as her cousin threw open the windows in their new room to take in the view. Charlotte gasped and squealed, and Ellie even cracked a smile. Lucy joined them at the window. In the distance, she could see Big Ben and the London Eye shining golden against the gray rain.

"This is perfect," Charlotte said. "Absolutely what I wanted."

"Good," Lucy said. "It was nice of Emerson to switch with us." She stepped away from the window and moved her suitcase out of the doorway. The lingering scent of male cologne unnerved her. Emerson wore something that smelled blue and fresh, like the sea, and she felt uncomfortable knowing this about him. She set her suitcase on the dresser and rummaged through until she found her body spray. She walked through the room spritzing the scent, a warm vanilla lavender, and watched for evidence of cameras or sharp blades. She might be a coward who ran from her problems, but she wasn't a victim.

"I'm still hungry," Charlotte said as she closed the curtains.

Ellie had moved to the vanity to fluff her hair. "Why don't we see if the pub next door has fish and chips," she suggested.

Lucy decided her search for murder weapons was useless, and a hidden camera would be . . . well, hidden. "Sure," Lucy said.

"I don't know," Charlotte replied. "I'm not sure we should go to a bar. That's what a pub is, right?"

"It depends," she said to Charlotte. "Some are bars, and others are more like a restaurant with a bar, sort of like an Applebee's."

Ellie snickered. "An Applebee's," she muttered.

Lucy gave her a look, but Charlotte seemed unfazed by her friend's rudeness.

"Why don't we go over and see what it's like," Lucy suggested. "If we don't like the atmosphere, we'll leave."

Charlotte agreed. The women put on their coats and left the hotel. The short walk over to the pub was staccatoed with puddles, and the air smelled of gasoline. A familiar feeling palpated in Lucy's chest—a mixture of awareness and excitement. She remembered feeling this way on her mission as she rode her bike through the streets of Berlin with her companion.

Lucy pulled open the heavy wooden door of the pub and stepped in, Ellie and Charlotte following behind. The space was swanky, with dim lighting and dark wooden tables and chairs. A bar with stools lined the back wall. Heavy yellow drapes hung in the picture windows that looked out onto the street. The air smelled bitter and yeasty, and the sounds of conversation and cutlery peppered the room.

Lucy turned to Charlotte. "What do you think?"

Charlotte nodded her head. "Not really like an Applebee's, but it's okay."

"Let's find a table, then," Ellie said.

They took a table in the back corner and draped their coats on their chairs. Soon a waitress appeared. They ordered drinks and a basket of fish and chips each, and Ellie and Charlotte discussed their plans for tomorrow—a Harry Potter walking tour and then dinner at a haunted mansion. Lucy's eyes wandered around the room as she people watched. It was something Charles loved to do. As a poet, the world was his source material.

A couple two tables away seemed to be on a first date. The woman was made up, and the man's hand trembled slightly as he took a drink of his lager. By the door stood a woman who appeared to be waiting for someone. Her skirt was a little too short for the weather outside, and she didn't wear a coat.

Up at the bar, the waitress flirted with a man. She laughed and touched his arm. Lucy couldn't see the man's face, but she imagined he was laughing and winking right back. The waitress left, and the man's shoulders quickly slumped, like he'd been defeated. Her interest piqued, and she continued to watch him. He ran a hand through his dark hair, and she caught a glimpse of his profile.

For a short moment, the air around her stilled. The warm expansive feeling she'd felt on the street reentered her chest. The man was Emerson. Lucy furrowed her brow, perplexed. Was he following them?

The waitress returned to their table with their drinks, and Lucy used that moment to look away and focus on the uncomplicated task of squeezing lemon into her water.

"It's so strange," Charlotte said, "that they don't put ice in their drinks here." She took a sip of her iceless Sprite.

Ellie swirled her Coke, and ice clinked against the glass. "You just have to ask," she said with one of her cool smirks.

Lucy peered back up at the bar. Emerson still sat there. If he had been following them, Lucy concluded, he would have already invited himself to sit with them. The bartender set an amber lager in front of him. Emerson nodded his thanks and then proceeded to stare at his drink. Warmth again expanded through Lucy's chest, and with it came a prompting: she needed to invite him to sit with them.

Emerson lifted his drink and examined it against the pale light in the bar, like he was weighing the risk. Or maybe he was one of those beer snobs who took in the color and smell before drinking. He set the glass back down, and his shoulders slumped even more.

Go, the feeling said. Lucy clenched her teeth. Charles would tell her she'd done enough for Emerson and let it be. But she knew if she ignored this feeling, she'd regret it. She stood. "I'll be right back," she said and walked away before Charlotte and Ellie could respond.

The distance across the pub seemed miles long, and the whole time, Emerson didn't take his eyes off the beer. Lucy slipped onto the empty bar stool beside him and said the only thing she could think of. "Fancy meeting you here."

Emerson started and turned his head toward her. "Lucy." He whispered her name, like the closing of a prayer. Her skin broke out in goose bumps. "What are you doing here?" He looked her in the eyes, and she felt a wordless plea pour from them.

She rubbed her hands up and down her arms. She didn't want to feel like she was saving him from something, but she did. "Ellie and Charlotte wanted fish and chips," she said. "We've in the back. If you aren't expecting someone, you should join us." She tried to act like she didn't feel unnerved. The expanding warmth came back, reassuring her that she was doing the right thing.

Emerson straightened his curved shoulders, a small smile appearing on his face. "You sure?"

Lucy nodded. "Yeah. Drinking alone at a bar is a little cliché."

He offered a chuckle but eyed the beer. "Thanks," he said and stood. He left a five-pound note on the bar top. "Lead the way."

He followed her through the dimly lit pub to her table, and she noticed he left his drink at the bar, which she thought was odd, but she didn't say anything about it.

"Look who I found," Lucy said to Ellie and Charlotte as she approached the table.

"Emerson!" Charlotte shouted. "What a coincidence!"

Emerson smiled, and Lucy felt his eyes on her. She didn't want to look at him and feel all those weird things she felt when their eyes met.

Ellie stood and stole a chair from an empty table, and they all sat, Emerson next to Ellie but across from Lucy. His foot tapped against hers under the table, and she couldn't tell if it was on accident or on purpose. She flushed regardless because he was ridiculously handsome, even if she tried not to notice. The corner of his mouth curved up, and he tapped Lucy's foot again. She moved her feet under her chair.

Emerson cleared his throat. "You ladies happened to pick the best pub in London for fish and chips."

"Did we really?" Charlotte asked.

Emerson nodded. "This is my third trip to London, and this pub has been my favorite, by far."

Lucy watched as Ellie examined him with a critical eye. "Interesting," Ellie said, the word heavy with implication.

Emerson's confident expression wavered a moment, like the comment was a continuation of a conversation they'd had previously. But Lucy had no idea when they would have had a chance to talk one-on-one.

The waitress appeared before things got too awkward and set three baskets of food on the table. The smell of grease and vinegar rose into the air.

"You'll be dining with these ladies, then?" the waitress asked Emerson. He nodded. "I'll bring your food over when it's out. Should I bring your ale over from the bar?"

Emerson shook his head. "Could I get a water with ice?"

Ellie's examination of Emerson continued, and Lucy was surprised to find she felt a little jealous at Ellie's interest in him.

"Anything else for you ladies?" the waitress asked.

"Some ketchup, please," Charlotte said. Her request was followed by a palpable beat of silence. "Sorry. I meant cat-sup," she tried again, this time with a British accent.

Lucy tried not to laugh, but Ellie didn't hold back.

"Did I still say it wrong?" Charlotte asked, her cheeks growing pink.

"Fish and chips aren't eaten with ketchup," Ellie said.

"No worries," the waitress interrupted. "I can bring you some."

Charlotte's face flamed as the waitress left their table. "I'm so embarrassed!" Charlotte exclaimed.

"Don't worry about it," Emerson said. "Is this your first time outside the U.S.?"

Charlotte nodded, her eyes shining with tears.

"Everyone does something embarrassing in a new country," he said. "When I was a teenager, my mom and I went to Eastern Europe. In Turkey, a lot of restrooms have attendants that you pay in order to use toilet. So when we got to Prague, I thought it would be the same way. My first day in the city, I went to use the bathroom at a train station, and there was a woman standing outside the door. I handed her a Czech koruna, and she said something in Czech that I thought meant 'Thank you' or 'Go ahead.' When I tried to open the bathroom door, she started hitting me on head with her purse. My mom rushed over to see what was going on. Finally, we figured out the woman wasn't a bathroom attendant. Plus, I was trying to enter the women's restroom instead of the men's, and the woman's sister was in there."

Lucy laughed louder than she wanted, and even Ellie offered a few giggles.

"So, Charlotte, you really have nothing to be embarrassed about," he assured her.

Charlotte exhaled and wiped a tear off her cheek. "Thanks. I do feel better now."

Emerson's kind, open smile at Charlotte endeared him a little more to Lucy. Maybe being good-looking didn't automatically make someone shallow and arrogant. But apparently being okay-looking and insecure did.

Emerson's own basket of fish and chips arrived, along with a bottle of ketchup, then the waitress left them to their food. Lucy was grateful for Charlotte's ability to never stop talking. Lucy felt like she was on a blind date; she wanted to get to know Emerson better since he was turning out to be surprising, but she didn't know where to start. And having an audience in the form of Charlotte and Ellie made it that much more difficult. So Lucy let Charlotte steer the conversation, and she asked him about being an airline pilot. Lucy was impressed that he didn't seem annoyed or bothered by her inquiries but seemed rather happy to talk about his work.

"Your girlfriend must really miss you being gone so much," Ellie said after a lull in the conversation. She squeezed Emerson's bicep, which was coming on a little strong, Lucy thought, even for Ellie.

Emerson noticed Ellie's hand on his arm and moved enough for her to get the picture to let go. "I, ah, don't have a girlfriend," he said, looking first at Ellie and then stealing a glance at Lucy.

Lucy fought to keep a neutral expression, although, for some reason, this information did make her heart flutter just a bit. But she didn't know him or like him, so it shouldn't matter to her what his relationship status was. Plus, she had a boyfriend.

Right. Charles. Lucy had a boyfriend named Charles, who wasn't actually her current boyfriend because they had broken up, but he'd proposed to her anyway. So the fact that Emerson was single shouldn't make Lucy's heart flutter at all.

Ellie side-eyed Lucy before returning her attention to Emerson. "That leaves you free to break hearts wherever you go," Ellie said.

Emerson chuckled. "Well, probably not this trip."

There was a beat of awkward silence before Ellie jumped up. "Oh! I love this song."

Lucy listened, and the music coming though the pub's stereo system was some generic club music.

"Charlotte," Ellie said, "let's go dance." She circled around the table as Charlotte tried to protest and pulled her to a stand, then dragged her over to a space by the bar and began dancing. Charlotte pushed an empty table aside to make more room for her. Lucy watched with slight mortification as Ellie pulled two young men from the bar to join them. Charlotte awkwardly partnered with one.

"Ellie's bold, that's for sure," Emerson said.

"That's not what I was doing in my early twenties," Lucy said.

Emerson shook his head. "Me neither."

"Oh?" Lucy hated the amount of disbelief in her voice. Even after all the small ways he'd surprised her, she kept resorting back to her initial impression of him.

He took a sip of his water and nodded. "I was deployed to Afghanistan."

Lucy imagined her face going pale as her eyes widened. "Oh, wow . . . Thank you for your service." She fumbled over her words.

Emerson shrugged like it was no big deal and took another drink of his water. She took a drink too. She wasn't usually this socially awkward.

"And what were you doing in your early twenties?" Emerson asked.

Lucy wiped her sweaty palms on her jeans. "I was serving a mission for my church," she said. *And this is where he makes an excuse to leave*, Lucy thought.

"I had a buddy from high school do that," he said.

Lucy exhaled a breath she hadn't realized she was holding. "Did you grow up in Utah?" she asked, silently cursing herself. Just because his dad lived in Salt Lake and he had a religious friend that served a mission did not mean the friend was LDS and certainly did not mean he grew up in Utah.

He shook his head and seemed to relax. At least one of them was enjoying the conversation. "I spent a few summers there after my parents divorced, but I grew up in Madison, Wisconsin."

"Really?" Lucy's heart pounded at the possibility. "I did my master's degree at UW Madison, and I lived there until two years ago."

Emerson's eyes brightened. "My mom is . . . was an English professor there. What did you study?"

"Food science."

"Let me guess," he said. "Your master's thesis was on how long it takes a chocolate bar to melt."

"Close." She wrinkled her nose in embarrassment. "I studied how protein affects the ice crystals in ice cream." She laughed sheepishly. "So basically, how long it takes high-protein ice cream to melt."

"How riveting." Emerson laughed, the sound resonating through her bones. "I can picture you sitting in front of a bowl of ice cream with a stop watch."

"That's unfairly accurate," she said, the tension finally leaving her shoulders. "How do you know so much about food science? Most people think it's a fake degree."

Emerson shrugged. "My mom was friends with a professor in that department. He'd always come around with his grad students' latest concoctions."

"And all the free fare didn't inspire you to study food science?"

He shook his head. "No. Maybe it was a little tempting, but I always wanted to fly." His eyes met hers, and electricity crackled in their shared gaze.

Lucy pushed her hair behind her ear and turned her head. Why did things with Charles never feel this exciting? "Did you learn to fly in the military, then?" Lucy asked after a moment.

Emerson nodded. "I attended the Air Force Academy right out of high school, then went through flight training after graduation."

The Air Force Academy? Lucy couldn't help feeling a little impressed. Getting into one of the military academies required equal parts brains and physical fitness. And he was definitely physically fit. So he was smart, handsome, and kind? Lucy didn't think guys like him existed anymore. At least not single ones.

She sighed and picked up a french fry. This was just a conversation in a pub. It wasn't her future. She didn't need to think catastrophically. When her eyes met his again, she tried to ignore the warmth blooming in her chest.

Chapter 7

THE WAITRESS CAME BY AND refilled their waters, disrupting their locked gaze. Emerson glanced over at Ellie and Charlotte, who had convinced a good number of people to dance with them. The music in the pub had been turned up. How had he not noticed that?

He squeezed the lemon into his drink as he debated if he should tell Lucy he was LDS. Well, kind of. Wasn't it sort of misleading for him to not mention it? Then again, Lucy hadn't asked, and how would he explain the ale at the bar?

Emerson had never said the words "I'm Mormon" out loud. In fact, he'd never thought that in his head until now. He hadn't assumed the religion as part of his identity yet because, honestly, he wasn't sure it was going to work out.

"Can I ask what it says?" She gestured at his arm where his sleeve had ridden up just enough to hint at his tattoo.

"Sure." Emerson dropped the lemon into his water and pushed the sleeve up to his forearm. He held out his inner arm to her and watched as she leaned in to take a closer look. In small block letters were the words "The moment you doubt whether you can fly, you cease forever to be able to do it."

"Did it hurt?" she asked, her clear eyes boring into his. The sweetness in her expression made him feel incredibly worldly.

"No, not as much as . . . other things." He rolled his sleeve back down so he didn't have to see Lucy's compassionate stare.

"Did you get it because you're a pilot?"

He swallowed and willed the ache to leave his chest. But will wasn't enough to get rid of that kind of pain. "It's a quote from *Peter Pan*," he said. "My mom's favorite book. I got it to commemorate her life."

Lucy nodded. "It's nice. I like it."

Emerson ran his hand through his hair, feeling baffled. "Really?" he asked. Weren't Mormons supposed to dislike tattoos?

"Yeah. I like the thought you put into it." He took in her gentle expression and absorbed her light.

"Thanks, Lucy."

Someone bumped into their table, breaking the spell. It was Ellie. Charlotte followed close behind her. "We have to leave," Ellie said, out of breath.

"Why?" Lucy asked, narrowing her eyes.

"The owner doesn't like what we've done with the place," Charlotte said.

Emerson glanced over to where the girls had been dancing. Half the pub, it seemed, was gyrating on the impromptu dance floor.

"Good grief," Lucy muttered as she stood.

She hadn't noticed either? he thought. He circled around to her side of the table and took her coat off the back of her chair, then he held it open for her. She looked confused, like no one had ever done this for her before.

"Thanks," she said before slipping her arms in.

His fingers pushed against her warm neck and through her soft hair as the coat settled on her shoulder. Her cheeks were pink when she turned around to face him.

"You're welcome," Emerson said, then busied himself with getting his own coat so he didn't have to think about why he felt so electric. Charlotte and Ellie scrambled, delighted that they were getting kicked out of a pub in London.

They each dropped some cash on the tabletop, and the four headed for the exit. Ellie blew a kiss to the stern-looking bartender as they left.

The night air hit Emerson's face with a welcome frigid blast. Ellie and Charlotte hurried ahead, leaving Lucy and him to walk alone.

As they neared the hotel entrance, Emerson's anxiety began to return. He again felt helpless, like this was his last moment with Lucy and he didn't want it to be. He couldn't decide which was scarier: never seeing her again or asking her if he could see her again. He took a deep breath. "So . . ."

Lucy looked over at him.

"What are you doing tomorrow?" He hoped the question sounded like a general question about her plans and not the prelude to getting asked on a date. He didn't want to freak her out since up until their conversation in the pub, she had acted uninterested in him.

They arrived at the entrance of the hotel, and Emerson opened the door for her. "I'm meeting up with an old friend," she said, stepping into the warm hotel lobby. He followed behind her, hoping his disappointment wasn't obvious. "What are you doing?" she asked.

They headed toward the elevator. Ellie and Charlotte were nowhere to be seen.

"I'm thinking of going to Kensington Gardens. My mom loved that place." Emerson pushed the up button, and they waited for the elevator to come. He wasn't really planning to go to the garden; in fact, he was putting off going to Kensington until his last day. But he didn't want Lucy thinking he didn't have plans.

"It's such a beautiful place," Lucy said. The elevator door dinged opened. They stepped in, and the door closed.

Emerson had seconds now to seal the deal. "It was nice running into you again." He pushed the buttons for their floors.

"Yeah, it was," Lucy said.

Emerson couldn't figure out why this was so nerve-wracking. He used to be good at picking up women while on layover. But none of them had been like Lucy. The women before were looking to be picked up. Lucy wasn't looking for anything.

A cold realization seeped through him. She probably had a boyfriend. That would explain her restraint.

The elevator stopped moving and settled on Emerson's floor. The door slid open, and he tried to swallow his heart as it attempted to jump out of his throat. He looked at Lucy, her face kind and open. "Maybe we'll run into each other again," he said.

"I'm sure we will," she said. "It's kind of a small hotel."

Emerson stepped out of the elevator. "Good night." Again, he felt like he was losing something.

"Good night, Emerson." Lucy offered a wave as the elevator doors shut.

That feeling of lost faith ebbed into the corners of his chest. He took a deep breath. He could make it through this night. He'd felt like this before and had survived. He could do it again.

His cell phone vibrated then, signaling a message. His pulse kicked up, and for a split second, he hoped it was Lucy. As he pulled the phone from his back pocket, he realized it was impossible for her to have his cell number; she hadn't asked for it, and he hadn't given it to her. He tapped the screen, feeling silly. It was a text message from Mindy.

I'm grounded, the message read. *Call me if you need me.*

Emerson pocketed his phone. Okay. Mindy would be there for him if he needed her. He unlocked the door to his room and stepped inside. A ghost-free room.

As he moved through the motions of getting ready for bed, he noticed the lingering scent of the women, a mixture of sweet perfumes. The scent was rather pleasant, and Emerson breathed deeply as he pulled the covers back on his bed.

He had said few formal prayers in his life, where he'd knelt and calmly communed with God. His bishop had been encouraging him to pray morning and night, kneeling by the side of his bed, but Emerson hadn't done it yet. Part of it was pride, but another part was this fear that if he did pray and felt nothing, he'd lose his way again. He hadn't been ready to put God to the test in such an intimate way.

Now, almost by external force, Emerson felt himself drop to his knees. His elbows rested on the bed as he brought his hands together and clasped them. He bowed his head and closed his eyes. The room felt beyond quiet, and his voice, even though it was a pained whisper, seemed too loud. "Dear God." He stopped and didn't know what to say next. He looked up at the ceiling, allowed himself to feel for one painful moment, and then bowed his head again. "Thank you for Lucy."

And then he listened. He heard his heartbeat and felt his breath on his arms. Air moved slowly in and out of his lungs. The heater clicked on. A light in the bathroom buzzed.

He felt nothing. No burning in his heart. No voice like a whispering of wind. But he felt still. For the first time since his mother died, his mind was absolutely blank. And maybe in that nothing, there was something after all.

Chapter 8

WHEN LUCY CAME IN, SHE found Charlotte standing at the window, watching London at night. Ellie was at the sink braiding her thick hair, her face makeup-less. She was still beautiful without all the gunk on her face, Lucy was surprised to discover. Her cheekbones were high and her lips full and round. Her well-groomed, arched eyebrows gave her face an elegant pose. But Ellie also looked older than Lucy had initially thought, maybe closer to twenty-five.

Lucy grabbed her toiletries bag from her suitcase and joined Ellie at the vanity. Ellie slid something across the marble countertop. "I got this from the front desk for you."

It was a new toothbrush, still in its packaging. Lucy smiled and picked it up.

"Thanks," she said, feeling a slight tolerance for Ellie starting to grow.

Ellie didn't respond and instead remained focused on rubbing moisturizer on her cheeks. She leaned in closer to the mirror and examined her immaculate skin before saying causally, "You and Emerson seemed to hit it off."

Lucy slowly unwrapped the plastic around the toothbrush, not liking how quickly her heart started to beat at the mention of his name. "He's a very nice man," she replied, trying to keep her voice neutral.

Ellie scoffed and put her hands on her hips, turning to face Lucy. "A man like that and all you can say is he's nice?" she said. "Are you blind?"

Lucy swallowed the lump in her throat. Of course she wasn't blind. That was part of the problem. "Mind if I use your toothpaste?" she asked.

Ellie pushed it over to her and let out an exasperated sigh. Lucy applied the toothpaste, and Ellie resumed her inspection of her face. "Since you *are* blind," Ellie said. "I'll tell you something helpful. From what I could tell, Emerson thinks *you* are a very nice woman." She gave Lucy a pointed look.

Lucy stuck her toothbrush in her mouth and gave her reflection the same kind of scrutiny Ellie was hers, but Lucy didn't have flawless skin, so she focused her gaze on her toothbrush and the task of cleaning her teeth.

"Oh, Lucy isn't interested in Emerson," Charlotte said, joining them at the sink. "She has a boyfriend."

Ellie cocked her head. "But didn't you come to London to get away from him?"

Lucy felt Ellie's eyes on her, but Lucy didn't want to engage her. She spit, rinsed her toothbrush off, and filled a glass with water. "It's complicated," Lucy said, taking a sip and swallowing.

"It's always complicated," Ellie replied.

"Oh, Lucy," Charlotte said. "Charles is so wonderful! How could anything be wrong?"

Lucy left the vanity and began searching through her suitcase for her pajamas. She didn't mind talking to Charlotte about this, but Ellie?

Lucy saw Ellie, who stood at the vanity, her arms folded across her chest and her perfect eyebrows arched. Charlotte sat on the bed beside Lucy's suitcase. Her innocent blue eyes gleamed like a begging puppy's.

Lucy hadn't said it out loud yet and wasn't really ready to, but maybe she needed to talk about it. She cleared her throat and lowered her voice, knowing Ellie would still be able to hear. "Charles wants to get married."

Charlotte's eyes widened, and she yelped. "You're engaged!" she shouted, throwing her arms around Lucy. "How is that a problem?"

Lucy gently shrugged off Charlotte's hold. "I'm not sure I'm in love with Charles," Lucy admitted, goose bumps breaking out on her arms. She for sure had never said *that* out loud. While Lucy loved Charles as a friend, she wasn't sure she was *in* love with him. How stupid! Why was there such a difference in those two things?

"How can you not be in love with him?" Charlotte asked.

Lucy's phone rang in her purse, and she used the interruption to end the conversation. She pulled her phone from her bag and saw that the call was from her boss. Lucy sighed and brought the phone to her ear.

"Do you have plans tomorrow?" Tanya asked without saying hello first.

Lucy cleared her throat. "I do in the morning. Why?"

"Since you left without notice, I'm still going to put you to work."

"Great," Lucy replied. "I was planning to work remotely."

"I've contacted some potential suppliers," Tanya continued. "It would be nice for us to add imported artisan chocolate to our ingredient offerings. I want you to do some taste testing while you're in Europe."

"Really?" Lucy stifled a laugh. "I thought you were going to punish me with some terribly boring task."

"I still could," Tanya warned.

That sobered Lucy. There were so many boring things Tanya could require, even from 5,000 miles away: invoicing, cost-analysis reports, social media marketing nonsense. "I'll taste as much chocolate as you need me to," Lucy said.

"Good. That's what I want to hear," Tanya said. "A chocolatier near Hyde Park has agreed to meet with you tomorrow afternoon. I've sent an email with the information."

After exchanging a few more details, the call ended. Lucy looked around the room to find Charlotte had fallen asleep on the bed beside her, and Ellie was doing something on her phone.

She looked up at Lucy. "Sounds like you have an interesting job," Ellie said.

"Yeah."

"So you're going chocolate tasting tomorrow?"

Lucy nodded slowly, not sure if Ellie was trying to finagle her way into an invite or if she was just making conversation.

"You should have Emerson go along with you," Ellie suggested.

Lucy swallowed wrong at the mention of his name and coughed. "What?"

Ellie laughed and gave Lucy a Cheshire cat smile. "I think I'm ready for bed. Mind if I turn off some lights?"

Lucy shook her head and got off the bed. Ellie turned off all the lights except for the one in the bathroom. Lucy changed into her pajamas, listing different types of vanilla in her head to keep her mind off Charles and Emerson: Madacascar Bourbon, Mexican, Indian, Indonesian, Thiahian, and Tongan.

Housekeeping had left an extra pillow and blankets, and Lucy settled onto the couch. She prayed and read her scriptures. Then she stared at the ceiling and mentally reviewed her reasons to marry Charles—returned missionary, ambitious, smart, attractive. He *was* perfect on paper, and what if this was her only chance to get married? It wasn't like she had a ton of other men interested in her. In fact, Charles was the only marriage-worthy man interested in her. For some reason, she didn't appeal to Mormon guys. If she thought too long about why, she'd grow cynical. And then there was the issue that she'd aged out of the eligible bachelor pool a few years ago and was now left with mostly the "single for a reason" types. Charles had everything going for him, and he was good-looking. What more could she ask for?

She rolled onto her side and looked through her purse until she found her father's handkerchief. He had worn it in his pocket the day he had married her mom. Shortly before he died, he gave Lucy the thin white square of fabric. He had carried it with him every day since his wedding day, and Lucy had carried it with her every day since he'd died. She used to hold it to her nose at night, trying to memorize the smell of his spicy cologne. His scent was long gone, but sometimes she could still convince herself she smelled him.

Lucy smoothed the handkerchief against her stomach and wondered for the millionth time what her father would have thought of Charles. Would he have approved? Would he have happily given his daughter's hand to Charles? A niggle of doubt crept in. Not because she thought her dad wouldn't approve but because she knew Charles wouldn't have liked her dad. Her dad hadn't been the type of man Charles would have found impressive. He had been a blue-collar worker, an electrician by trade, and had owned a successful small business. But Charles valued high education and liked to talk about ideals. While her father had been a smart man, he hadn't been smart in the way Charles would have appreciated.

She then thought of Emerson and his charming smile. Her father would have liked Emerson; that was obvious. A military-academy graduate. The kind of guy who could paint his grandma's cabin. A man's man. That was the type of person her father would have instantly hit it off with. But it was foolhardy to even entertain the idea of Emerson since they had just met and a marriage-bound relationship with him was impossible for logistical and spiritual reasons. So it was Charles or no one.

For hours, Lucy's mind remained unsettled. Sometime around 2:00 a.m., she fell asleep, her fist clutching her father's handkerchief. Her last thought was of Emerson and his caramel-colored eyes. An eye color, she realized, she had seen before.

Chapter 9

EMERSON FOUND ELLIE IN THE dining room the next morning. It was late, near the end of breakfast, and she was alone. He loaded his plate with eggs and ham from the buffet and approached her table. "Mind if I join you?"

She looked up from the magazine she was leafing through and met his eyes with a cool expression. She gestured with her hand for him to sit.

Emerson pulled out the chair and noticed a half-drunk cup of coffee. A cold uneasiness went through him. Should she be drinking coffee? She took a sip from the mug, like she had read his mind, leaving another lipstick stain on the brim.

"You and Lucy seemed pretty chummy last night," Ellie said, palming her coffee cup.

Emerson suspected Ellie was the conniving type, and he didn't want to play into whatever trap she was setting. He kept his expression and response neutral. "Lucy is a very nice woman."

Ellie rolled her eyes. "She said the same thing about you. Both of you are so noble." She leaned forward and set her coffee down. "What I want to know," Ellie continued, with narrowed eyes, "is why you haven't told Lucy you're LDS."

Emerson laughed. "Asks the Mormon girl with coffee breath."

"Who said I'm Mormon?"

"Who said I was?"

She leaned back in her chair, still sipping her coffee, watching Emerson over the cup. "As a bad Mormon, I'm pretty good at picking out others like me."

Emerson felt surprising anger flare inside him. "That's where you're wrong, Ellie." His heart hammered loudly in his chest. "I'm not a bad Mormon." He'd finally been forced to pick a side, and there it was: Emerson was not only a Mormon, but he was a good one too.

She chuckled. "Right. Neither am I." She put her coffee cup back on the table, wiped the lipstick off the brim and pushed it over to him. She stood and waved at someone. "Lucy, over here."

Emerson stared at the coffee mug, a condemning piece of kitchenware, as Lucy took a seat at their table. She seemed nonplussed by the coffee, but why should she be? She didn't know Emerson was LDS. And now he felt like he could never tell her. How would he explain the ale at the bar last night and now this half-drunk cup of coffee that appeared to be his?

"See, I knew we'd run into each other again," Lucy said to Emerson. She wore her hair loose around her face today. It had felt so soft when he'd touched it last night. He moved his gaze away from her hair and focused on her face.

"I think I'll see what's keeping Charlotte." Ellie stood and walked away with swinging hips.

A beat of silence moved between Lucy and Emerson. She smiled, and Emerson thought about touching her hair. That wasn't a productive train of thought, so he said the next thing on his mind: "This coffee isn't mine." He bit his tongue. *Idiot.*

"What?" She glanced down at the mug. "Okay."

"It was here when I sat down," he continued, heat rising to his face. Lucy nodded and gave Emerson a confused look, taking a sip of her orange juice.

"How are the eggs?" she asked.

Emerson looked at his plate of uneaten food. He loaded his fork and took a bite. "Good," he said between chews. What happened to the smooth Emerson? The pilot who was good at talking to women? The man who fought in wars and skydived for fun? Why was sitting with this beautiful woman, sharing an impromptu meal, so difficult?

"Want to know a fun food-science fact?" she asked.

Almost too happily, Emerson nodded. Lucy was leading the conversation, which meant his stupid coffee comment hadn't put her off.

"Most restaurants use eggs from a carton, which are really just egg whites with beta carotene added to make them yellow." She pointed at Emerson's plate with her fork. "Those eggs are definitely from a carton. You can tell because it's just one yellow lump."

Emerson considered his lumpy yellow eggs. "Is the ham real?" he asked.

Lucy's eyes went wide. "Oh no. Did I ruin your breakfast?" she asked. "Things that I find interesting about food sometimes gross people out."

Emerson shook his head and took a bite of his eggs to reassure her. "Have you ever eaten powdered eggs?" he asked.

Lucy gagged.

"Exactly," Emerson agreed. "I think I can still enjoy eggs from a carton after the garbage I ate in the military."

Lucy took a forkful of hash browns and made a face.

"Let me guess," Emerson said. "Also from a carton?"

"No . . . I mean, yes." Lucy put her fork down and met Emerson's eyes. The heaviness in her gaze stilled him. "This is going to sound really strange, but I think I met your mother once."

Emerson gulped. "What?"

"When I was in grad school, I attended a thesis writing workshop taught by a woman from the English department."

"Do you remember her name?"

Lucy shook her head. "She was friends with my thesis advisor though. And she was tall and had curly brown hair, and . . . she had your eyes."

A bittersweet sense of nostalgia tugged at Emerson. "That was probably her," he said. He again felt that nothingness he'd felt last night. But maybe it wasn't really nothingness but rather stillness. Emerson had never believed in fate until this moment. He could have met Lucy years ago. If he had been active in the Church, they might have been in the same singles ward in Madison when he'd gone home to visit. Everything might have been different for him.

"She was so funny. And smart," Lucy said.

"Yeah, she was." Emerson and Lucy shared a smile that soon turned sad. Pain ebbed in the chambers of Emerson's heart.

"It's terrible, isn't it?" she said.

Emerson nodded and cleared the thickness from his throat. Instead of offering some trite platitude, Lucy took another bite of hash browns. And Emerson took a drink of his juice.

"It's kind of remarkable," Lucy said after a long moment. "How connected our lives seem to be, but this is our first time meeting."

"Lucy, I . . ." The words died in his throat. She looked so incredibly gentle. And good—like she had spent most of her life trying to do the right thing for the right reason. Emerson didn't know what he was supposed to do with someone like her. "Thank you," he finally said. "Thank you for everything."

Chapter 10

LUCY WAS OFFICIALLY LOST, AND the empty residential street offered her no help. She wasn't about to knock on a random door to ask for directions, so she kept walking, trying for the hundredth time to get the GPS on her phone to work. She was already running late because lunch with her former mission president and his wife had gone longer than she had anticipated. And now she couldn't even pull up the directions to the chocolate shop for her afternoon tasting.

She continued walking, her legs beginning to ache from the fast pace. Up ahead, she saw an intersection with an *M* marquee jutting up into the sky. Perfect. She'd ask someone at McDonald's for directions. She jogged until she reached the intersection. There was a Starbucks across the street from the McDonald's, and she thought about what Charlotte had said: she could be in any city in the world.

Lucy waited at the crosswalk for the light to change. A man walked up and stood beside her. Way too close. They were the only two people waiting at the intersection; it wasn't like there was a reason to crowd in. His shoulder brushed against hers, and Lucy took a small step away, uneasiness pressing up from her stomach.

The walk signal changed, and Lucy took a step forward, exhaling a saved breath.

"You dropped something," the man called.

Lucy paused, turned toward him, and realized her error instantly. With big, quick hands the man grabbed her purse. He yanked the strap off her shoulder, and Lucy stumbled with the force. Her hands hit the pavement, gravel digging into her palms. She tried to right herself, the sounds of the man's footfalls matching the quick beat of her heart. He was getting away.

Lucy sprinted after the man. "Hey, come back here," she yelled, reaching for the collar of his denim jacket. Her pointer finger caught for a split second before the man swatted at her and her finger slipped. As she passed the Starbucks, another man stepped in front of her, stalling her pursuit. "Excuse me," she said, trying to get around him.

Starbucks Man handed her his drink. "Hold this," he said.

Lucy took the cup, her head growing foggy. What about her purse? Once she had the drink, the man took off. She watched as he turned the corner after the purse grabber. Exhaling deeply, she slumped against the wall of the coffee shop. She felt like she was treading water while waiting for a life buoy. Adrenaline pounded loudly in her head. Her body shook, and the corners of her vision began to go fuzzy. She'd been robbed.

Her breath grew shallow, and she felt the blood draining from her head. A coldness swept through her. Her father's handkerchief was in her purse. The last piece of her father, the thing that connected her to him through his long absence, was gone.

The chill in her body turned to heat. Her heart throbbed loudly and impossibly fast in her chest. More adrenaline coursed through her body, and her limbs began to shake, and her breath became short and uneven. She'd been robbed. She'd lost her dad. Again. It was too much. It was all too much, and she felt her body shutting down. Her legs grew heavy and her head light.

She tried to remember what she had done when she had felt this way before. She hadn't had a panic attack in nearly five years and its sudden appearance frightened her, causing her heart to beat even faster. She knew she needed to find something to ground her. Or she needed to go to her happy place. Or she needed to calm her breathing. Or not focus on her breathing. Or . . .

She saw the shadow of a man and heard his voice: "Lucy, I . . ."

And just like that, she dropped the man's drink and everything went black.

* * *

A familiar blue scent roused her. A strong arm and a solid chest supported her body. Lucy's eyes fluttered opened to find Emerson's wide caramel eyes staring at her. His free hand touched her cheek gently, and he brushed the hair out of her face. He smiled, and her vision almost went out again.

"Are you okay?" he asked.

His words bounced around in Lucy's head like a pinball. Mmmm, the pressure of his arm holding her waist was absolutely perfect. Her eyes drifted to his mouth. He was saying something else, but Lucy still couldn't process the words. His lips did look awfully enticing though. Why was he holding her? Were they about to kiss?

Her heart started beating fast again, and then she remembered. The robbery. The stolen handkerchief.

"Do you think you can stand?" he asked.

She understood that question.

"I think so," she said. As Emerson helped move her to a more vertical position and Lucy's vision blurred and then cleared, she realized how incredibly humiliating this was. She steadied herself by placing her hands on the wall behind her instead of on Emerson's broad shoulders.

"Here, drink this," he said, picking up the Starbucks cup from the ground, which had remarkably not spilled out when Lucy had dropped it.

"I don't drink coffee," she said through parched lips as he handed her the warm drink.

"It's hot chocolate," he replied. He studied her face carefully and touched her hair again like he couldn't help it. She noticed they still stood awfully close to each other. His presence felt safe, reassuring, and just a little exhilarating, so when he took a step back and the air around her grew colder, her heart ached a little. She took a sip of his drink, resting her head against the wall, and closed her eyes.

She couldn't believe she'd fainted.

"I didn't catch him," Emerson said.

But you caught me.

"He turned a corner, and I lost him."

Lucy's eyes popped open. It all clicked into place. Emerson was the Starbucks man who had handed her the drink and chased after the thief. She touched her face with her free hand. Her cheeks felt unbelievably hot. She probably looked like a cherry.

"Did you have anything valuable in there?" Emerson asked.

She couldn't bear to look at him, so she stared at the Starbucks cup with his name scrawled on the outside. If she hadn't fainted, she probably would have realized it was him chasing after the thief sooner.

"Just my phone and . . . something of my father's."

"Oh," Emerson said. "What about your wallet?"

Lucy shook her head and fished the travel wallet out from under her shirt. "Believe it or not, this isn't my first trip to Europe." She let the wallet go, and it hit her chest with a light thump. It contained her credit cards, a photocopy of her passport, and a little cash. But, really, she wouldn't have felt this devastated had it been stolen. What she should have kept hidden was the thing that mattered most. She pictured the thief digging through her bag and tossing the handkerchief to the side. It was almost too much.

"We should call the police," he suggested. "Are you okay to walk? Let's sit down inside." Emerson put his arm gently around her shoulder to support her. His touch made her feel light-headed again. He led her through the door, and the air in the shop felt hot on her already-too-warm skin. He pulled a chair out for her at the nearest table and helped her sit, his hands lingering on her shoulders a moment before he circled the table and took the chair across from her.

"Drink up," he said, pushing the cocoa across the table.

Lucy took a sip and suddenly wanted to cry. She'd been a victim of a petty crime. And her father's handkerchief was gone. And Emerson was being so kind.

Lucy felt a hand on hers. She looked down at her fingers intertwined with Emerson's—his worn and hers small. His thumb ran over the knuckles of her hand, causing goose bumps to break out on her skin. "Are you okay?" he asked.

And that was when the sobbing started. The humiliation and loss were too much, and Emerson's concern was so perfect and necessary that she couldn't stop herself, even though it added to her embarrassment. He moved next to her and put an arm around her. "You're safe now, Lucy," Emerson said.

Lucy allowed herself to soak up his warmth and kindness. It was nice to be physically comforted and to be given a chance to be emotional. She couldn't help but think of what Charles would do in a situation like this. He would have left her sobbing while he figured out the 911 equivalent in London. Helpful, but not what she'd need from him.

Emerson handed her a napkin, and Lucy wiped her eyes and blew her nose, trying not to care that he watched her the whole time.

"Okay?" he asked.

Lucy shook her head and took a deep breath. "My dad's handkerchief was in the purse," she said. "He gave it to me before he died."

He hesitated and then said, "Shucks," but it sounded like he meant a different word.

Lucy laughed because the word sounded so strange coming from his mouth. "Yeah, shucks is right." She met his eyes.

He touched her hair again. His fingers stayed tangled, and Lucy felt something electric pass between them. Their faces sure were close, and Lucy's gaze drifted down to Emerson's mouth again. He pulled back a little, his fingers slipping from her hair. "Are you ready to call the police?" he asked.

Lucy could feel her cheeks beginning to heat up again. She tucked her hair behind her ear. "Can you do it? I don't even know where I am."

Emerson squeezed her shoulder before letting go. "Yeah, sure."

Lucy wiped a stray tear. "Thank you."

He pulled his phone from his pocket and dialed 999. Lucy could faintly hear the line ringing as Emerson held the phone to his ear, and soon someone picked up. "I'd like to report a crime," he said. "My friend was mugged."

A surge of gratitude rushed through her chest.

"Her name is Lucy . . ." He glanced at her. "Lucy . . ."

"Kappal," she finished.

"Lucy Kappal," he said. He exchanged a few more details with the dispatcher and ended the call. "An officer should be here within an hour to take a statement."

Lucy frowned. An hour? What about her meeting with the chocolatier? And in an hour, her purse and her father's handkerchief would be long gone. "Do you mind if I borrow your phone?"

He shook his head and slid it across the tabletop.

"Does it have an international plan? I don't want to run up a huge bill."

He smiled. "I'm a pilot. Of course I have an international plan. Call whoever you need to."

As Lucy tapped the phone's screen, she took a few calming breaths. Emerson excused himself to the ordering counter. She first called her phone company to put a hold on her mobile account. Then she googled the phone number to the chocolate shop. She explained her situation to the owner and was told to come over when she finished with the police. Next, she called her boss and left a voice mail letting her know if she needed to get ahold of her, email was the only option.

She placed the phone on the table and finished the hot chocolate, which was now tepid. Exhaustion like liquid lead moved through her veins. Her father's handkerchief had always offered so much comfort in moments like this. Her fingers clasped the empty air.

* * *

Emerson returned to the table with a fresh cup of cocoa for himself and an ice water for Lucy. She took a long, eager drink. "Should I get you something else?" he teased.

Lucy stopped drinking, and her eyes widened. He found it amusing how easily she got embarrassed. "No, this is perfect. Thank you." She set her drink down. "Really, Emerson, thank you . . . for everything. I'm so grateful you're here."

He met her gray eyes and enjoyed the pressure building in his chest. "I'm glad to be here." He couldn't get over how pretty she was, even with tear-stained cheeks. He took a drink of his hot chocolate and, for the first time, didn't wish it were coffee. "So . . ." Emerson said, "your last name's Kappal?"

Lucy nodded.

"That means 'chapel' in German, right?"

"Oh, yes," Lucy said. "*Sprechen Sie Deutsch?*"

"*Nein.*" Emerson laughed. "I took two years in high school and can hardly speak a word. But I suspect you do."

The slightest tinge of pink still colored her cheeks. "I served a mission for my church in Germany."

Emerson's heart began to pound loudly in his chest. He could easily admit right now that he was a returning member of the Church. And he could explain the ale as a moment of weakness. Lucy seemed like someone who wouldn't judge him. She might even understand. He swallowed hard. "You're Mormon, right?" he asked.

Lucy laughed. "What gave it away?"

Emerson felt his courage waiver. She hadn't guessed he was LDS, and it suddenly felt like such a huge bomb to drop.

The full-time missionaries in his ward had given him all the lessons already, but he hadn't had a big moment of spiritual witness. At least, not in the way he'd hoped. He feigned a flirty smile and leaned in a little. "On your mission, you probably had a little spiel you gave people, right?"

Lucy laughed again, and Emerson found he kind of loved the sound. "I guess you could call it that," she said.

"Tell it to me."

"In English or German?"

"English."

She stopped grinning. "Oh. You're serious?"

"Yes," he said. "If you ran into me on the streets of Germany, what's your two-minute elevator pitch?"

"Well." Lucy set her cup down and sat back, pushing her hair behind her ear. The amusement melted off her face as she closed her eyes. They stayed closed for a few long seconds, and when she opened them, her gaze was unguarded. The hair on Emerson's arms rose. He'd never been looked at that way, like she was honestly trying to figure out who he was and what he needed. "Emerson . . ." His stomach did a funny little flip. She looked him in the eyes, and her brows knitted together. The air between them felt gravid and impossibly warm. "You'll see your mom again." She spoke slowly and softly, her voice like heavy cream. "I know she feels impossibly far away, but God designed families to be together forever."

He felt a sharp, hot pain in his chest. Lucy continued in a steady voice. "You are a son of a loving Heavenly Father. And even though life is hard and we all make mistakes, He's prepared a way for us to be happy. That way is Jesus Christ. Because of Him, it doesn't matter what we've done wrong or what challenges we might face, He has overcome it all. Because of Christ, death has no victory and sin cannot consume us. In the Bible, we read that it is through His stripes that we are healed. I have felt the redeeming power of Jesus Christ in my life. And I know through Him, you can find true joy and hope too."

Something settled inside Emerson like sand slipping through rocks to fill in the empty spaces. He'd been so focused on all the rules of being Mormon that he'd forgotten what it was really all about. He'd forgotten Christ's part in it all. "Do you really believe that?" His voice broke like glass.

Lucy's expression remained earnest. "I do."

He turned away, and his sigh sounded like a muted laugh. "You must have broken a lot of hearts in Germany."

"Why do you say that?"

"You, with your message of love and hope. Plus . . ." He met her eyes. Emerson found himself utterly entranced. "You're beautiful."

Lucy looked away and then everywhere but back at him. The warmth between them began to dissipate. "Oh, the police are here." She quickly stood and approached the officers.

Emerson's heart hurt again but for a different reason. He'd never met anyone like her and was afraid he never would again. He wanted someone like her in his life, someone with faith, someone he could borrow light from until he had his own. He wanted someone like her whom he could come home to.

Chapter 11

AFTER REPEATING HER STORY TO two different officers, Lucy wanted to collapse. The squashed adrenaline mixed with a sugar crash from the hot chocolate she'd drunk left her limbs feeling like sandbags. The beginnings of a headache whispered in her brow, and she rubbed her chest where a tiny ache pulsed. It was just a handkerchief, but how could it be gone? If she didn't have a chocolate tasting, she'd go back to the hotel and bawl her eyes out.

Her legs almost too weak to stand, Lucy rose from her seat. On the other side of the coffee shop, she saw Emerson shaking hands with one of the officers. Part of her had hoped he had finished before her and left. Not only was she mortified that he'd seen her totally break down, but something had also changed between them after she had shared her testimony, and she wasn't sure what was going to happen next.

Emerson had called her beautiful.

Just thinking about it sent a bunch of dumb butterflies flitting through her stomach. Lucy could count on one hand the number of men outside her family who had said she was beautiful. How was she supposed to act with him now that she knew he was attracted to her?

The officers left, and Emerson made his way over to where she gripped the back of her chair for support. "I guess we're done," he said, his eyebrows raised, his hands stuffed in his coat pockets.

"Yup." Lucy nodded, her eyes bouncing from his face to her hands to the wall and back to his face. How much eye contact should she be making right now?

He untucked his hands. "Where are you headed? Let me walk you."

"Uh . . ." Lucy swallowed. Her stomach did a slow agonizing flip. "I'm headed to a chocolate shop."

"Great," he said, touching her elbow and leading her to the exit.

"But I need to stop at a grocery store first."

"Sure, let me look one up."

They stood on the sidewalk near where Lucy had fainted as Emerson typed away on his phone. He showed her a map with little red flags marking where stores were located. "Any of these on the way?"

Lucy tapped one of the flags. "This one."

Side by side, they walked down the street. Emerson's nearness mixed with the devastation of the stolen handkerchief caused Lucy's heart to palpitate and flex in an uneven rhythm, like a sudden summer storm. Trapped in her own headspace, surviving the rest of the day seemed almost impossible.

Lucy felt a little knock on her arm. "You okay?" Emerson asked.

"No."

His arm came around her shoulder, and Lucy settled against him. She fit perfectly in the crook of his arm. She absorbed his warmth and the solid strength of his body.

They walked like that for a few paces before he spoke. "I'm so sorry, Lucy." He gave her a short squeeze before releasing her. Lucy stifled a sigh. His blue scent lingered in her nose. "Is there anything on earth that would make you feel better?"

The uneven pattering of her heart picked up again, and she felt like a cliff jumper standing on the ledge. With an exalted lurch of her stomach, she realized she was about to be brave. She grabbed his arm and put it back around her shoulder. "This," she said.

Emerson laughed and pulled her close. "Yeah, me too."

* * *

After a quick stop at a grocery store to get vanilla ice cream, a green apple, and a bottle of sparkling water, Emerson and Lucy arrived at the chocolate shop. The thick air inside made him feel heady and a little homesick. As Lucy spoke to the person at the counter, Emerson studied the fancy candy in the glass cases: colorful squares of chocolate; chocolates embossed with powdered gold; white, milk, and dark chocolate sculpted into fragile figurines. A white-and-gold swan with a dark-chocolate bridle sat in a brown paper moat. The price tag read fifteen pounds.

"We're going back to the kitchen," Lucy said to him.

We? So he was allowed to stay? He felt stupid in his relief. Being with her felt comfortable, and he hadn't felt comfortable in a long time. He didn't want to have to say goodbye to her just yet.

He followed her and the employee whose name tag said Bernard through two corral doors behind the counter. The air in the kitchen was much cooler than the air in the shop. Two large metal tables stood in the middle of the open space. Three gas stoves lined the back wall. Industrial-sized refrigerators hummed. Pots in all sizes, measuring spoons and cups, wooden spoons, and other gadgets he didn't know the names of hung on walls or were stacked on racks. Emerson breathed deeply, and the bitter dust of cocoa stung his nose.

Bernard wheeled a tall rack of cookie sheets over to one of the tables. Lucy set her grocery bag down. Bernard said something in broken English that Emerson didn't quite understand, but Lucy nodded and the man left.

Lucy went to the rack and slid out a cookie sheet halfway. She lifted the wax paper to reveal rows and rows of bite-sized chocolate squares, then she selected two and set them on the shiny tabletop. "Have you ever done a wine tasting before?" she asked him.

"Yeah," Emerson answered, feeling a little crushed by the question. It was pretty clear she didn't think he was Mormon. It was seeming less and less likely that he would ever tell her; there would be too much he'd have to explain.

"Great," she replied. "This will be a lot like that. We'll mostly be considering the mouthfeel, complexity, and aftertaste of the chocolate. My boss wants something really smooth and well-balanced."

"Wait," Emerson said, putting his hands out. "Are you working on your vacation?"

Lucy picked up the square of milk chocolate and held it up against the light, examining it a moment. The chocolate looked sleek and shiny. "Yes," she replied, breaking the piece in half. It made a distinct snap. "I sort of left the country without telling my boss first." She smelled the chocolate and then examined the residue on her fingers after rubbing her fingertips together. She looked very much like a scientist.

"So as punishment you have to do research in the form of chocolate tasting?" Emerson asked, a smirk on his face.

"Something like that." Her eyes flickered from him back to the chocolate.

He wanted to ask what made her leave on such short notice. From what Emerson could tell, Lucy was cautious and precise. Something awful must have made her run. He swallowed the question whole. It was none of his business.

Lucy selected another piece of chocolate from the rack and held it out to Emerson. He opened his palm, and Lucy dropped it in his hand. "Okay, here's the procedure," she said. "Place the chocolate on your tongue, and let it begin to melt. After it gets soft, you can chew to release more of the flavor, but don't chew more than three times."

Lucy placed the chocolate in her mouth, and Emerson stared at her lips. Her mouth looked incredibly enticing: soft and pink. To distract himself, he put the chocolate in his mouth. As the square melted, smooth sweetness spread over his taste buds. He first tasted the rich flavor of the chocolate, then the sweetness of the sugar. The soft creaminess of milk soon followed. And then he tasted something else. It was fragrant and almost herby. Lucy was chewing, so Emerson did the same thing, making sure to chew only three times. The flavor heightened ever so slightly. "Is that lavender?" he asked.

Lucy's eyes brightened. "Hey, you're a natural."

"In Madison, did you ever go to Gail Ambrosius Chocolatier?"

"Are you kidding me? I probably spent half of my grad student stipend on her chocolate."

"My mom would take me there for my birthday and let me pick out four pieces of chocolate," Emerson said.

"So you've probably tasted them all." Lucy opened the grocery bag and pulled out the apple. "Which one is your favorite?"

"I'd have to say it's a tie between the orange almond and the lemongrass ginger truffle."

"Mmm, the lemongrass." Lucy found a knife by the sink and returned to the apple. "I loved that one. And the blueberry truffle." She cut the apple into thin, even slices. "I still have dreams about Madison."

"Why did you leave?" Emerson asked, moving to her side of the table.

She handed him a slice of the fruit. "To cleanse the palate."

Emerson chewed while he waited for her to answer his question.

She pulled the sparking water out of the bag. "So, I was dating this guy." She spoke flippantly, like if she sounded like she didn't care, then maybe she wouldn't. "He was in medical school, and he got matched with a hospital in Oregon for his residency, and he wanted me to come with him."

Emerson furrowed his brow. But she lived in Utah, not Oregon. Lucy went to a rack of dishes and selected two measuring cups.

"It was kind of this awful fork-in-the-road moment for us." She returned to the table and set the cups down. "He wasn't a member of my church, which already made things complicated, and he wasn't asking me to marry him by coming out to Oregon with him. He was hoping to wear me down once I got out there so I would just move in with him." Lucy sighed. "I realized if I wanted to marry a Mormon, I was going to have to leave Madison and go somewhere where I'd have more options. So I moved back to Utah, got an apartment with my little brother, and two years later, I'm still not married. So . . ." She shrugged.

Emerson reached for another apple slice. He ran his finger over the waxy green skin before eating it.

"You got any sad stories?" she asked.

Emerson looked down and shook his head, letting out a small laugh. "More than I can sometimes bear."

He felt her hand settle on his arm. "You know the best part about being broken?" Emerson looked up to meet Lucy's eyes. They picked up the metallic sheen of the steel tabletop, turning into pools of liquid mercury. "You get to be someone new when you're put back together."

Six inches separated them, and Emerson could sense the warmth of her skin and smell the chocolate on her breath. Their eyes stayed on each other as a palpable energy brewed between them like thunderclouds rolling in. Her hand moved up to his shoulder, and his fingers braved her hair. As she leaned forward ever so slightly, Emerson's heart ran like a wild horse.

How do you kiss a Mormon girl?

* * *

Before their lips touched, Lucy heard the sound of shuffling feet and a door closing. She opened her eyes—when had she closed them?—and took a small step back from Emerson. His fingers slipped through her hair, sending delicious goose bumps down her arms. The static in the air began to settle, leaving her feeling flat.

"Do you need anything, madam?" Bernard asked.

She answered too quickly. "Nope, we're fine. Thank you."

He nodded and returned to the front of the store.

Emerson had moved to the other side of the table, away from her. Was he embarrassed? His gaze wandered around the kitchen, and Lucy's overanalytical mind raced off when he didn't look back at her. Had he even wanted to kiss her? Had she thrown herself at him? Was his standing that close and touching her hair a gesture of extra-friendliness? She exhaled, reached for the bottle of Pierre, and silently scolded herself. *This isn't going anywhere, so it doesn't matter.* She wasn't thinking rationally. It had been an emotionally draining day with the mugging and the loss of her father's handkerchief. Plus, she was trying to sort through all the Charles stuff. She was feeling extra vulnerable. That was all. Combine her overwhelmed emotions with a handsome stranger who also found her attractive and chocolate almost-kisses were bound to happen.

Lucy screwed the lid off the bubbly water and poured it into the two metal measuring cups. She glanced up to find Emerson's caramel-colored eyes watching her in careful appraisal. The atmosphere still felt a little charged, and even though a steel table separated them, Lucy couldn't deny the pull she felt for him.

He came around to her side of the table and picked up one of the measuring cups. "Should we toast?" he asked.

Okay. If he could act normal, so could she. "To what?"

"Sad stories." He lifted his cup, and Lucy clanked her cup against his. "To sad stories."

They each took a drink.

"What's next?" Emerson asked, eyeing the rack of chocolate.

"Ice cream is next," she said. She reached for the ice cream carton and pried off the lid. The dessert was melted on the edges, but the middle was still pretty solid, so she could use it. "So the challenge of putting chocolate in ice cream is maintaining the chocolate's flavor," Lucy continued, and Emerson nodded in encouragement. She wasn't used to guys being interested in her work. "Chocolate's flavor changes when it gets cold, so one of two things usually happens with ice cream: either it appears in really small pieces— think of mint chocolate chip ice cream, for example—or it's turned into a fudge or sauce. I'm looking for a chocolate that could be used both ways."

"Chocolate and ice cream?" Emerson said, revealing a dimple. "Lucy Kappal, you keep making my day."

Lucy's stomach did another roller-coaster flip. "Find me some spoons?"

He went to the rack of dishes and returned with spoons, handing one to her.

"Most people eat ice cream wrong," Lucy said, digging her spoon into the vanilla ice cream. "To get the optimal flavor, you'll want to turn your spoon over and place the ice cream directly on your tongue." Lucy demonstrated, Emerson watching. "Your turn."

Emerson got a scoop of ice cream and flipped his spoon over so the ice cream touched his tongue first.

"Better, right?" Lucy said. "The first thing you taste is the ice cream instead of the spoon."

Emerson nodded. "I'll never eat ice cream wrong again."

"Good." Lucy couldn't help but smile. "Let's add the chocolate."

Chapter 12

When Lucy and Emerson stepped out of the chocolate shop, the sun was beginning to set. Lucy inhaled the wet spring air and reveled in the orange light reflected in the puddles. It had rained while they were inside, and now the sky was beginning to clear.

"We aren't far from the hotel; should we walk?" Lucy asked.

Emerson nodded, and they walked side by side, their arms and hands brushing every few steps. Their silence felt amiable, at least to Lucy, but she glanced over at Emerson, and he appeared to be chewing something over. She wasn't sure what to make of him. At times, he seemed so ambivalent and preoccupied. And at other times, he exuded confidence and awareness. She thought of her first few encounters with him, on the airplane and in the hotel lobby. How charming and predictable he seemed. Served her right for passing judgment. "Most people are complex," Charles liked to remind her. She had a tendency to categorize and hypothesize. It was what she did so naturally as a scientist, and it extended to all aspects of her life, even to people.

They stopped at an intersection and had to wait for the traffic light to change. Emerson nudged her with his elbow. "You seem to have recovered well."

It took her a moment to realize what he was talking about. Oh. The mugging. Perhaps she had recovered remarkably fast. But really, being with Emerson had been a wonderful distraction. "If I don't think about it, I won't feel so devastated," she said.

He pulled her into a sideways, one-armed hug again. She leaned into him, and he let go much sooner than she wanted. A feeling of gratitude warmed her, like the sun peeking out from behind the clouds.

"Emerson," she said.

"Hmm?" He had a contented smile on his face.

She had this silly thought that it felt like they'd known each other forever. "I'm really thankful for everything you did today."

"It was nothing," he replied.

"Really, Emerson, thank you." She stopped walking and put her hand on his arm. "I wish I could do something to make it up to you because I must have ruined your plans today."

His smile wavered. "Believe me, Lucy, spending the day with you was much better than what I had planned."

Lucy's eyebrows shot up. "And what did you have planned?"

He stilled and, clearing his throat, said, "I was trying to talk myself into depositing my mother's ashes in Kensington Gardens."

"Oh," Lucy breathed, feeling the weight of his burden settling in her chest cavity. A final burial. She grabbed his hand, surprised again by how worn his palm felt. "I'll go with you if you want me to."

His eyes met hers. "You would?"

"We can go tomorrow. You shouldn't have to say goodbye alone."

His mouth moved into a thin line, and he studied her face for a long moment. She couldn't quite read the expression there, but she sensed he was holding something back. "Thank you, Lucy," he said.

Her heart thumped, and she squeezed his hand. As they started walking again, his fingers laced with hers.

When they reached the hotel, Lucy went to her room to see if Ellie and Charlotte were there. Emerson stood in the doorjamb with his hands shoved in the pockets of his jeans while Lucy stepped in and turned on the lights. She called out for the two girls, but no one answered. She shrugged and went to the phone on the bedside table. Pressing one, Lucy called down to the front desk. The concierge said there weren't any messages for her. It didn't worry Lucy too much since she knew the girls had a full day. A guided Harry Potter walking tour and then a murder mystery dinner at some haunted mansion.

"Can I use your phone again?" Lucy asked. "I don't want to have to pay for a long-distance call on the hotel's phone."

In a languid movement, Emerson pulled his phone from his pocket and held it out to her. He looked almost too comfortable leaning against the threshold, waiting for her. It didn't escape her that a man she hardly knew was standing just inside her hotel room door. She closed the space between them and took the phone.

She couldn't look at him right now. Something about him at this very moment was *too* appealing. Her stomach twisted into knots, and not all of those knots felt like bad ones. Maybe it was the hand holding, which had felt innocuous at first, a friendly gesture, one to connect two sad people, but as they'd walked, the connection had grown more pronounced. Heated even. And it was just from a handhold. She'd never felt that with Charles. Even if they'd held hands for an hour. It had become sweaty, not tempting.

Lucy exited into the hall, and Emerson followed, the door closing behind him. She took a few steps away from him and dialed Charlotte's cell, one of the few numbers she had memorized. When Charlotte didn't pick up, probably because she didn't recognize the number, Lucy left a voice mail telling Charlotte to call the hotel or Emerson's number if she needed anything and she'd see the two girls later tonight.

Hanging up, Lucy turned back to Emerson. He was staring at the carpet and gnawing on the inside of his cheek, his lower lip puckered out a little. His hands were back in his pockets. Lucy held the phone out to him, and he took it back. "I told them to call your number if they need me," Lucy said. "I hope that's okay."

He took his phone. "So, are Charlotte and Ellie out for the evening?"

Lucy felt a charge move through her. His words held so much promise. She nodded and rocked back on her heels. She felt certain she was going to have a heart attack.

He continued biting the inside of his cheek and rotated his phone around in his hand, his gaze unsure. "Would you like to have dinner with me?" he asked.

Lucy's stomach unknotted and did a backflip. She totally felt her cool slipping as a wide grin appeared on her face. "I'd like that," she said.

"Great. I know a place."

* * *

The restaurant felt sultry and much more romantic than Emerson remembered. The walls were painted a deep crimson, and orange and yellow scarves decorated the room, dividing each dining section into secluded spaces. The air smelled of curry, cardamom, and burning sage. Emerson placed his hand on the small of Lucy's back as the hostess led them to their table in the back corner of the restaurant.

The long, thin table sat low to the ground, surrounded by red and orange silk throw pillows. Emerson gestured for Lucy to sit first, and she took a seat against the wall. He moved in beside her, and they settled into the pillows. The hostess left them with menus.

"Have you ever eaten Middle Eastern cuisine before?" he asked.

Lucy nodded. "I went to Israel last summer with a friend." She scanned the menu. "Well, he was actually my boyfriend . . . I guess now an ex-boyfriend."

Emerson found himself puzzled that she brought up the subject of a boyfriend. Maybe this was her way of letting him know she was single? "What happened between you?"

She shrugged. "We broke up. A few weeks ago."

Before Emerson could really digest this information, the waiter appeared and delivered their water. Lucy ordered with alacrity, and Emerson, once again, was impressed. He liked that she wasn't afraid to show how smart and competent she was. She handed the menu back to the waiter and settled back against the wall.

He put in his order and gave back the menu, then watched Lucy as she took a sip of water. If she and her ex-boyfriend had broken up a few weeks ago and had been dating since last summer, that meant they had probably been together at least nine months. Maybe that was why Lucy had acted so aloof at first. She was just getting out of a serious relationship, maybe one she had even hoped would lead to marriage, and she wasn't looking for a rebound.

She pushed her hair behind her ears. "I don't know why I mentioned my ex-boyfriend. I guess it's been bothering me," she said, unrolling her silverware from the napkin. "Okay, your turn to tell me something that's been bothering you that you had no intention of telling me." She looked like she expected him to laugh it off.

"I was raised Mormon," he said. The words came out as involuntarily as an exhale.

Lucy responded with a quick blink and a frown. "Really?"

Emerson nodded, swallowing the lump in his throat. But a weight he'd been carrying began to lift. He could now be totally honest with her. "My dad is a member, but my mom wasn't. They divorced when I was fourteen, and I lived with my mom most of the year, so I stopped going to church."

Lucy didn't say anything but examined him in careful assessment, like she had done earlier at the Starbucks. He felt like she was stripping back layers and layers of him to get to the center. "How do you feel about the Church now?" she asked, a deep furrow in her brow.

Emerson looked away and exhaled, his cheeks puffing out. "I'm trying," he said, feeling like the response watered down all the complications he felt.

"Is that why you asked me for my two-minute pitch?"

He laughed, wondering if she was upset. Her gray eyes gave nothing away. "I thought if I heard it from you, someone who seemed so normal and intelligent, I would believe it. That there'd be hope for me yet."

She covered his hand with hers and shook her head like she didn't like his answer. "Emerson, there's always hope."

He felt a small warmth spring alive in his chest at her words.

"Do you want to talk about it?" she asked.

He shook his head and brushed his thumb over her small hand. He wanted to talk about it. Sometime. But not right now. "I'd rather talk about you."

* * *

No male had ever looked at Lucy like Emerson was looking at her now. His eyes had turned to molten caramel. Her pulse kicked up. Emerson shifted in his seat and angled himself toward her, his knee pressing briefly into her thigh before he moved it. Lucy gulped, enjoying the attraction between them.

Emerson was Mormon.

She tried not to let that change how she felt about him, but it did. It sort of changed everything. The seventeen-year-old inside her imagined this three-day fling turning into a long-distance relationship, with him eventually moving to Salt Lake, where they would live happily ever after. She wouldn't have to marry Charles.

"I have this theory," he said, pulling her out of her head. "Every interesting person has a secret passion." His eyes flickered over her face in a quick study. "What's yours?"

Lucy wanted to steer the conversation back to him. She hated talking about herself; she really wasn't interesting, so she shrunk back and shrugged.

Emerson's gaze softened a little. "Let me guess."

The waiter arrived and delivered their appetizers. Lucy tried to regulate her breathing to get her heart rate under control. She took a piece of pita and dipped it in the hummus. The creamy texture of the garbanzo beans spread over her tongue as she chewed, followed by the nutty taste of olive oil and tahini, then the garlic and a hint of lemon at the end.

"You're passionate about food," Emerson said. "But that's too obvious." He dipped a piece of pita in the hummus and took a bite. "Maybe you're a world traveler?"

Lucy's lips quirked up, but she played coy. "Maybe."

He looked pleased with himself. "You've been to England, Germany, and Israel. Where else?"

"Ireland, France, Italy, Egypt, and Canada," Lucy replied. "But I'm sure you've been to a lot of places."

"One of the hazards of being a pilot." He leaned closer and lowered his voice. "I have a very messy passport."

Lucy laughed and felt like she was in high school again, flirting with the cute boy in math class. When was thirty-year-old, grounded-in-reality Lucy going to show up? "I don't think you'll ever guess my secret passion."

A slow smile spread across his lips, and Lucy felt transfixed by his stare. "Want to help me out?" he asked.

"Beethoven," she said.

He raised his eyebrows. "Beethoven?" He appeared to think a moment and then gave a mocking gasp. "You wouldn't be a Mormon girl who also plays piano, would you?"

She laughed again. "Guilty." She raised one hand. "Lessons since age five."

"And you like to play Beethoven?"

"He was my first love," Lucy said.

Emerson's smile was so big and bright, she felt like a moth drawn to a flame. She took this opportunity to eat more pita and drink some water. She needed to cool off.

"Tell me yours," she said, glancing over at him.

"Bookworm," he answered.

"Bookworm?" She tilted her head to the side in surprise.

Emerson dipped a piece of pita and popped it in his mouth. "I'm a huge reader," he said after a few chews.

"A hazard of being the son of an English professor?" she asked.

"Not a hazard," he said. "A benefit."

"Do you have a favorite book?"

He nodded. "Two actually: *The Things They Carried* by Tim O'Brien and *Slaughterhouse 5* by Vonnegut. Have you read them?"

Lucy scrunched her nose and shook her head. "I don't read," she confessed.

Emerson gasped again. "No!"

Lucy swatted him. "Don't you start too. The ex-boyfriend always got after me for not reading." She bit the inside of her cheek, cursing herself for bringing up Charles again. "A hazard of dating a writer," she muttered.

The waiter returned then with their food, and Lucy exhaled gratefully. She could tell by the puzzled expression on Emerson's face that he was itching to ask her more about her ex-boyfriend. She didn't want to talk about him. But maybe the reason she kept bringing him up was that she didn't quite feel single, especially with Charles's proposal out there. Maybe she even felt a little guilty for being attracted to Emerson and flirting with him and planning a fictional future with him.

She dug into her shawarma and hoped she appeared too wrapped up in her food for Emerson to ask her about Charles. After a few bites, she glanced at Emerson to find he was also eating.

"Did you eat this food while stationed in the Middle East?" Lucy asked, taking over the conversation.

"Not too often," he replied. "I usually ate whatever was served at base camp."

"Can I ask what you did in the war? It's just, I've never really met a veteran before."

He took a large bite of his kabsa, then drank some water. "Sure," he said, but she sensed he didn't really want to talk about it. He shifted in his chair again, this time angling himself away from her ever so slightly. "I did cargo and troop transport and some reconnaissance stuff."

"It must have been scary, flying over a war zone."

"I was one of the lucky ones, Lucy," he said but must have seen her skepticism. "Really, I was lucky. I never had to kill anyone. My mom found me a good therapist once I got home, so I got the help I needed. It could have turned out really differently, but I'm in a good place now. As good a place as I can be, anyway." He shrugged and resumed eating.

Lucy didn't feel hungry anymore. If she spent a million years with Emerson, she probably still wouldn't know everything there was to know about him. He was like a monolith, seemingly on display but impenetrable. "You've been through a lot," she said tentatively.

He shook his head in disagreement. "My mom had this quote posted on the refrigerator." His eyes were luminous in the red light. "It said 'Be kind, for everyone is fighting a battle you know nothing about.' Everyone has something. Don't discount your experiences. You've been through a lot too."

She saw something intensely good and kind in his eyes. He was someone she could fully trust. Someone she could care for deeply. She felt like she was teetering on the edge, in danger of slipping and falling head-over-heels. Was it safe for her to let go? What would happen if she did? And if she didn't, would she ever find someone like him again?

Chapter 13

EMERSON GRABBED LUCY'S HAND AS they left the too-warm restaurant. The cool evening air entered his lungs with a welcome pull. She wove her fingers in between his and gave his hand a little squeeze.

The conversation at dinner had been intense and much more intimate than he was used to. She had a way of drawing information from him. It was the way she asked her questions, with curiosity and concern. Her gray eyes would shine with understanding and implore him to answer. There was nothing he wouldn't tell her. It was both alarming and liberating.

When they reached the hotel, they meandered through the lobby, weaving between chairs and couches and talking couples holding drinks. Emerson was in no hurry for the night to end. He wanted as much time with Lucy as she would give him.

They neared the entrance to the hotel bar on their walk to the elevators. Under normal circumstances, he would have asked if she wanted a drink. Instead, he planned to continue on to his room.

But Lucy stopped, pulling on his arm. She gestured to the grand piano just inside the bar. "Since you know my secret passion, should I play you something?" she asked.

He felt relief. She didn't want the night to end just yet either.

"I'd love that," he said.

They walked into the bar, the lights low and cool. She positioned herself on the piano bench and patted the space next to her. "Sit," she said. Emerson settled beside her, shoulder to shoulder. "Do you have a request?" she asked.

Emerson opened his mouth to speak, but Lucy stopped him. "Anything but 'Piano Man.'"

"I would never suggest that," he said. Of course that was the song he was going to suggest. "I mean, how cliché."

Lucy laughed. "Do you sing?"

He shook his head.

"Me neither. I'll play something without words, then."

Emerson watched as she set her fingers lightly on the keys. When the notes sounded, Emerson recognized them immediately. He had heard those notes countless times while listening to the classical music station with his father as a child. She continued and then glanced at him out of the corner of her eye. "Too pretentious?" she asked.

"If you can play Beethoven, you've earned the right to be pretentious," he replied.

And then her fingers were off, flying over the keyboard with an impossible assurance. His heart swelled with the music, and his soul zoomed within the small confines of his body. He felt light, like anything and everything were possible.

When she finished, Emerson was not alone in his applause. A small crowd of bar and hotel patrons had gathered around the piano. Lucy stood and took a deep, exaggerated bow, her face alight. She returned to the keys and played a slow, smooth melody. Emerson looked at Lucy's face again. Her eyes closed, and her breath deepened. Her body swayed slightly as she pressed and released the pedals at her feet. She seemed to be falling into the music. And as slowly and softly as the music played, Emerson found himself falling too.

* * *

They left the piano hand in hand and rode the elevator to Lucy's floor. As they walked down the hall to her room, his heart rate picked up. This wasn't a normal first date for him, if this was a date at all. He didn't know what the rules were with Lucy. All he knew was his old rules didn't apply.

They stopped outside her room, and she let go of his hand. She peered around the hall and lowered her head, avoiding eye contact. Emerson knew he wasn't going to be invited in, but he hadn't had to end a date at the doorstep since he was a teenager. He suddenly felt very childish. Dating as a Mormon would be like going back to high school.

Lucy pushed her hair behind her ears and looked up at him. Her features appeared soft in the sconce lighting of the hallway. "Thanks for taking me to dinner," she said. "I had a nice time. You're a really interesting person."

Emerson chuckled. "You make it sound like a bad thing."

He heard noise on the other side of the door: shuffling and light laughter. He grabbed Lucy and pulled her to the side, out of the view of the peephole. She looked bewildered and opened her mouth to speak. He brought his finger to her lips and walked her over until they were against the wall. "Charlotte and Ellie are trying to spy on us."

Lucy rolled her eyes and laughed. She stood close enough that Emerson could sense the soft vibration of her laughter in his body. "They're just jealous," she said, glancing up at him. Her eyes connected with his, and the air around them became charged. She blinked slowly, her eyelashes dark and long. He felt like he couldn't breathe and didn't want to breathe. The electricity between them was better than air.

Emerson had a dangerous thought: would one kiss be enough for him now? He took a small step back from her. "I'm going to say good night," he uttered, his voice feeling rough in his throat. "See you tomorrow?"

Lucy visibly swallowed and nodded her head. Did she feel the attraction too? Was she as confused by this feeling as he was?

"Good night, Emerson." She squeezed his arm, released it with mild hesitation, and went to the door of her room. He watched her slip inside, his heartbeat erratic. Chatter on the other side of the door signaled he should leave. Unless he wanted to overhear what Lucy had to say about him.

He turned on his heel and entered the elevator, his body still buzzing. As he stepped onto his floor, he realized it was his cell phone ringing. He quickly pulled it from his pocket, and the caller ID indicated it was his cousin. His face split into a huge grin as he answered.

"Mindy!"

"Emerson?" He could hear the confusion in her voice. "Is everything okay?"

He swiped his key card through the reader and entered his room. "Everything is fine," he replied. "Why?"

"It's just, you sound . . . happy."

Emerson laughed. Yeah, he did feel happy. Happier than he had in months. "I've met someone," he said, a giddy feeling rushing through him.

"You met someone?" Mindy echoed. "Like your usual version of 'meet'?"

"No," Emerson replied. He wouldn't want it that way with Lucy. This was much better. "You remember that woman on the flight over who was eavesdropping on our conversation?"

"Vaguely," she replied.

Emerson sat on the edge of his bed and proceeded to untie his shoes. "I ran into her again at the hotel." He hesitated, not sure how Mindy would react. "She's Mormon."

"Really?"

"Yeah." He kicked off his shoes and laid on the bed.

"And how are you doing with the Church rules?" Mindy asked. "I was a little worried when I didn't hear from you last night."

Last night. That seemed like a lifetime ago. He remembered how desperate he had felt sitting at the bar with his ale. He felt like an entirely new person now. It wouldn't even be a temptation anymore. Well, almost. "Really good," he said, warmth spreading through him. "Lucy's been really supportive."

"The woman from the plane?" The doubt in her voice was unmistakable.

"She's incredible. You'd like her, Mindy. She went to grad school in Madison and knew my mom. I don't know. Part of me feels like this is . . ." He stopped, afraid if he said it aloud, the magic would stop. It felt too personal to think God had sent Lucy to him.

"Emerson, are you in love?" Mindy teased, and he could picture her freckled smile.

He wanted to laugh, but the sudden pounding of his heart overrode his ability to speak. Was he in love? Is this what love felt like? He hadn't been in love in so long, he wasn't sure if this even felt the same way. And it was ridiculous to think he could fall in love in only twenty-four hours. He liked Lucy, and he found her attractive, and the thought of never speaking to her again caused him some anxiety, but surely this wasn't love. Whatever it was, though, felt really good.

"Your silence is concerning," Mindy said. "Have you kissed her?"

"No," Emerson replied. "I'm not sure what the rules are."

Mindy laughed, and Emerson was grateful she couldn't see his reddening face. "It's good that you're overthinking this," she said. "Just make sure your motives are in the right place."

His motives? He chewed on this for a moment and knew Mindy was using female double-speak. "Just tell me what you really mean to say," he said.

He heard her exhale, the breath rattling through the phone. "It can be really easy to do the Mormon thing for another person," Mindy said. "If Lucy wasn't around, what choices would you be making right now?"

Emerson stilled and gripped the phone. Mindy never minced words. She was always really good about telling him the truth and giving out advice. Often, it was hard to hear. And right now, Emerson didn't want to think about the direction this trip would have taken if he hadn't met Lucy. A shudder ran through his body. If Lucy wasn't here, would he still not want to drink? Would hot chocolate and hand holding be enough? Would he not miss his old, easy habits? But more importantly, was he doing this all because of Lucy? When he went back to Georgia in a few days, would he still feel this strong and determined?

"I know this isn't what you want to hear," Mindy continued, "but you still need to figure out the Church thing. And on your own. Don't makes changes for a girl. She won't be enough in the long run."

Emerson made a noncommittal noise. He knew she was right.

"Really, Emerson. What do you want?" she asked.

The question hung in the air, heavy and palpable. What *did* he want? His head spun with the millions of things he wanted, all of them seeming equally impossible. He wanted his mom back, or at the very least, he wanted closure. He wanted a guiding light. He wanted a less itinerant lifestyle. He wanted to repair the strained relationship with his father. He wanted someone to come home to at the end of the day.

This thought struck him. He had never pictured himself married. For the most part, he liked being unattached and able to seize whatever moment was thrown his way. His mother's death was causing him to reexamine everything, and he suddenly thought a wife and a family might fill the gap his mother had left.

He closed his eyes and tried to imagine what his life might be like in five years if he continued on his new path, one in the Church. He pictured a house with a pitched roof and flower beds. He wouldn't fly international flights anymore. And he'd have a wife and child who would be excited to see him when he came home from work. He tried to imagine his wife, what she would look like and how she would be. He wanted someone kind and careful, someone with enough faith for both of them in case his doubts returned, someone he felt he could anchor himself to.

He couldn't stop the next thought from coming: he wanted to marry someone like Lucy Kappal.

"I want a different life," he told Mindy. "I want everything to be different."

* * *

If Ellie and Charlotte hadn't pounced on her the second she'd entered the room, Lucy would have leaned against the door and clutched her hands to her chest, her heart feeling lovesick and her body tingling. Instead, Charlotte pulled her over to the bed and pushed on her shoulders so she'd sit. The two girls hovered around her, shooting off questions. "What happened today?" "Where did you go?" "What are you doing with Emerson?" "Did he kiss you?"

The last question came from Ellie, her brow quizzical. Lucy flushed, and her heart clenched. "No, he didn't kiss me," she answered, sounding outraged at the suggestion.

Charlotte sat in front of Lucy, and Ellie crossed her arms over her chest, looming nearby. "What happened today?" Charlotte asked. "You said you lost your cell phone?"

Lucy sighed. "My purse got stolen."

Charlotte gasped. "Are you okay?" she asked.

"I ran into Emerson shortly after it happened, and he helped me," Lucy replied.

"What a blessing." Charlotte said.

"And he spent the rest of the day with me," Lucy said with a shrug to mask her delight. Being with Emerson felt so exhilarating. It was both comfortable and delicious. She wished she could feel this excited about seeing Charles.

"Did he go to your chocolate tasting?" Ellie asked.

"He did," Lucy answered, trying to keep her face neutral, but she felt a smile breaking through. "Which reminds me," she said, standing up. "My boss needs my notes from the tasting."

Lucy fished her iPad from her suitcase. Charlotte and Ellie went about their evening routine to get ready for bed. Lucy typed up her notes from the tasting and sent the email off to Tanya. She already had an idea for a flavor. The lavender milk chocolate had been interesting, and it might appeal to the foodie demographic a potential client was wanting to tap into.

Then Lucy joined Ellie at the sink, Ellie's nighttime regimen seeming endless. She was rubbing some green goop into her cheeks. Lucy grabbed her toothbrush. "I assume you'll spend tomorrow with Emerson too?" Ellie said.

"Actually, we're going to Kensington Gardens." Lucy stuck her toothbrush in her mouth.

In the mirror's reflection, she saw Charlotte sit up in bed. "Can I go?"

"It's supposed to be just a me-and-Emerson thing."

"It's a big place," Charlotte said. "We'll stay out of your way. You won't even know we're there."

Lucy couldn't say no to that logic, but she didn't want Emerson thinking she'd invited the girls to intrude on what was supposed to be a private experience. She turned away from the bathroom mirror to see both girls. "Okay, only if you promise to give us space."

"It's not like you could stop us," Ellie said. "It's a public park."

Luckily, adult Lucy was running the show right now, so she didn't stick her tongue out at Ellie like she wanted.

"Are you sure you should be spending so much time with Emerson?" Charlotte asked. "What about Charles?"

Lucy shrugged. What about Charles? She didn't know.

Chapter 14

EMERSON CARRIED HIS MOTHER'S ASHES in a small metal box wrapped in a red scarf. It was made of silk and slipped against the smooth exterior of the box, making him feel like it would fall from his hands. Or maybe it was because his hands shook. He stood outside the door of Lucy's room, trying to draw out the courage to knock.

He was a woven ball of emotions, some good, some bad, and some just hard. Today he'd lay the last piece of his mother to rest. Today was his last day with Lucy. Tomorrow he went back to his regular life, with long flight plans and an empty condo to return home to at the end of the day. He knew it was foolhardy to pursue a romantic relationship with Lucy, but he couldn't imagine her not being a part of his life anymore.

He knocked on the door of her room, and she soon answered, greeting him with a bright smile that caused his heart to crack a little more. "The girls have invited themselves along," she said in a low voice. "I'm really sorry. But they promised to leave us alone." She ushered him into the room. "I think I need a few more minutes. Have a seat."

Emerson took a seat by the window and observed the activities of the women. Ellie stood at the vanity, brushing her hair. Charlotte searched through her suitcase for something. Lucy sat on the edge of the bed, putting on a pair of heels. The white knee-length summer dress made her look soft and feminine. Her hair fell over her shoulders and down her back in curls. Her eyelashes looked dark and long, and her mouth was painted pink. He felt his heart constrict, and he gripped the box of ashes tighter, hoping to displace the ache.

"Is everyone ready?" Lucy asked as she stood and smoothed down the front of her dress. Ellie and Charlotte made sounds of affirmation and headed for the door. Emerson stood slowly as Lucy approached him. She was almost eye-level with him in her heels. She reached out and brushed the shoulder of his sports coat, her touch sending his stomach into a free fall. "You look handsome," she said. "I'm sure your mother would be very pleased."

He glanced down at his outfit, a pale-blue button-down shirt and a charcoal sports coat. He wore slacks and a pair of black Chucks. His mother always hated these shoes, and he imagined her shaking her head and tutting, all the while smiling. Lucy offered her hand, and Emerson slipped his fingers through hers. He clutched the red-wrapped box to his side. He could do this. With Lucy, he could do anything.

* * *

Emerson felt hot and uncomfortable in his jacket. The day was uncommonly warm and cloudless, the sky blue and the sun radiant. Emerson and Lucy walked through the garden paths, their hands connected, their steps slow.

"Where did she want her ashes?" Lucy asked, her gray eyes picking up the blue of the sky. The color looked like rain clouds.

"There's a little grove near the statue of Peter Pan." He pointed down the path. Up ahead, he could make out Ellie and Charlotte. The two left the path and wandered into a rose garden.

The box of ashes grew heavier with each step Emerson took in the direction of its final resting place. This burial had gone on too long—spanning ten months and two continents. His mother hadn't wanted to be forgotten. She'd wanted tiny pieces of her left everywhere. She didn't believe that there was anything after death, and the request to have her ashes strewn so many different places forced her memory to remain vital and alive inside Emerson. After this final burial, the pressure of the task would be gone, and perhaps Emerson would find the closure he'd been seeking. But would moving on betray the memory of her?

When they reached the statue of Peter Pan, Lucy let go of his hand and moved toward the sculpture. She examined it from all angles, circling the flying boy, her head cocked to the side in contemplation. She reached out with a tentative finger and touched one of the bronze rabbits sculpted into the thick base of the statue. Lucy's curiosity and admiration endeared her further to Emerson. She peered up at him with an unguarded expression. He couldn't believe how lovely she looked.

He approached her, a mix of emotions competing in his chest. He felt sad and heavy and a little guilty for finding Lucy attractive at a time like this. But also deep gratitude that she had come, that he didn't have to say goodbye to his mother alone.

"Are you ready?" she asked as she held out her hand to him. He nodded his head. Warmth traveled up his arm as their hands connected and she followed him into the nearby grove of trees. The air cooled significantly in the shade. They were surrounded by hundreds of blue flowers.

Emerson took a deep breath and felt his eyes sting with tears. He unwrapped the tin box and handed the red scarf to Lucy, and she took it and ran it through her hands.

"It's very beautiful," she said.

"My mom wore it on the first day of school for as long as I can remember," Emerson replied. An image of his mother popped into his head. She often wore reds and browns and heeled boots. Her smart-looking glasses were tortoise-shell frames. She allowed her curls to be untamed around her face. Her smile was most often an ironic one.

Emerson popped the lid off the box. Less than a handful of ashes still remained. The rest had been scattered at Lake Michigan, the Philosopher's Camp, Walden Pond, and her parents' grave.

Lucy peeked inside and then looked up at Emerson. "Do you want to say a few words first?" she asked.

Emotion caught in his throat before he even opened his mouth to speak. An oppressive sorrow settled in his chest, pressing the air out of his lungs.

She reached out and stepped closer to him, touching his arm in a light, reassuring gesture. "Remember, Emerson," she said. "This isn't the end."

Emerson released the ashes. The small dark particles drifted to the ground like snowflakes. How strange that her body could have fit into such a small box. And how strange that she was now finally gone, her remnants in the air and trees and dirt below. Did this really not have to be the end? Did she live on in more than just his memory? Could believing really be as simple as making the choice to do so?

A hoarse sob broke through his chest, and his shoulder's shook as he tried to hold back more. It hurt so much. He caught a glimpse of Lucy, her eyes filled with tears. She took the tin box from him, set it at his feet, and pulled him into her arms. She didn't say anything, just held him tight like she was afraid he'd collapse if she let go. He probably would.

He buried his face in her shoulder and let himself be weak. Her embrace invited it, and he cried like he did when he was alone. Like he had in the time between his mother's last breath and the arrival of the ambulance. The kind of tears that left him sadder and more exhausted than before. But this time someone was there. Lucy was there, touching his hair and rubbing his back, telling him it was okay to feel this way.

And sooner than he thought possible, the tears subsided. The crushing ache in his heart let up. He took in slow, deep breaths. The smell of lavender and vanilla filled his nose. He noticed the soft pressure of Lucy's body against his, and her hair tickled his face. He pulled back so he could see her face. Her cheeks were tear-streaked, and he traced the line with a slow finger.

Lucky. He felt so lucky to have Lucy in his life, even if it was only for this tiny moment. The warmth that he felt whenever he was with her returned to his chest, pushing back the ache until it was a dull throb, thumping with his heartbeat. He looked into her storm-cloud eyes and ran a finger gently across her bottom lip. "My mom always said you needed only two things in life," he uttered. "And if you have them, everything else will fall into place."

Lucy's eyes stayed fixed on his. Her fingers gripped the lapels of his jacket. "What are they?" she asked. Something built up inside Emerson that he didn't want to control anymore.

"Courage and love," he replied and kissed her.

* * *

The kiss tasted blue, like the cornflowers around her and the smell of his cologne and the wetness of their tears. His hands on her cheeks held her in place as the kiss deepened. She tightened her grip on his jacket to steady herself on her weakening knees. Lucy could have lived and died in that kiss.

Like an echo, she heard her name being called. "*Lucy!*"

She felt the spell and connection with Emerson fading as the familiar voice pulled her out. She heard her name again, this time closer. Lucy ended the kiss and turned her head toward the caller. Charlotte stood among the blue flowers, her face ashen and her mouth open.

"Lucy, how could you?" Charlotte asked before turning and disappearing into the trees.

Lucy looked up at Emerson, his face reflecting her own bewilderment. Her fists clung to his jacket. His hands moved slowly from her face. She imagined what this looked like to Charlotte.

"I should go talk to her," Lucy said. She slipped away from Emerson, not wanting to look back. She wasn't sure if looking back meant she'd never leave or never return. She could still taste blue on her lips.

She caught up to Charlotte a few yards down the path from the Peter Pan statue. Lucy stepped in front of her since calling her name did nothing to slow her down. Charlotte crossed her arms over her chest, the hurt evident on her face. Lucy drew her eyebrows together, puzzled at Charlotte's visceral reaction. Kissing someone wasn't that big a deal, was it? Lucy didn't even know what to say.

"What were you thinking?" Charlotte asked.

Lucy gaped, staring at Charlotte's smooth, young face. She looked airbrushed. Everything was black and white for Charlotte. How could Lucy begin to explain how complicated things were with Emerson and how strongly she was beginning to feel for him in such a short time?

"How could you kiss Emerson?" Charlotte demanded.

Lucy recalled how beautiful and sorrowful he'd looked, like an imperfect hero on a long journey. Her heart had broken for him and then swelled far beyond its size. And there had been so much blue around them. Eye-blurring blue. It was like a fairy tale, so different from how her life had been up to that point that she would have done any reckless thing in that moment. How could she have kissed him? "He looked like something out of a book," Lucy finally said.

"Something out of a book?" Charlotte asked, frustrated. "Lucy, what about Charles?"

At the mention of his name, Lucy felt the blood draining from her face. She imagined her cheeks growing pale. Charles? Was this about Charles? Charles, who in Charlotte's mind, was Lucy's fiancé or, at the very least, boyfriend?

Guilt ebbed in the corners of Lucy's conscious. But why? She wasn't Charles' fiancée or girlfriend or anything else. She'd broken up with him weeks ago. He was the one who had proposed out of nowhere. Plus, she hadn't given him an answer, and twenty-four hours later, she'd put an ocean and a continent between them. That should have been answer enough and a final end of things. But Lucy couldn't deny the guilt she felt now or in certain moments with Emerson over the past two days. Did the guilt mean she was still harboring feelings for Charles? Or was it because part of her still felt like things weren't completely finished between them?

"Charlotte, I broke up with Charles," Lucy said, sounding sure, much more so than she felt. "Emerson is a kind, attractive, *single* man. I am allowed to kiss him if I want."

"But Charles wants to marry you," Charlotte replied. "Charles, who you've dated for over a year. Charles, who can take you to the temple and provide you with the type of life you want. You can't seriously be willing to throw that away because you met some hot guy while on vacation, can you? You have no future with Emerson. And Charles is at home waiting for your answer."

Lucy felt sick to her stomach. The adrenaline from the kiss had tanked, and a heavy weakness was settling in her limbs. She wanted to collapse. Could sweet, naive Charlotte be right? Was Lucy really going to say no to Charles for good when she got back? Could she maintain a long-distance relationship with Emerson? Would he figure out the Church stuff and be able to take her to the temple if their relationship even went that far? That was ultimately what she wanted, a temple marriage. And that was what Charles offered.

Lucy turned her face upward, the sky golden as the sun moved down the horizon. "Charlotte, it's complicated." In the distance, coming down the path, she saw Ellie, and behind her, Emerson. Lucy's heart started to pound. She grabbed Charlotte by the shoulders and leveled her gaze. "Don't say a thing to Ellie about what you saw," Lucy ordered. "This is my business. I don't want her opinion. I don't want her tainting this."

Charlotte gulped and nodded her head.

"What's with the death grip, Lucy?" Ellie asked as she joined them.

Lucy released Charlotte's shoulder. "Just giving Charlotte some serious life advice," Lucy replied.

Ellie eyed them suspiciously.

Emerson reached them before she could say anything else. "Is everything okay?" he asked, looking solely at Lucy.

She wanted to grab onto his jacket again and never let go. Instead, she nodded her head yes.

Chapter 15

THE WALK BACK TO THE hotel after dinner was slow. Lucy dragged her feet, and Emerson seemed to be doing the same. She watched as Ellie and Charlotte disappeared down the street, and then she slipped her hand into his. Electricity moved through her fingers and up her arm at the contact. She thought of their kiss, how beautiful and powerful it had felt. So unlike any of her kisses with Charles.

Dinner had been enjoyable, with Ellie and Charlotte talking nonstop as usual. It wasn't the romantic last meal she'd imagined having with Emerson, but maybe it was better that way. Maybe it was best if they parted as friends—friends who'd shared one incredible kiss. A vacation fling. A happy memory.

Emerson squeezed her hand, and she glanced over at him, feeling overwhelmed that this amazing man liked her. But did he actually like her? Had he kissed her only because he'd felt sad and needed physical comfort? Wasn't she trying to convince herself it was better that they be just friends?

"Penny for your thoughts?" he asked.

Lucy sighed, and like the sound was a cue, it started to rain. Big, cold London drops of rain. Lucy shrieked, and hand in hand, they ran the remaining block back to the hotel. They stumbled into the lobby. A bellboy greeted them with towels, and Lucy and Emerson headed to the elevator. He smiled at her, big and boyish, as he pushed the call button. Lucy wrapped the towel around her shoulders in case the rain had made her white dress see-through.

In a panic, she realized the rain had cut short the few minutes she'd had left with Emerson. Everything between them still felt incomplete. A tenuousness hung between them. They stepped into the elevator and began the short ascent to their rooms.

"When do you leave tomorrow?" Lucy asked. It felt like something precious was slipping through her fingers.

"I have to be at the airport at 9:00 a.m.," he said, his face giving nothing away. He stared down at the tin box in his hand, the red scarf sopping wet. "I need to get eight hours of sleep tonight before I fly," he added.

They were already to the third floor. Lucy was running out of time. "What happens after you go?" she asked, a quiver in her voice. His caramel eyes locked on her gray ones. There was so much vulnerability in his face that Lucy almost lost her balance.

"Let's meet for breakfast tomorrow," he said. "Early, without Ellie and Charlotte. We'll make a plan."

Lucy nodded her head and broke contact with his intense stare. She looked over his shoulder and noticed the mirrors on the walls. They reflected an infinite number of Emersons and an infinite number of Lucys. He looked young with his wet hair plastered to his forehead. And Lucy wore white, like a bride. The mirrors reminded her of those in the sealing room of the temple, the two mirrors facing each other that repeated the newly married couple an infinite number of times.

Lucy wondered if this moment was the closest she would get to an eternity with Emerson.

* * *

They reached the seventh floor and stepped off the elevator. Emerson took Lucy's hand again as they walked down the hall to her room. His heart beat erratically. He still had maybe an hour with her tomorrow morning, but it felt like this was it. He'd never met anyone like her before, and he knew he didn't want to say goodbye to her permanently. But she'd been acting differently since their kiss. She'd become quiet and a little distant. She was thinking hard about something, and he was afraid it was him. *Don't overthink this*, he wanted to tell her. *Let's see where it goes.*

They stopped at her door. Lucy held the white towel around her shoulders, with one hand bunching it at her neck. She looked like a sopping-wet child, white and pure. She searched his face, the scrutiny making him feel vulnerable and transparent. What did she really see?

"Emerson." She said his name slowly, and goose bumps broke out over his rain-chilled skin. "Did you kiss me because you were sad?"

A strange feeling of relief washed through him. Was this what she'd been thinking about all evening? "No, I didn't kiss you because I was sad." He took a small step closer. "I kissed you because I finally got brave enough." She grabbed his shirt and pulled him the rest of the way to her.

Their lips connected, and the kiss felt reckless, like Lucy had given up on something.

"In case I never get another one," she whispered as their lips parted. This was a goodbye kiss, and it had ended far sooner than Emerson had wanted.

She stepped away from him, and her back hit the door. "See you tomorrow morning?" she asked. "Will 6:00 a.m. give us enough time?"

He wanted more time with her, but it wasn't possible at this point. He shoved his hands in his pockets so she wouldn't see that he shook. "Meet you in the lobby?" he said.

"In the lobby," she replied. She met his eyes, and the look was bittersweet. "Good night, Emerson."

He felt a crack forming in the chambers of his heart. "Good night."

Lucy stepped into her room. Emerson let out the breath he was holding and went back to his room. Once there, he removed his wet clothes and changed into dry ones for bed. As he grabbed his toothbrush, he heard a knock at the door. His heart kicked into high gear. It had to be Lucy. But why would she be coming to his room? She was proper. She had standards. Emerson was afraid he wouldn't stop her from coming in.

He opened the door a crack with the chain lock still intact. He frowned when he saw who it was.

"Charlotte?"

She looked small and angry, with her arms folded tightly across her chest. "I'd like a word with you, Emerson," she said. "Can I come in?"

"Yeah. Sure." He closed the door, undid the chain, and reopened the door. Charlotte stepped into his room with tentative steps. He closed the door behind her and gestured for her to have a seat. She shook her head and remained by the door.

"What can I do for you, Charlotte?" he asked, growing more and more puzzled by her visit.

She unfolded her arms. "I don't know what your intentions are with Lucy, but I suggest you stop."

Oh. Of course. The kiss Charlotte interrupted.

An amused smile crept onto his lips, doing nothing for his ethos. "I'm afraid you're only seeing half of the picture," he said.

"No, Emerson. *You're* only seeing half the picture. I don't know what story Lucy told you, but before she left for London, her boyfriend proposed."

A cold lump formed in his throat. Her boyfriend? "Lucy said she broke up with someone a few weeks ago . . ." Emerson started.

"Lucy has cold feet," Charlotte said. "She's just getting one more fling out of her system before she gets married." She crossed her arms over her chest again, and Emerson could tell she was trembling. He felt pretty shaken up himself.

This didn't make any sense to Emerson. Was Lucy really engaged? Had she lied to him about her relationship status? Was this really just a fling to her? He remembered one of the first things she'd said to him. She'd sarcastically proposed they have a week-long fling. And the first few times they had interacted, she'd seemed so guarded. He had initially suspected she had a boyfriend but had dismissed that theory once she'd seemed to warm up to him. And at dinner last night, she had admitted she'd just gotten out of a serious relationship.

Charlotte slumped her shoulders and creased her brow. She looked so upset it was hard for Emerson to believe she was lying. But he didn't think Lucy had lied to him either. So what was Charlotte's motivation for telling him this?

He ran a hand through his hair and exhaled. "Charlotte, I appreciate your concern, but this is really between Lucy and me."

"Fine," Charlotte said. "But you seriously had no business kissing Lucy." She spun on her heel and left his room with an air of self-righteousness. He put out his Do Not Disturb sign and chained the door.

As he went through the routine of getting ready for bed, he tried to shake off the weird encounter, but he became more and more agitated. He stared at himself in the bathroom mirror, something he rarely did. He assessed himself, taking in the color of his eyes, the line of his jaw, the shape of his mouth. He stared until he didn't recognize himself anymore, like saying a word over and over again until it lost all its meaning. His face simply became shapes and features. When he blinked and opened his eyes again, he saw a stranger.

Familiar loneliness crept in. He thought of Lucy and how good she was at making him feel secure. How reassuring her presence felt. How uncomfortable he was with the thought of never seeing her again.

How Charlotte's implications muddled things.

He didn't have time to think this over, to call Lucy to get her version of the story. He needed to get to sleep so he could fly tomorrow morning.

He sat on the edge of his bed and took a few deep breaths. Charlotte's words came unbidden into his mind. *She's just getting one more fling out of her system before she gets married.* Could this really have been a fling for her? It felt so real to him. So important. So much like fate . . . or God.

He was overwhelmed with the sudden need to pray; it almost knocked him to the ground. He knelt by the side of the bed and allowed his mind to race with all the things in his head: The final burial. His doubts. His gratitude. His anger. And what to do about Lucy.

* * *

The phone rang. Emerson roused from sleep, and it took him a minute to realize where he was. The bedside light was still on. His knees were folded beneath him. He'd fallen asleep praying. His phone went off again. The clock on the bedside table read 4:50 a.m. Had he really fallen asleep praying? And stayed in that position most of the night?

He grabbed his phone. It was work. "Hello?" His voice held the distinct sound of sleep.

"Emerson, are you sober?"

"Yeah," he replied. It was the flight scheduler.

"When was the last time you had a drink?"

"Um . . . three months ago." Emerson blinked his eyes, trying to wake up. Why was his flight manager calling this early to ask about his alcohol consumption?

"Really?" she asked. Emerson blinked some more. She continued speaking when he didn't say anything. "What time did you get to bed?"

That was a harder question to answer. He wasn't sure when he'd fallen asleep. "About eight thirty," he guessed. Emerson tried to stand and winced as his stiff knees unbent. He sat on the bed and worked his legs, trying to move the soreness out.

"I need to change your flight plan," his manager said. "Do you think you can be to the airport by six thirty this morning?"

He'd have to leave the hotel in less than an hour if he was to make it to the airport by then. That would mean no breakfast with Lucy. Emerson exhaled long and slow. "What's going on?" he asked his flight manager. "Why the last-minute change?"

"Two pilots have called in sick this morning. Everyone I've contacted so far isn't sober or hasn't had enough sleep to take the flight."

Emerson rubbed his hand over his face. He really didn't feel like he could say no. He was still fairly new with the company and saying yes to everything was how someone made it up the ranks. As much as he wanted to see Lucy, he also had this weird feeling brewing in his chest, a feeling that was pushing him to take this new flight. Suddenly, Mindy's words echoed in his head. *Don't do the church thing for a girl. You've got to figure this out on your own. What do you want, Emerson?*

"Okay," he said, his heart slamming. "I'll take the flight."

"Great," his manager replied. "I'll update your schedule with the details."

Emerson hung up and clasped the phone tightly in his hand. What was he going to do about Lucy? He thought about his prayer last night—how he'd asked for direction. Maybe this was his answer. As serendipitous as Lucy's entrance into his life was, perhaps her exit would be just as fated.

He thought again of his conversation with Mindy. He couldn't do the Church thing for Lucy. He needed to figure out what he really wanted. And if Lucy was in his life, he was afraid he wouldn't ever be objective. Plus, Charlotte said Lucy was engaged. Whether that was true or not, having Lucy in his life long-term might not even be a possibility.

The weird feeling in his chest expanded further. This realization didn't hurt as much as he'd anticipated. It stung, but he felt like this was what was supposed to happen. He felt like something much bigger than himself was making decisions, and he wasn't going to fight it. He was going to find comfort in it.

* * *

At five thirty, he stood outside Lucy's hotel room door. In his hand, he held his parting gifts. He knocked on the door, wincing, afraid he'd wake up Charlotte and Ellie. After a few long moments—moments in which his heart rate doubled—he heard the sound of the lock sliding out of its place and the door opening. Ellie stood in the doorway, wearing pajamas and looking bleary-eyed.

"Emerson?"

"Is Lucy awake?"

Ellie glanced behind her, then back at Emerson. "She's in the shower."

He bit his lip to keep from swearing.

"Are you leaving?" Ellie asked. "I thought you were supposed to meet Lucy for breakfast."

"My flight plan changed." He shifted his weight from one foot to the other. He was hoping to at least see Lucy for a few minutes, to give a preface to the letter he'd spent the past hour writing. "Can you give these things to Lucy?" He handed two envelopes over to Ellie. "I don't have time to wait."

Ellie nodded. "Yeah, sure." She took them and held them gingerly in her hands.

Emerson took a step back, feeling an ache growing in his chest. "Don't worry about moving back to your room. I've paid the difference through the rest of your stay."

"Thanks," Ellie said.

He took a deep breath and moved to leave.

"Hey, Emerson?" He stilled and turned back around. Ellie stepped into the hall, and the door shut behind her. "Sorry about the coffee thing the other morning. I don't know why I do stuff like that."

"Don't worry about it," he replied.

Ellie looked down, and her facade crumbled. "I think we're probably going through a lot of the same things right now," she said, glancing up, her eyes clear and surprisingly vulnerable. "Mind if I steal your number off Charlotte's phone and call you sometime? I think we can help each other."

He wanted to be annoyed with her, but the look in her eyes made him believe she was sincere. She needed someone to talk to, and for some reason, she wanted it to be Emerson.

"Yeah, sure, Ellie. That's fine."

She squared her shoulders and tipped her chin up. Her cool veneer returned. "Don't crash the plane." And she disappeared back into her room.

Emerson swallowed the lump forming in his throat as he stared at the closed door. This was it. This was the end to a marvelous, brief affair. He placed his pilot's hat on his head, grabbed the handle of his suitcase, and left, each step a small fracture in his heart.

Chapter 16

LUCY EMERGED FROM THE BATHROOM, wrapped in a thick white robe, compliments of the hotel. She'd thought all night about what she would say today, what her plan with Emerson would be. She wanted to know him better. She didn't want to say goodbye. She felt willing to sacrifice a future with Charles for a little bit more time with Emerson to see if they could work. The year plus with Charles had proven they didn't need to be together. There wasn't the same urgency to be with him that she felt with Emerson. Lucy owed it to herself to see where this could go.

Ellie joined her at the vanity, her face ashen without all the makeup. "Emerson stopped by."

"What?" Lucy stopped toweling her hair and stared at Ellie.

"His flight plan changed. He asked me to give these to you."

Lucy looked at the two envelopes Ellie held out for her. Her pulse jumped in her throat. "How long ago did he come by? Why didn't you come get me?"

"It was about ten minutes ago." Ellie shook her head. "He was in a big hurry and said he didn't have time to wait."

Lucy felt her legs weakening. She dropped the towel on the vanity and took the two envelopes from Ellie. She couldn't take the sound of the blood rushing in her ears, the feeling of dread spreading through her. She made her way over to the chair by the window.

She didn't want her fingers to tremble, but they shook as she examined the envelopes. They were from the hotel's stationery—thick, beige, marbled paper with the hotel's emblem embossed on the envelope's lip. They were numbered one and two. Envelope two was thicker than the first but still light as air. The paper gave into a softness beneath when Lucy squeezed the envelope in her fingers.

She opened the first envelope, sliding her finger along the crease at the top. The ripping of the paper mirrored what she felt was going on inside her. Her still-shaking hands unfolded the letter, and she held it for just a moment before reading the words.

Dear Lucy,

I'm sorry we weren't able to have a last morning together like we hoped. I was looking forward to eating fake scrambled eggs with you and coming up with a way to stay in each other's lives. Because that is what I want very much, Lucy—to stay in your life.

I know I risk sounding dramatic, but I feel like meeting you has changed my life. In January, I returned to the Church as a final effort to find peace after my mother's death. I started living the Church's standards, trying to reintegrate myself back into a religion and culture I had left fifteen years before. I didn't really know what I was looking for or what I expected to happen. I was just going through the motions, waiting for something to click, for it to start feeling like it was really me and not just some act I was putting on. Because of you, I felt that click. That day in the coffee shop, when you gave me your two-minute pitch for the gospel, something settled inside me that had been out of place. I felt like something quiet but significant had happened. And I started thinking maybe everything could be different. Maybe I could be different. Maybe my life could be different. Maybe I could be with you.

But I feel like I have to stop myself. It is my life and your life I have to consider. I have this crazy feeling I would do anything for you. But I don't want to do this for you. I want to do this for me. I have to figure out the Church thing on my own, without the possibility of you. And I suspect you also have some things you need to figure out too.

So this is where I have to leave us. I will forever be grateful to have met you, for the strange circumstances that brought us together and kept pushing us toward each other. I will never forget your influence. And maybe one day I'll be your pilot again and we'll see where we've ended up. I hope we're both happy there.

Forever,

Emerson James

P.S. Open the second envelope. I know it won't replace your father's hand-kerchief, but maybe it can become something meaningful to you.

Lucy tore open the other envelope as a million different emotions competed for attention inside her. Beneath the paper, she saw red and felt the slight stickiness of real silk under her fingers. It was his mother's scarf, Lucy realized as she pulled it from the envelope. The scarf his mother had worn the first day of class every year. The scarf he had wrapped around her ashes.

Lucy felt her heart crumbling, imploding. A deep pain ran down her breastbone, knocking the air out of her. As she struggled to take in a breath, she realized she loved Emerson. A crushing sob escaped her lips, and she knotted the red scarf through her fingers. She loved him. And maybe he loved her too. *Because that is what I want very much, Lucy—to stay in your life . . . But I feel like I have to stop myself.*

Lucy watched as her tears fell onto the scarf, leaving crimson specks. She felt Ellie and Charlotte surround her in a tight embrace. They said the things people say in situations like this: "I'm so sorry." "He doesn't know what he's giving up." "I can't believe he left like that." "At least you still have Charles."

The last comment came from Charlotte. Lucy's eyes flew up to her face.

Charlotte looked young and earnest. She touched Lucy's wet hair. "You can still have Charles," she said again.

Lucy shook her head and felt a fire ignite in her chest. She tried to breathe slowly and deeply. She didn't want Charles. Hadn't coming to London proven that? She clenched her fists until her nails dug into her palms. She reread the letter, hoping she had misunderstood Emerson. Did he really want her out of his life for good?

So this is where I have to leave us . . . maybe one day I'll be your pilot again and we'll see where we've ended up. I hope we're both happy there.

He wasn't asking her to wait. He wasn't saying, "Call me in six months, and we'll pick this back up." He was saying goodbye and leaving any reunion up to chance.

Lucy wiped her eyes with the palm of her hands, and she felt the horrible crack of her heart as it crumbled. Slowly, she folded the letter and slid it back into its envelope. Her fate felt final. Emerson was gone, and in four days, she'd be back in Salt Lake. What would her happily ever after look like now?

PART TWO

End of August
Salt Lake City

Chapter 17

FIVE MONTHS AGO, LUCY WOULD have been on Emerson alert as she walked through the Salt Lake airport. But as she pulled her rolling suitcase behind her today, the only thing on her mind was Charles. The dairy commodities convention in Philadelphia had been only four days long, but Lucy had missed her new fiancé with an intensity that surprised her.

After London, she had wanted to move on. She had tried to live her life without Emerson and without the possibility of him. He'd wanted her cut from his life, so she needed to cut him from hers too. It had been hard at first. She had thought of him often and had looked for him in airports whenever she had traveled for work, which was becoming more and more frequent. She had tied his mother's scarf to her purse, and the silky token had become a constant reminder that he was somewhere in this world without her.

Instead of continuing to torture herself by wondering about him, in May, on the anniversary of his mother's death, Lucy found Emerson on Facebook. In London, they never exchanged contact information, and Charlotte, whom Lucy had called from Emerson's phone after the mugging, was never going to give up his number. Lucy wanted Emerson to know she was thinking about him on a day that would be hard for him. It was the sight of his profile picture that had broken her again—he stood shirtless, a beer in one hand and his arm around a buxom blonde. He wore sunglasses and a backward baseball cap. The scene was beachy and blue. Emerson looked happy. With a lump in her throat and a roaring pain in her chest, Lucy had clicked on the photo. The caption read "Livin' easy in Belize."

It hurt her to see him like that. The picture was two years old, but it was snapshot of who Emerson could be if he hadn't figured out his feelings for the Church. While he would still be the kind, caring man she'd met in London, he wouldn't be able to give her what she wanted most: a temple marriage and a forever family. She realized she shouldn't count on him. She couldn't. He didn't want her to. So she'd cried over him one last time and had really opened her heart to Charles, someone who could give her everything she'd ever wanted. He had proposed a week ago, and she had said yes, throwing her arms around him after he'd slipped the heavy ring on her finger.

Lucy's skin chilled as she walked through the airport. When she reached the junction, she situated herself on an escalator to go to baggage claim. Knowing Charles, he'd probably been sitting in the park-and-wait lot before her flight had even landed. She'd call him after she got her luggage.

A crowd of people at the bottom of the escalator waited with balloons and flowers and signs that read "Welcome Home, Sister Allred." Lucy smiled and remembered her own mission homecoming at the airport. She'd felt so excited and sure of her future. She almost felt that way now.

She pushed through the crowd of welcomers, muttering "Excuse me" every few feet. When she finally broke through the large group and pulled her suitcase out of the masses, she looked up, and a small niggle of happiness zoomed through her. She stifled a laugh with a hand over her mouth and moved toward Charles.

He stood with a small sign that read "Welcome Home, Lucy" and a bouquet of pink daisies. She let go of her carry-on and took the last few steps to him without it, then fell into his arms, exhausted from traveling. He smelled of the essential oils he wore in place of cologne, a woody aroma of spruce and frankincense. His return hug was awkward because he still held the sign and flowers, both of which pressed her from behind. She pulled away. He wasn't much taller than her, and she could see right into his clear blue eyes. She gave him a kiss on the lips, one long enough that it required her to pull him closer. She'd been gone only a few days, but gosh, it felt good to be home.

His cheeks instantly turned ruddy as the kiss ended. "*Lucy*," he said, moving the daisies to the crook of his elbow and adjusting his glasses with his freed hand. "You know how I feel about public displays of affection."

She grinned. Part of her loved how embarrassed he got, which was why she did it. She didn't respond to his statement. "Are these for me?" she asked, gesturing to the flowers.

He adjusted his black-framed glasses again. "Why, yes, they are." He presented her the bunch.

Lucy smelled the flowers, and something like love bubbled through her. She thought about kissing him again and then decided against it. One PDA was about Charles's limit. "Thank you."

Hand in hand, they walked to the baggage claim. Her suitcases were the last ones, circling lonely on the carousel. She hefted the two bags off and set them at her feet. They had been filled with dry ice and ice cream on her flight back East for the conference but were now empty. She extended the pull handle on one of the bags and hooked the two together. Charles slipped his free arm around Lucy's shoulder, and they headed to the parking garage, where Charles's car waited.

"I'm glad you're home, my dear," Charles said, kissing her on the temple. Lucy leaned against him. "Me too."

* * *

Lucy lived at Windy Corner, a trendy apartment complex in Sugar House that used to be an old school. The exterior was brick and gothic, the grounds kept like a garden. The courtyard where Lucy imagined the children used to play had a pool, ramada, and sand volleyball court. Her apartment was in the building that used to house the elementary-level grades. The classrooms had been fully renovated and upgraded to create two-bedroom, one-bathroom apartments. Each included a full-sized kitchen with granite countertops, an induction stove, double ovens, and a large farmhouse sink. The kitchen was what sold Lucy, even though the rent was twice what she wanted to pay for an apartment.

Charles lived in his parents' house, which was across the street from Windy Corner, while they served as mission president in the Netherlands. His parents were due home around Christmas. Lucy and Charles would get married after the New Year and move down to Lehi, so they'd be halfway between each of their workplaces: Lucy in Salt Lake City and Charles in Provo at BYU. On top of wedding planning, they were also house hunting.

As they climbed the steps to her apartment, Lucy's apartment manager, Harry Otway, came down. "Oh, Lucy, excellent!" he said. "Just who I was hoping to see."

Lucy furrowed her brow. Had she forgotten to pay rent? Harry stopped on the step above her. He was famous in the ward for violating personal space. She got a noseful of his cologne and body odor. She felt Charles slip a possessive arm around her shoulder, and she held back a laugh. Like Lucy needed protection from Harry Otway.

"What can I do for you?" Lucy asked.

"Apartment 202B, you know the one?" Harry said. "It's two doors down and across the hall from yours."

Lucy nodded.

Charles sighed impatiently beside her.

"Well," Harry continued. "It's vacant. Do any of your friends need an apartment? I want the next tenants to be the right kind of people. You know, people who would enhance the ward and not detract from it. I have a feeling you'd know people like that." He gave Lucy a slow once-over. Lucy shuddered and moved the daisies from one hand to the other to hide her reaction.

Charles sighed again beside her. "Just be direct, Harry," he said. "You want to know if Lucy knows any single young ladies who are looking for a place to live. Preferably ones who don't know you yet."

Lucy thought she had grown accustomed to Charles's directness, but then he'd do something like that. Embarrassment and anger simmered over his being so rude. She at least had the manners to try to cover up when she was annoyed.

"Actually, my cousin might be looking for an apartment," Lucy offered, trying to offset Charles's blatant disrespect.

Harry's face grew hopeful.

Charles squinted at Lucy. "Do you mean Charlotte?" he asked.

Lucy nodded.

"Oh, Charlotte wouldn't be a good fit at all."

Lucy elbowed Charles in the ribs. "Do you have a business card I can pass along to her?" she asked Harry. "I'll be seeing her this weekend."

Harry pulled a card from the front pocket of his shirt, a smarmy smile on his face. "It's a two-bedroom with a max occupancy of five, so encourage her to fill it up with her friends."

Lucy took the card, then she and Charles made their exit.

"I don't understand how he gets away with it," Charles said once they were in the safety of her apartment. "Using his position as apartment manager to build himself a harem." He sat on her couch and crossed his legs.

Lucy sorted through the mail on the table by the door. Credit card offers, two birth announcements, and a wedding invitation. She set the mail back down.

"It's housing discrimination," Charles continued. "I don't want you telling Charlotte about the apartment."

Lucy picked up the two suitcases Charles had left by the door. "It won't do any harm to mention it to her," she said, retreating to her bedroom and setting the suitcases on her bed. She unzipped one and took out a small Styrofoam box. "Want some free conference swag?" she shouted to Charles.

He appeared in the doorway. "Always."

Lucy took a moment to drink him in: his graceful posture, his bright-blue eyes, the neatness of his short blond hair. He wore sports coats and slacks or suits with neat button-down shirts, like life was his lecture hall. He was probably one of the skinniest men she had ever met. Although it sometimes made her feel insecure, she couldn't help but admire his lithe-ness and the sure way his body moved.

"Let's see if this ice cream survived." Lucy pushed by Charles and went to the kitchen. After retrieving two clean spoons from the dish-washer, she set the box on the countertop. She pried the top off, and the cold steam of dry ice puffed into the air. Perfect.

Careful not to burn herself on the ice, Lucy extracted the small ice cream carton. She felt Charles come up behind her and slip his arms around her waist. "This is some of the best ice cream I've ever tasted," she said.

"Freddy's not home," he muttered, nuzzling into her neck. He spun her around and kissed her soundly. Sometimes he could be wonderfully affectionate.

"You keep kissing me like that and we'll have to elope," Lucy teased.

His cheeks turned red. He released her and cleared his throat. "You're right." He adjusted his glasses. "Forgive me."

Disappointment tightened in her chest. She didn't want the man she was going to marry to apologize for kissing her. She wanted him to kiss her again despite the risk and then share a carton of ice cream with her and then kiss her some more. She collected the spoons and the ice cream, and Charles followed her to the living room. They settled onto the couch.

"Tell me about this ice cream," Charles said as Lucy pried the top off the carton. Inside was a butter-colored ice cream swirled with caramel. Lucy handed him a spoon and kept one for herself.

"It's a *dulce de leche* ice cream from this tiny ice cream shop in New Jersey." Lucy dipped her spoon in and scooped out some of the creamy mixture. She angled the carton toward Charles, and he took a spoon-ful. Lucy flipped her spoon over and placed the ice cream right on her tongue. The coldness melted through, revealing a smooth, buttery cara-mel flavor with a rich sweetness. She watched as Charles stuck his spoon in his mouth like he was eating cereal. She held back her critique. How many times had she shown him the correct way to eat ice cream? His face appeared thoughtful as he slowly worked the ice cream in his mouth.

"That *is* very good," he said. "So the conference was productive, then?" He took another spoonful.

"It was amazing," Lucy said. She'd spent the last four days in Pennsylvania at a dairy commodities convention. Every day she'd had her fill of ice cream, cheese, yogurt, snacks dipped in sour cream, and butter-topped breads. She had probably gained ten pounds, but the convention was her favorite one of the year. It gave her a chance to network and meet potential clients and *eat*. "The owner of this shop is interested in getting his ice cream into some supermarkets in his town. I told him I could probably formulate his recipe for mass production." Lucy felt almost giddy at the prospect, but Charles only smiled politely. He didn't really understand her work or how someone could be passionate about something he didn't consider "art."

"Good for you, darling," he replied and took another spoonful of ice cream. They finished off the carton in silence over the next few minutes.

Lucy had to work in the morning, and the past four days and the travel were starting to catch up to her. She felt a heaviness settling in her legs and arms. After stifling a yawn, she glanced over at Charles, who had a far-off gaze in his eyes. He tended to look spaced out whenever he thought hard about something. Lucy often felt wary about bringing him back to the present, afraid she'd interrupt something almost brilliant. "Charles?" she finally said softly.

He blinked and turned his attention to her. His eyes softened as they focused on her face. "Yes, my love?"

She melted a little at the endearment. "What were you thinking about?"

"This whole thing about Charlotte moving in down the hall," he said, angling himself closer to Lucy. "I don't like it at all."

"She's not moving in down the hall," Lucy replied, feeling disappointed that he'd not been thinking about her or one of his poems or world hunger or the political divide or the origin of the Bible or one of the other big things he often thought about. Instead, he'd been thinking about Charlotte. "I just told Harry I'd pass the information about the apartment along to her. Anyway, I think she said she wanted to live at home her first year of medical school so she wouldn't have to worry about cooking for herself or doing laundry." Things had been tense between Charlotte and Lucy since London. Soon after arriving home, they'd had a falling out after Charlotte had admitted she had told Emerson that Lucy was engaged. Lucy didn't want to be angry anymore, especially now that she really was engaged to Charles. Maybe if she saw Charlotte more often, they could start to repair their relationship. But she didn't want to tell Charles this because then they would have to talk about London again.

"Do you really think we should subject Charlotte to the likes of Harry Otway?" Charles asked. "She's such a sweet, lovely young lady. You know she wouldn't have the grit to say no to a date with him."

"Why does everyone think they need to protect Charlotte?" Lucy asked, bristling. "Shouldn't we give her a chance to grow a backbone? She's going to be a doctor. Don't you think she'll see a lot of shocking things?"

Charles scoffed. "What a horrible profession for a woman."

Lucy's eyes widened, and anger like flames shot through her. "Excuse me?"

"Oh, you know I didn't mean it like that." He adjusted his glasses. Lucy crossed her arms over her chest and waited for him to explain. "What I meant is being a doctor would be a challenge to motherhood. It would make it harder to have and raise children."

Lucy could have argued with him, pointed out that many doctors in private practice worked only a few days a week and could create their own hours—that sounded pretty mother-friendly to her—but instead, she sighed. She wasn't in the mood for a fight. "I suppose it could be hard."

Charles looked at her like she was a young child. He tucked some loose hair behind her ear. "I don't like Harry Otway using you as his personal Match.com."

"If I tell Charlotte about the apartment, it will be because I think Windy Corner is a nice place to live, not because I want to do Harry a favor."

"Good." He pecked her softly on the lips. "Now, I'd better let you get some rest." He took Lucy's hand and pulled her to a stand with him. They walked to the front door together. "I won't see you tomorrow—I need to spend the day revising my manuscript—but I'll be at the party on Saturday."

"You better be," Lucy said. "It would be a strange engagement party if one of the *affianced* weren't there."

Charles pulled her into his arms, and Lucy settled into the familiar embrace—the light pressure of his hands, one on the small of her back and the other at her shoulder, the slow way their breathing synchronized, the stiffness of his collar against her cheek, the soft tickle of his breath in her ear. How glorious it was that he was here, that he wasn't just an idea or a memory. She pulled back so she could see him. "I love you, Charles."

He touched her cheek with a slender hand. "I love you too."

Chapter 18

"DID CHARLES ASK YOUR PERMISSION before he proposed?" Lucy heard her brother, Freddy, ask their mother. Lucy had left them in the kitchen preparing the food for the party while she oversaw the setting up of tables in the backyard with her uncle. She stopped in the hall before entering the kitchen and listened, even though she knew this wasn't a conversation she was supposed to hear.

"Which time?" her mother asked.

"The first time, I guess," Freddy replied.

"Yes, he asked my permission the first time," their mother replied. "And the second time too."

"He asked my permission too," Freddy said. "He told me he didn't know who to ask since Dad is dead, so he asked all of us."

"What did you tell him?" she asked. "I know you aren't fond of Charles."

Lucy felt a sharp stab in her chest at hearing this. She already knew it, but it killed her that her brother didn't approve of the man she was going to marry. But he had never said anything overt about his lack of fondness.

"The first time, I told Charles it didn't matter to me. Lucy could make her own decisions. The second time, Charles didn't really ask me for permission; he wanted to know if I was happy for him because he was sure Lucy would say yes this time."

"Well, did you tell Charles you were happy for him?"

"No, I didn't," Freddy said. "I told him I thought Lucy had given him the right answer the first time and to not be surprised if she jetted off to Timbuktu this time."

Anger and heavy resignation settled in Lucy's stomach. Her brother knew her better than anyone else, and if this is what he had expected of Lucy, then perhaps she'd made the wrong decision.

"Freddy!" their mother scolded. "I can't believe you said that."

"I couldn't help it!" Freddy said. "He shouldn't have asked me in first place. I didn't think it would stay a secret very long that I don't like Charles. I just didn't want him telling Lucy what I said."

And Charles hadn't. This was the first of any of this—Charles asking her mother's and brother's permission for her hand—that Lucy had heard. Doubt niggled its way into her heart. There were moments when she was so certain Charles was the right person for her. Like Thursday night in her apartment when he'd held her for a slow goodbye. It had felt so right and exquisite to be so cherished. But if Freddy didn't like Charles, what was she not seeing that he *could* see?

"I like him well enough," their mother said. "He's stable and dependable, and he loves Lucy deeply. That counts a lot in my book. He's also patient, and Lucy needs someone who will be patient with her."

Lucy wished she'd never heard any of this conversation. Served her right for eavesdropping. How could she enter the kitchen now? How could she attend this engagement party that her mother insisted on throwing when some of the people she loved most didn't approve of her match? What did everyone see in their relationship that was such a disaster? And why didn't anyone care enough about her to say this to her face?

* * *

Lucy's mom had invited everyone from her ward, plus all of Lucy's friends, in addition to various aunts, uncles, and cousins. The backyard was filled to capacity. Lucy held her plastic cup of lemonade in a vise-like grip as everyone she had ever known congratulated her on her engagement and expressed their relief that she was finally getting married. "We figured it was never going to happen," her old Laurel advisor, Sister Martian, said. "Especially after you went off to graduate school in Wisconsin." Lucy kept her lips pressed together in a thin smile. Charles, who had shown up twenty minutes late, stood at her elbow, acting aloof. She doubted he was even listening to the conversation. "But here you are, engaged and everything," Sister Martian continued. "I don't think I heard the wedding date."

"January 16," Lucy said.

Sister Martian laughed. "Why, that's five months from now. You'll never make it to then, dear." She winked, and Lucy felt a red flush of embarrassment reaching her cheeks. "You'll be married by Thanksgiving, I guarantee it."

"Actually, we won't," Charles said, his voice tight. "My parents don't return home from their mission until December, and I could never get married without them present. I am the last of their children to get married, and I wouldn't deprive them of the joy of seeing me wed."

Sister Martian's lips moved into a thin line of distaste. "Well, good for you, then." She side-eyed Charles. "If you'll excuse me."

Although Lucy was glad to see Sister Martian go, she wasn't happy about how her exit had occurred. "Charles, why did you have to be so rude?" She grabbed him by the forearm because she sensed he wanted to leave.

He adjusted his glasses. "I just think our engagement and the matters of our married life should be personal, between you and me. Instead, it seems we have to share intimate details about our relationship with all your mother's friends. It's simply irreverent."

While Lucy agreed with everything he said—she definitely didn't want commentary from other people about the obvious challenges of their long engagement—she didn't think Charles had to go about it in such an obtuse way. Tugging on the sleeve of his sports coat to bring his focus back to her, Lucy gave him a pleading look. "Be nice, okay?"

He let out a short laugh. Touching her cheek gently, his gaze grew tender. "Then it's best if I don't speak at all."

"That would be even better." She kissed him because she loved the crooked shape of his mouth when he smiled like that.

When the short kiss ended, Lucy saw Charlotte approaching them, Ellie with her. Charles seemed unfazed by the kiss, even though he was the one who usually protested, but Lucy felt embarrassed for some unknown reason. She touched the back of her hand to her mouth as if to erase the kiss.

"Charlotte, it's good to see you," Lucy said, then offered Ellie a terse "Hi." Lucy hadn't seen the two girls since London. She hoped by offering Charlotte the apartment down the hall from her, it would let her know she wasn't angry anymore.

Charlotte gave Lucy a hug and then gave one to Charles. "Charlotte, always a delight," he said to her.

Charlotte beamed. "Charles, have you met my friend Ellie?" she asked.

"No, I don't believe I have," Charles said, giving his full attention to Ellie.

She extended her hand to him, which he took. "Eleanor Lavish," she said in her cool voice, her posture rigid and confident. She withdrew her hand in a slow, seductive way. Lucy bit the inside of her cheek to keep the annoyance from her face.

"I feel like I've heard your name before," Charles said, his brow creased and perplexed. "Are you someone I should know?"

Ellie preserved an air of mysteriousness by offering a small smile and an arched eyebrow. "I'll be attending your poetry workshop in October."

"Ah." Recognition dawned on his face. "You wrote those moving poems about adoption."

Lucy could sense they were about to delve into a poetry discussion, which she wouldn't know how to participate in. She tugged Charlotte on the arm and drew her away. "How have you been?" Lucy asked. Charlotte shrugged, and Lucy felt the strain between them building. "Are you excited about starting medical school in a few weeks?"

"You didn't hear?" Charlotte asked.

Something jolted in Lucy's chest. "Didn't hear what?"

"I'm not going to medical school," Charlotte answered.

"You're not?" The revelation hit Lucy harder than she would have expected. The image she'd drawn of Charlotte crumbled in her mind. Charlotte, who was sweet and naive but wildly intelligent, a young woman smart enough to get into every medical school she had applied to.

"I realized what I really want to do is deliver babies. I was talking to Ellie's friend Audrey, and she's a midwife. I don't have to go to medical school to do that. Instead, I'm starting classes at the Midwives College of Utah."

The glow on Charlotte's face told Lucy she didn't need to feel bad that Charlotte was giving up medical school. For a change, Charlotte was plowing her own path and asserting herself. "That's really great," Lucy said.

Charlotte beamed, and Lucy hoped some of the walls between them were starting to break down for good.

"Are you still planning to live at home?" Lucy asked.

Charlotte shrugged. "Ellie wants us to get an apartment together somewhere in Salt Lake. But I'm not sure . . ."

Lucy could sense that what Charlotte wasn't sure about was living with Ellie. "Well, there's an open apartment in my complex, if you're interested," Lucy said.

"Oh, we should take it," Ellie said from a few steps away.

Charles was no longer with her; he appeared to be heading into the house. Lucy swallowed her annoyance with him. He couldn't just leave the party—*their* party. And Lucy knew him well enough to know his intention was to leave, not that he needed to use the bathroom or take a break from the August sun.

"I don't know . . ." Charlotte said.

"Come on," Ellie interrupted. "Lucy's ward is known for having older, good-looking single guys with ambitious career goals. We'll find ourselves rich husbands." She sounded like she was reading the plot summary of a Regency romance novel. Lucy moved her annoyance from Charles to Ellie. "Plus," Ellie continued, "you'll be really close to school."

Charlotte sighed and appeared to be relenting. "I guess it wouldn't hurt to take a look and apply."

"It will be nice to have a friend down the hall," Lucy said. "And Freddy will still be there after I get married."

Charlotte perked up. Freddy was everyone's favorite cousin.

"Did someone say my name?" Freddy asked, slinging his arms around Lucy and Charlotte's shoulders.

"I'm trying to convince Charlotte to be your neighbor." Ellie's voice was cool and even. With the sunlight behind Ellie, Lucy thought she looked like a Calvin Klein model—a sharp, angular face; slender hips; dark, smoldering eyes; wind-tamed hair. The purse of her red lips was both alluring and cruel.

"Eleanor." Freddy released Charlotte and Lucy. "It's been a few months."

Ellie's look grew a little heated. Lucy felt a weird vibration in the space between them. She stole a glance at Freddy. His jaw was working, and it was very possible there was murder in his eyes. Lucy excused herself, saying she needed to go find Charles, and made her escape to the house. She had no idea what was going on between Freddy and *Eleanor*, but she knew if Ellie was involved, it was probably bad.

After a quick search of the house, Lucy discovered Charles had in fact left.

* * *

That night as Lucy wrote in her journal, trying to spin the day's events into something funny (because one day Charles leaving their engagement party would seem funny, right?), her phone chimed with a new text message. Hopefully it was Charles, apologizing again for embarrassing her. She picked up her phone and saw the text was from an unknown number. As she tapped open the message, her blood froze.

Hey, Lucy. It's Emerson.

She closed her eyes and tried to swallow. Her heart ricocheted through her chest as she leaned back on her headboard. This wasn't possible. She opened her eyes and read the rest of the message.

I got your number from Ellie, hope that's okay. I'll be in Salt Lake on Monday and Tuesday next week and would love to catch up. Maybe we could meet for lunch?

Lucy had to close her eyes again. Her mind zoomed with so many questions she could hardly keep up. Why was he contacting her now, after five months of radio silence? What did he want? How did he get her number from Ellie? Should she reply to his text? Should she meet up with him? What would be the point of reconnecting?

A headache grew between her eyes. This didn't seem fair. After Lucy had worked so hard to move on, he couldn't expect her to come running back to him after one text message. Granted, that wasn't at all what he was asking. He was wanting to catch up. To meet for lunch, the most casual of all meals. Lucy's heart started to pound as she imagined seeing him again. She felt excitement and relief at the prospect. This wasn't good. She couldn't still have feelings for him. It wasn't right to pursue this. She was with Charles now and didn't need any complications. She had finally convinced herself Charles was the right person for her, and one little text wasn't going to undo that.

Lucy decided to do what she was best at: avoid the problem. She picked up her phone, and with two taps, she deleted the message. There. The temptation had been eliminated. Now she could go about her life without Emerson, as planned. She finished her journal entry about the engagement party, made no mention of the text from Emerson, and opened her bedside table to store her journal. Inside, she saw the edge of his mother's scarf sticking out from underneath some sheet music. She pulled it out and smoothed her hand over the silk. The ache of memory came with the motion. Lucy could hide his mother's scarf and delete his text, but a small part of her would always care about him. It was naive of her to think she could simply avoid those feelings away.

Maybe because she was still mad at Charles, or maybe because Emerson had texted her, she didn't put the scarf away. She stood from her bed, found her purse, and tied the scarf to the shoulder strap. For just a moment, she allowed herself to feel everything she wasn't supposed to. Both the pain and the joy. She acknowledged what she was giving up. She had once loved Emerson so much.

Chapter 19

EMERSON STOOD IN FRONT OF the housing board at the University of Utah's Institute building. It was Mindy who had suggested he find an LDS roommate to help him stay on the strait and narrow. Moving to Utah was the last thing Emerson had ever pictured himself doing, but he'd become tired of flying long international hauls, and when the opportunity had come to fly domestic flights, he felt his prayers had been answered. He took the job, joining a flight crew out of the Salt Lake International Airport. He had a week to find an apartment and move across the country.

He took pictures of the more promising ads with his phone. He didn't want to be in a singles ward with mostly college students, so he was looking for an apartment that wasn't right by the university. Mindy had suggested he live in the suburbs. He took a picture of an ad for an apartment in Sandy, then read the next ad. His phone chimed with a message, and his heart leaped into his throat. Was it Lucy? He'd sent her a text Saturday night and still hadn't heard from her. Ellie had already told him Lucy had recently gotten engaged. He'd been surprised to hear this and more than a little heartbroken. But what could he really expect? In his letter, he'd told her he didn't want the possibility of her in his life affecting his decision to figure out how he felt about the Church. She was right to move on. At this point, he just wanted to see her again for closure so he could see for himself that she was happily engaged to someone else and move on with his life. But she hadn't texted back yet. And she hadn't accepted his friend request on Facebook.

He unlocked his phone and saw the message was from Ellie. *How's apartment hunting going?*

He typed back a quick, *Good. Call you later?* and continued scanning the board.

He didn't even notice someone had approached him until the man spoke. "I see you're looking for housing."

Emerson glanced to his left and saw a thin blond man standing beside him. He wore a charcoal sports coat with a red bow tie. His slacks had a stiff crease down the front, and it looked like he'd polished his shoes. Even though he looked to be about Emerson's age, he couldn't help but think the guy dressed like his father.

"I know the perfect apartment for you," the man continued, adjusting his black-framed glasses.

"Yeah?" Emerson thought he looked a little familiar, but he couldn't place him.

"I happen to know a fantastic apartment that is available in Sugar House," he said. "Are you familiar with the area?"

Emerson nodded. Where had he seen this guy before?

"The ward is fantastic. I should know—I'm the elders quorum president. Lots of quality women too, if you're hoping to find a wife. In fact, I met my fiancée there."

"I'm sorry, what did you say your name was?"

"Oh, forgive me." He extended his hand. "Charles Buffington."

It all came into focus. Emerson *did* know who this guy was. He'd seen his picture on Lucy's Facebook page. This was her fiancé. What a strange coincidence.

"Emerson James." He shook Charles's hand. Maybe he wouldn't need a roommate if he had a "fantastic ward." "Tell me more about this apartment."

* * *

After a week of back and forth, Lucy was able to convince the owner of the ice cream shop in New Jersey to give her a shot at reformulating his recipe for mass production. And during that week, before she'd even won the bid, she had spent her free time working out some of the potential complications. Instead of deciding on wedding colors, where to hold the reception, and if she wanted an ice-cream cake or a regular wedding cake, in her spare time, Lucy had thought through ways to maintain the ice cream's density, richness, and flavor while also reducing the ingredient cost to seventy-five cents a pint. When Lucy finally got the owner's recipe in her inbox Friday afternoon, she almost canceled dinner with Charles so she could start on the reformulation. But dutifully, when five thirty rolled around, she shut down her computer, locked the lab, and headed home.

Lucy found Ellie sitting on her couch when she walked into her apartment. Ellie glanced up from the magazine she was leafing through, gave Lucy an impatient look, and resumed her perusal. Puzzled, Lucy hung up her purse on the hook by the door. Before she had a chance to ask Ellie what the heck she was doing in her apartment, Freddy emerged from his bedroom. He was freshly shaven—he had the type of facial hair that grew back in by noon—and was wearing a button-down shirt that looked *ironed.*

"Sorry for making you—" He stopped when he saw Lucy standing in the doorway.

Ellie closed the magazine and rose, her posture swan-like. "Not a problem," she said. "*The Journal of Food Science* kept me occupied." The look she shot Lucy was one of boredom.

Lucy tried to make eye contact with Freddy, but he was doing an excellent job of avoiding it. He wasn't going on a date with Ellie, was he? There was definitely some weird chemistry between them, but Lucy thought it seemed a lot like hatred or anger, not attraction or affection.

"Ah, um, Eleanor and I are going now," Freddy said, gesturing for Ellie to follow him.

"By the way, Lucy," Ellie said as she went to the door with Freddy. Lucy stepped out of their way. "You can tell Harry Otway that even if another apartment opens up, we won't be interested."

"What?" Lucy asked, her confusion increasing. "I talked to Charlotte two days ago, and she said you two were going to pay the deposit yesterday."

Ellie shook her head. "Harry gave the apartment to someone else. Some guy who wanted to pay month to month. Harry charges through the nose for that kind of contract. Apparently, he cares more about dollar signs than having eligible females in the ward."

"Oh shucks," Lucy said. "I was really looking forward to Charlotte living down the hall."

Ellie narrowed her eyes, clearly noticing Lucy hadn't mentioned she was happy to also have Ellie as a neighbor. "I'm surprised you hadn't heard," Ellie added. "Harry said the guy is a friend of Charles."

"A friend of Charles?" Lucy echoed.

Ellie shrugged, then looked to Freddy, her face softening a little. "Shall we?"

Freddy opened the door and placed a hand on the small of Ellie's back, directing her out the door. "I'll be back in a few hours," Freddy said to Lucy.

When the door shut, Lucy let out a long exhale. That was weird.

She spent the next half hour getting ready for her evening with Charles. She reapplied her makeup and wove her hair into an elaborate braid. She then changed into a pair of skinny jeans and heels. Lucy did her best to not let the irritation she felt for Charles grow. Ellie liked to create drama. For all Lucy knew, Ellie had made it up that the new tenant was Charles's friend because she was angry about not getting the apartment.

At six thirty on the dot, Charles rang her doorbell. "*Mi amor*," he said when she answered, presenting her with a single white flower. He wore skinny khaki slacks and a light-blue sports coat. Lucy wondered how many sports coats he owned since she'd never seen him wear the same one twice in the same month.

She accepted the flower, got her purse from the hook, and locked the door behind them. Hand in hand, they walked across the street to his parents' house.

It was an old cottage-style structure with a steep, pointed roof. In winter, with Christmas lights up and snow covering it, it resembled a gingerbread house. It was the type of house Lucy had always wanted to live in, but she doubted she'd be able to convince Charles to buy a cute old home in Sugar House. He would tell her it would be better if they both had to commute to work; it would make things equal. "Plus," she could picture him saying, "what if you decide to quit working once we have children? We can't buy a house close to where you work if you are going to be a stay-at-home mom. We need to be closer to mine."

Lucy rolled her eyes at the fake but very likely conversation. She had no intention of quitting her job once she had a baby. Plenty of women worked and raised children. She hoped Charles wouldn't pigeonhole her dreams or goals.

"Is there a problem, love?" Charles asked. "What's that scowl doing on your face?" He led her into the kitchen, where he'd set out ingredients for pasta carbonara.

She didn't want to talk about what she was really thinking. "Ellie said she and Charlotte didn't get the apartment."

A self-satisfied smirk appeared on his face. "No, they didn't," he replied.

"She said you helped one of your friends get it instead."

Charles took a moment before answering, filling a large pot with water. "I wouldn't call him a friend," he said as he placed the pot on the stove and turned on the heat. "Will you mince that onion?"

Lucy took the knife, surprised by the amount of anger coursing through her. She placed the onion on the wooden cutting board and felt a little better as she forcefully cut it in half. "Charles, Ellie is really upset about it."

He stood at the stove with his back to Lucy, placing pieces of bacon in a frying pan. "Do the garlic next, will you?"

Lucy steadied the knife and began mincing the onion. "If he isn't a friend, then who is he?"

Charles turned to her with a gleeful laugh. "It was the most random thing," he said, his eyes bright with mirth. "I was at the Institute building, on a whim, and I saw this man standing at the housing board. He was in his late twenties, at least, and had an air of professionalism about him. I told him about the apartment and how great our ward is for older single adults with *careers*. He said he'd take it."

"But, Charles, you knew Charlotte wanted to live there."

"No," he said, emphasizing the word with a swish of his spatula. "Ellie wanted to live there. Plus, Harry Otway needs to stop leasing only to females. That kind of discrimination is illegal." He turned back to the stove. "And the elders quorum's attendance is abysmal. Perhaps this fellow will attend and I can get the home teaching numbers up."

Lucy felt her jaw drop. Was he serious? Home teaching numbers? She quickly snapped her mouth shut before Charles could catch her. "Do you even care about how this could affect my already strained relationship with Charlotte?" Lucy asked, her exasperation rising. "Ellie is angry, and I'm sure Charlotte is disappointed."

He turned the heat down on the bacon before returning his attention to Lucy. "Charlotte will recover, and you don't like Ellie anyway." His tone was so dismissive Lucy felt like she'd gone invisible. Something small and fragile shriveled up in the pit of her stomach. A strong feeling of rejection echoed against the emptiness left there. Lucy focused on chopping the onion, tears stinging the back of her eyes. She knew Charles could be shrewd, but it had never been at her expense.

The urge to run swept through her with startling force. Charles's first proposal played in her head—his unexpected arrival at her apartment, the presentation of a ring, the words he'd said: "Make me happy, Lucy. Marry me. Be my wife." Instead of hearing a declaration of love, Lucy had heard a prison sentence. And she'd run away to London. To Emerson. Emerson, who had never chastised her or made her feel small or silly.

"Are the onion and garlic ready?" Charles asked.

"Yes." Lucy's voice cracked.

He joined her at the cutting board. She could feel his eyes on her. "Are you crying?"

She took a deep breath. "No. It's just the onion."

Charles tipped her chin up with a long finger. She met his clear, blue eyes. He cupped her face with his hands and wiped her tears with his thumbs. He smelled of bacon grease and fennel essential oil. "I've gone and behaved selfishly again, haven't I."

Lucy nodded and sniffed pathetically.

"This is why I need you, Lucy," he said. "You make me better than I have to be."

* * *

Five days later, on September 1, Lucy noticed that the door to the vacant apartment down the hall was open. She resisted the urge to walk by and steal a peek at her new neighbor. Instead, she slung her purse over her shoulder and went out to the parking lot. Pulled up to the curb was the moving van. Lucy glanced into the truck on the way to her car and saw boxes and boxes labeled "books." She rolled her eyes. Of course her new neighbor, handpicked by Charles, would own a library.

At work, she lost herself in the formulation of rich ice creams and cost-reduced novelties. If she worked hard enough, she could ignore the anxiety pressing heavily on her chest.

Chapter 20

"COME OUT OF THE DRESSING room, dear," Lucy heard her mother call from outside the door. This was her mom's second inquiry into Lucy's progress on trying on the wedding dress. Lucy had already confirmed that she wasn't having problems putting it on or zipping it up. It was anxiety that kept her in that small space, surrounded by a cloud of billowing white tulle. This was dress number thirteen, and still, no dress felt right.

She stared at herself in the 360 mirror. The dress fit like a glove, the fabric snug at her curves, the sweetheart neckline neat and flattering. The dress was beautiful, and Lucy looked like a bride. But for some reason, she couldn't shake the image from her mind of being sopping wet in a white sundress, seeing herself repeated an infinite number of times in elevator mirrors. In that tiny moment, she had felt the infinity and the possibility. She wanted *that* forever. It didn't matter that she had looked terrible; she'd been utterly happy. That was what she wanted on her wedding day. The dress didn't matter as much as the feeling.

She swallowed the lump forming in her throat and left the dressing room. She stepped up on the pedestal and shrugged her shoulders. She looked from her mother to Charlotte. Charlotte loved everything about weddings, and Lucy knew the best way to make peace with her was to involve her in the wedding plans.

"Oh, Lucy," her mother said, bringing her hand to her chest. "You look lovely."

Lucy's eyes darted to Charlotte. "Yes or no?" Lucy asked.

"Yes," Charlotte said. She'd said yes to the previous twelve dresses too. "You look like a cupcake," she added, as though looking like a baked good was a desirable trait for a bride.

"What do you think?" her mother asked, the creases on her forehead giving away her impatience.

"I think Charles will say it's too poofy," Lucy replied, her hands brushing across the skirt.

Lucy's mom sighed, and her expression grew pained. "No, what do *you* think?"

Lucy stared at her reflection for a moment. "I guess I always thought I would get married in the spring and have a shorter gown," she mused as she knotted a fist in the tulle. "I'm having a hard time accepting that I'm having a winter wedding and need a gown for cold weather." Lucy turned a little and looked at the mirror over her shoulder to see the back of the dress. Maybe if she saw the dress from a different angle she'd like it more. "Do you think I can convince Charles to wait until March to marry me?"

The expression on her mother's face relayed her discomfort. "Don't you think January is already too long to wait?" her mother asked.

The tight fabric of the dress stifled Lucy's sigh, so it wasn't as deep as she wanted, leaving her feeling unsatisfied.

"Aren't you just dying to marry him?" Charlotte asked, her eyes big and round and hopeful.

"Sure, Charlotte," Lucy replied. "Charles is perfect, isn't he?"

Lucy had once been like Charlotte—a hopeless romantic, devoted to getting her happily ever after. Lovesick with the notion of one day marrying her Prince Charming in the castle-like Salt Lake Temple. But Lucy had put those notions to rest somewhere in graduate school when she had crossed the threshold of twenty-five. And even after dating Charles for over a year and the possibility of finally getting her happily ever after loomed, she didn't feel as idealistic as Charlotte looked in that very moment. If Lucy were to be completely honest with herself, lately, she felt resigned or like she'd settled. She'd been thinking of Emerson more since she'd received that text from him and then his friend request on Facebook. She never responded to either, trying her best to forget him again. She had already committed herself to Charles, and she was determined to not let an old fling come between her and the future she had always dreamed of.

She didn't think she believed in fairy-tale love anymore. Her and Charles's love was slow. It had never been explosive and passionate, but it had always been tender and reliable. By the end of life, that was what love usually felt like, so it couldn't be a bad thing for it to start that way too, right?

Lucy was getting older, and marriage to a worthy priesthood holder was the right thing to do.

She stole a glance at her mother, which she instantly regretted. Her mother's face betrayed her reservations about her daughter's pending marriage. Her lips sat in a strained neutral line, neither smile nor frown, but her brow lay heavy with creases of worry.

Charlotte was saying something about Charles while Lucy and her mother held a silent but weighty conversation.

Lucy, are you sure?

But who else is there?

And like a physical force, Lucy felt electricity sweep up her body as she remembered a kiss in a grove of trees surrounded by blue cornflowers.

* * *

"Did I miss anything at church today?" Lucy asked Freddy at Sunday family dinner.

He smirked. "It was fast Sunday; of course you did."

Lucy had been camping out at her mother's house since the failed dress-finding excursion yesterday. She didn't want to see Charles and have to admit to his face that the dress was yet another detail of the wedding she couldn't commit to. A short phone call was much easier. So far, the only thing decided for the wedding was the date and place: January 16 in the Salt Lake Temple. Lucy was hemming and hawing over the announcements, the location of the reception, the wedding theme and colors, the photographer, and anything else related to the wedding. Part of her just wanted to elope. But Charles was the last of his siblings to get married, so his parents wanted it to be a big to-do. There were certain things Lucy could pawn off on her mother, who seemed to be having a delightful time leafing through wedding magazines and creating myriad boards on Pinterest. But the selection of the dress really did fall on Lucy. So, for now, Lucy would remain dress-less.

"Does that mean you had a good game of Testimony BINGO?" Lucy asked her brother. They sat across from each other at the dining room table in their mother's house. Freddy's plate was loaded with pot roast, mashed potatoes, and steamed carrots. Gravy dripped over the edges and onto the pink tablecloth.

"Sobbing Susie for the win," he replied, thrusting his fork into the air triumphantly.

Lucy shook her head with both amusement and disapproval. Freddy had corrupted the activity designed to help children pay attention during testimony meeting into a cruel game. Instead of watching for a speaker with a red tie or listening for the name Joseph Smith and marking the game board, Freddy had spaces for "Cry-imony," where the person cried the whole time; "Stor-imony," when the speaker tells a long story rather than testifies of anything; "Overshare," "Blasphemy," "RM," "Mission Story," "Improv Musical Number," and then he even had specific spaces for people who went up every month, like Sobbing Susie or . . . Charles.

"You would have had a field day in Mom's ward today," Lucy said. "Sister Hutchings was at the pulpit for fifteen minutes rambling. The bishop had to pull her off."

"Now, Lucy," her mother interjected. "Sister Hutchings has dementia. She probably didn't even know where she was."

"Which is why I was surprised it went on so long," Lucy replied. "It was clear after thirty seconds that she was *confused*."

"I love that stuff," Freddy said. "Testimony meeting is better than any open-mic night I've ever been to."

"Other than the usual testimony meeting nonsense, anything else I should know about? Did Charles behave himself?"

"Elders quorum was interesting, but you wouldn't have been there anyway to rein him in," Freddy replied.

"Do I even want to know?"

Freddy shook his head. "I'll just say our new neighbor isn't as orthodox as Charles had hoped."

Lucy had forgotten about their new neighbor. She'd been meaning to stop by and welcome him to the complex but had gotten caught up with things at work. Then she'd ended up spending the weekend with her mom. She hadn't even bumped into him in the hall or parking lot. She'd just noticed his car, a blue Jetta with Georgia plates, and had had the irrational thought that maybe he knew Emerson.

"Tell me exactly what happened," Lucy said, pointing her fork at him.

"Well," Freddy said, his eyes alight with mischief. "Charles was teaching the lesson, and the discussion *devolved* into the topic of deification. And the new guy was all, 'Why are we talking about becoming gods when we can't even do our home teaching every month? Wouldn't a more productive conversation center on keeping basic commandments?' I love controversy, so of course I stepped in and agreed with New Guy, and he and I sort of hijacked the lesson, which resulted in Charles's pulling us aside after the meeting to let us know how much he"—Freddy made air quotes—"'disapproved of our actions' and 'expected more from us.'"

Lucy did her best to hide her smile by taking a bite of roast. "Freddy, you shouldn't have," she scolded because she was supposed to stand up for her fiancé.

"Lucy, I hate to say it, but your Fiasco is a piece of work. Just for marrying him, you're going to be granted admittance into the highest kingdom."

Lucy balled up her napkin and threw it at his head. Freddy ducked and laughed, the napkin missing him.

Their mom looked on with disapproval. "Both of you," she said, "behave yourselves."

"Fine, fine," Freddy said, adjusting his tie.

Lucy's eyes dropped to her plate of food, and she realized she'd lost her appetite. Freddy had finally told her what he thought of Charles. The worst part was that Lucy agreed. Charles *was* a piece of work. He could be difficult. She was going to have to put up with that difficulty for the rest of her life and eternity. She took a deep breath. She didn't want to think about this.

"So, tell me about our new neighbor," Lucy said.

Freddy shrugged. "He doesn't like Charles, and he lives down the hall from us. That's about all I know."

"Well, does he have a name?"

"Ah, Lucy. You know how bad I am with names." He put a huge forkful of potatoes in his mouth and kept talking while he chewed. "It was some philosopher's name or something."

"Like Plato or Socrates?"

"I know it wasn't one of those. I would definitely remember that. It wasn't a super weird name, but it was a last name. Just ask Charles if you want to know."

Lucy shook her head. She was going to have to talk to Charles at some point. Maybe her inability to commit to wedding details was cold feet, and if she had an honest conversation with him, she'd feel better.

At the thought of being honest with Charles, anxiety swelled within her. She got up from the table and set her plate on the counter. As she walked down the hall to her childhood bedroom, she heard her mother ask her to put the dish in the sink. Lucy kept walking and shut the door behind her, settling onto her old bed. She grabbed the red scarf from her purse, smoothing the fabric between her fingers.

* * *

When Lucy returned home to her apartment later Sunday night, she discovered that every surface of her bedroom was covered in paper hearts. She slumped against the door, her legs feeling brittle.

"Charles," she breathed into the phone when he answered.

"How do I love thee?" he replied. "Let me count the ways."

Lucy took a step forward and plucked a heart from her bedside lamp. On the heart, Charles had written, "#137 You are always kind."

"Charles, can we talk?" she asked.

A few minutes later, he was in her room, holding her as she cried into his neck. She couldn't tell him what she was really thinking. She didn't want his judgment or to hurt him. Instead, she told him how overwhelmed she felt with the wedding planning. It was kind of the truth and seemed like a reasonable thing a girl would cry about. "I know you said you wanted a reception with a formal dinner, but . . ." Lucy hiccupped. Geez, she needed to pull herself together, especially since it wasn't really the reception she was crying about. "But I think I want something more casual."

Charles chuckled and patted her hair. "My love, we don't have to do a dinner. It's just what my parents preferred."

Lucy nodded, and he handed her a tissue from the box on her nightstand. She dabbed her eyes and blew her nose.

He grimaced at the sound. "I have an idea," he said. "Why don't we make a list of the top five things we want for the wedding, and then we'll start compromising from there."

"Yeah, okay." This would be a good distraction. Lucy stood and took paper and pens from her desk. She returned to her place on the floor beside him, and they made wedding plans, surrounded by the paper hearts, until it was almost morning.

Chapter 21

WHEN LUCY ARRIVED HOME FROM work on Monday, the courtyard of her apartment complex swarmed with swimsuit-clad young single adults—an FHE pool party. Since Lucy had gone into work late, she'd had to stay late, so FHE was in full swing. As she passed by the hot tub, packed beyond capacity with YSAs, she wondered why pool parties were permitted. Lots of skin touching skin for a Church activity.

That was something Charles would think.

Wandering over to the veranda, she spotted Freddy seated with one of his friends. The smell of charcoal and burning meat wafted through the air as she approached her brother. He saw her and made room for her at the picnic table. His friend said something about a girl and left.

"You should get some food," Freddy said, his mouth full of hamburger.

"I will in a minute," Lucy said, still scanning the crowd. For the first time in a few days, she was actually looking forward to seeing Charles. Their talk last night had been very cathartic. And humbling. She'd realized she didn't need to hold back from Charles and she could trust him. He understood and loved her. They'd been open and honest as they'd planned their wedding, and they'd also shared their anxieties and concerns. Lucy had realized she was happier with Charles than she was without him. She was just getting cold feet. It was perfectly normal, Charles had assured her.

"You look *rough*," Freddy said, wiggling his eyebrows. "Charles sure left early this morning. Didn't get much sleep, did you?"

"Knock it off," Lucy scolded. "You know my life is G-rated."

"Yes, Lucy, it is," Freddy replied. "But as Charles would say, 'Appearance counts for a lot.' And your life sure doesn't look G-rated with the Fiasco leaving your apartment at four in the a.m."

Lucy narrowed her eyes at Freddy, knowing he was right.

"Speak of the devil," Freddy mumbled.

Lucy turned and saw Charles approaching. He took slow, long-limbed steps, looking like a freshly sharpened pencil. Lucy narrowed her eyes at Freddy and went to Charles.

"Ah, Lucy," he said and greeted her with a quick kiss on the cheek. "I've been looking for you. Come, I want you to meet your new neighbor."

Disappointment niggled in her stomach. This was not the reception she had wanted from him. After their talk last night, she felt much closer to him. She had expected a more enthusiastic greeting than a quick kiss and a "Follow me." Charles placed a hand on her lower back and steered her over to the sand volleyball court.

She scanned the court, trying to pick out the person she didn't know. And then there he was, like an impossible dream with fuzzy edges and woozy improbability. Emerson served the ball just as Charles called his name. He turned and saw her, and Lucy felt herself growing small and very still as he locked eyes with her and made his way over to them.

"Emerson," Charles said. "Meet my fiancée, Lu—"

"Lucy Kappal," Emerson finished for him, his lips curling into a dimpled smile.

Lucy couldn't take her eyes off him. She couldn't believe he was standing right in front of her. And he was shirtless. And tan. And had many more tattoos than she'd imagined. Her heart began to beat erratically, and her stomach couldn't decide if it belonged in her body or on the moon.

"Oh, you two have met already?" Charles asked, touching his glasses.

Lucy stole a look at Charles out of the corner of her eye and then looked back at Emerson.

"Yes," Emerson replied. "We met in London."

She probably imagined it, but she saw heat flicker in his eyes for the briefest moment.

"In London?" Charles asked. Did she look like she was seeing a ghost? Because that was exactly how she felt. Charles let out a short laugh as recognition dawned on him. "London?" He looked from Emerson to Lucy. "Lucy, is this the man you kissed in London?"

Emerson had a smirk plastered on his face. How was he playing this so cool? She was losing her cookies, and he was *smirking*. "Um, yes," Lucy said, looking back at Charles.

He chortled and adjusted his glasses. He seemed delighted by this coincidence. "How awkward this must be for you!"

Lucy tried to laugh, but it sounded like a dry cough.

Someone behind Lucy caught Emerson's attention. "Hey, let's catch up later, okay?" he said. He touched her on the arm as he walked past her. Lucy turned to watch him go, baffled, then saw Emerson scoop up Ellie in a long, full-bodied hug.

* * *

Lucy had a bad habit of being the last one to leave a party, even if the party was totally lame and she spent most of it watching an ex-love flirt with a girl she didn't like. When had Ellie and Emerson reconnected? He'd been living in her complex less than a week, but they sure did look chummy.

"Love," Charles said by her ear. "I need to call it a night."

Lucy turned to him and examined his face in the light of the bonfire. His features looked especially angular in the flickering shadows. She nodded and kissed him quickly on the lips.

"I'll see you tomorrow?" he asked.

"Yeah. Tomorrow."

Lucy watched him go, his posture graceful, and she ached. She fiddled with her engagement ring as thoughts of another man clouded her mind. She was never supposed to see Emerson again. But he was here, and it made her nauseated.

The night air began to chill, and more and more people left the courtyard, pairing off into temporary couples. The bonfire slowly lost its strength, and Lucy worried on her red silk scarf. This didn't change how she felt about Charles. She was still going to marry him in January. Emerson being here didn't mean anything. It was not a reprisal of fate but rather a cruel coincidence.

Freddy was leaving the courtyard for the parking lot, Ellie with him. Lucy rolled her eyes. Emerson. Freddy. Who didn't Ellie flirt with? And she wasn't even in this ward, so what was she doing at FHE? Lucy had gone months without seeing the girl, and now she appeared to be everywhere Lucy was. Freddy needed an intervention. So did Emerson. Why did guys even go for girls like Ellie?

"Mind if I join you?"

The voice beside her felt like silk on her skin, cool and soft. She swallowed the huge lump that had formed in her throat and peeked at Emerson to make sure he had a shirt on, which he did, before looking at him full on.

The smile Lucy offered felt brittle. "Sure."

An itchy uncomfortableness grew as Emerson took a seat on the bench beside her. They didn't touch, but she could feel his energy vibrating near her. Her heart began to pound erratically, and a fight-or-flight response kicked in. But she didn't move. Wasn't this why she'd stuck around so long? So that Charles would leave and she could talk to Emerson alone?

Slowly, she brought her eyes to his. The red glow of the fire's coals made his caramel eyes appear the color of lava. As she examined his face, she realized how much of him she'd forgotten. Her memory was all she'd had these past months, since she had never taken a picture of him. And memory had lost the small things. She'd forgotten the dimple in his left cheek and the hint of crow's feet around his eyes. His hair was a little longer and curled around his temples and ears.

"So, how have you been?" She tried to sound friendly, but she wasn't sure she was successful.

"Good," Emerson replied, his dimple reappearing. "And you? Things are good?"

"Yeah, things are good." Should she explain why she never returned his text message?

"You're engaged," he said, gesturing to her hand.

Lucy nodded and focused on her ring. It was heavy on her hand, a two-carat gray sapphire with a diamond-encrusted white-gold band.

"When's the big day?" he asked.

"January 16."

He nodded, and his eyes roved over her face. She wished he'd stop looking at her so intently. She wished seeing him again felt comfortable, like there wasn't a wall of pressure between them. Like she wasn't about to hyperventilate or turn to dust.

The silence between them grew as he continued to examine her. She felt like she was being slowly stripped down to the bone. She blinked and sighed slowly. "I was never supposed to see you again," she finally said.

There was a long pause. "Yeah," he agreed.

"What are you doing here?" She sounded upset. Was she?

"I applied for a job transfer and got it," he replied.

"I'm sorry I didn't text you back," she said. "I didn't think it would be appropriate to see you again since I'm engaged."

Emerson nodded. "Ellie thought the same thing."

"So you stayed in touch with Ellie?" *But not me?*

He frowned and looked ashamed. "Yeah."

Lucy waited for him to explain, and when he didn't, a fresh hurt sprang. An awkward silence grew between them. Lucy wanted to hit rewind. This wasn't how she wanted their reunion to go. Then again, their reunion couldn't play out as she had fantasized. She was engaged to someone else. And though she'd told herself she had extinguished the flame she'd carried for Emerson, seeing him again made it clear the flame wasn't all the way out. Lucy very much felt like she was on fire.

"I probably shouldn't say this," he said slowly. "But I'm going to."

Lucy's heartbeat went into overdrive. She tried to swallow, but her mouth was too dry.

"I'm glad to see you again," he said, his eyes no longer on her. "I felt like I left a lot of loose ends with you in London." He shook his head. "I know it's selfish of me because you've clearly moved on . . ."

Lucy's heart jumped in her chest. *But I haven't moved on,* she wanted to say. *You were supposed to be the one who got away, but now you're here, and I don't know what to do.*

"But now I feel like I can get some closure," he continued. "You ruined dating for me, Lucy." He laughed. "I basically haven't been able to date anyone the last six months because no one has measured up to you." He stole a glance at her out of the corner of his eye but returned his gaze to the fire pit.

"What about Ellie?" *Really, Lucy? That's what you choose to say?* She wanted to slap her hands over her mouth for blurting out such a stupid thing.

Emerson let out a long exhale. "Ellie is just a friend."

Lucy held in a scoff. It wasn't her place to be jealous.

Again, the silence stretched out. Maybe it was best that this was awkward. It made it easier to never want to talk to him again. And then she could continue to love Charles and marry him in January like she was supposed to. She wouldn't have Emerson charming her and changing her mind.

"I'd better go in," she said.

"Oh, yeah, me too," Emerson said.

They stood and walked around the fire to their building, up one flight of stairs and down the hall. They paused at her door for a curt good night, and Lucy disappeared inside. Her jelly legs managed to get her to her bedroom, where she finally collapsed. What was she going to do?

* * *

Emerson let himself into his apartment, his fingers tingling and his head feeling cloudy. He'd finally seen Lucy. He'd been waiting five days to run into her, anticipating what it would be like to see her again. And now that he'd seen her, he felt . . . light, high. Almost punch-drunk. He paced in his living room and ran his hand through his hair. He shook slightly with adrenalin. He didn't want to feel this way. The electricity racing through his body wasn't supposed to be there. Lucy was engaged to another man. She had moved on.

And he should too.

Instead of feeling like the door he'd left cracked was slamming shut, he felt it creaking open. He felt exactly like he had that night in London after Lucy had rescued him from the ale at the pub. It felt so much like fate, he couldn't stop the hammering of his heart or the racing of his thoughts toward images of Lucy and him together.

This was not good. He bit his knuckle in an attempt to ground himself and keep himself from swearing. This was not good at all. He needed an intervention, someone to act as the voice of reason. Whipping out his cell phone from his pocket, he speed-dialed Mindy. She'd know what to do.

She answered on the second ring, and Emerson's sigh rattled through the phone.

"What's the matter?" she asked, alarm sounding in her voice.

He stopped his pacing. "You'll never believe this," he said. "But I live in Lucy's apartment complex."

There was silence on the other end for too long. "London Lucy?" Mindy finally asked, like she was piecing together a puzzle. "That's crazy."

"I know."

"Have you talked to her yet?"

"Yes," he replied. "For just a minute." He had to sit before he said the next part aloud. "She's engaged."

"But you knew that already," Mindy said. "Didn't Ellie tell you a few weeks ago?"

Emerson knew very well Mindy's opinion about him staying in touch with Ellie. Mindy had warned him that if he truly wanted to get over Lucy, he needed to cut ties with everyone he'd met in London. If he heard things about Lucy, she'd stay on his radar. He'd keep pining for her, even if she wasn't there and there was no possibility they'd be together. He had to admit, cutting her out was what he'd wanted when he'd written Lucy the letter. And when he'd first started talking to Ellie, he'd made it a point to never ask about Lucy. But Ellie would mention her occasionally, and Emerson wouldn't stop her. He'd maybe even encouraged it at times.

"Yeah, I knew about the engagement," he replied. "But part of me hoped Ellie was exaggerating. Charlotte sure had been." When he'd written the letter to Lucy, it had been under the assumption that if she wasn't engaged, as Charlotte had suggested, she was at least trying to figure out her relationship with someone. It wasn't until months later, when Lucy was officially engaged to Charles, that Emerson learned the whole story about Lucy and Charles's on-again, off-again year-long relationship and how Lucy had come to London to get away from Charles and they had in fact been "off" when Emerson had kissed her in Kensington Gardens. He couldn't dwell too long on his decision to cut Lucy out of his life. At the time, it had felt right, and he never would have figured out the Church for himself if he'd had her influence. He'd come to the gospel on his own . . . well, Ellie and Mindy had been a big help. But he wasn't doing the Church thing because he was in love with Lucy; he was doing the Church thing because his life felt so much better that way.

Mindy's voice broke up his thoughts. "Now you can fully move on," she said. "Lucy's completely unavailable, you are in the land of single Mormon women, and you'll have plenty of opportunities to date. I bet the female population of your new ward is dying to get to know you."

Emerson laughed. He had gotten a lot of cookie deliveries by highly made-up females. But none of them had caught his eye or sparked his interest. "Do you think I can be friends with Lucy?"

The sigh on the other end of phone was unmistakable. "Emerson, you'd better leave her alone."

He was about to ask why, but the answer was perfectly clear. He was still in love with her. It would be too hard on him to be around her but not have her. Plus, if *he* had a fiancée, he wouldn't want her hanging out with a guy she had once kissed, even if they were "just friends" now.

"Yeah," Emerson agreed and left it at that.

Chapter 22

ALL THE HOUSES THEY'D VISITED smelled of pumpkin pie Scentsy wax. In the first house, Lucy had almost believed a pumpkin pie was cooling in the kitchen. But now, on house number four, she could instantly identify the artificial sweetness of the scent, and she found it pretentious and nauseating. Or maybe it was the slate-green paint on the wall of this kitchen that was making her nauseated. Or the fact that her pretentious future husband was totally okay living in a cookie-cutter mini-mansion in Lehi.

"There are four bedrooms on the second floor," their real estate agent said. "And two more in the basement." Lucy looked up at the high ceiling in the open kitchen and wondered how much it would cost to keep this house warm in the winter. "Plus, there is a den on this floor that can be used as a guest room or an office."

"Oh, Lucy," Charles said. "We could have a library. How regal." He shared an enchanted looked with the agent. Dollar signs flashed in the woman's eyes, but Lucy figured Charles hadn't noticed.

"I don't know," Lucy said stepping into the family room adjacent to the kitchen. "Do we really need a house this big?" The three previous homes they'd seen had been three- or four-bedroom homes in nice enough neighborhoods, though all of them had underwhelmed Lucy in their ordinariness. But this home overwhelmed her and her sense of practicality. "Who's going to live in all those bedrooms?"

"Our children, of course," he said, putting an arm around her waist.

Lucy noticed the agent watching them.

"I'll just step out while you talk things over." Her stiletto heels clicked out of the kitchen.

"How many kids do you think we're going to have?"

Charles shrugged. "I don't know; four, at least."

Lucy laughed, and he stepped away. "Charles, I'm thirty years old. I don't think there's enough time left for me to have four children."

"Of course there is. We have time for you to have ten children if we wanted."

"You seriously want to have kids right away?" Lucy asked. They'd had variations of this conversation a number of times, but now that they were talking about their real life together, it felt like the first time any of this had ever been said.

"Like you said, we're thirty." He adjusted his glasses. "I thought that would be obvious."

"Don't you want some time with just the two of us?"

He reached out and touched Lucy's face, but the gesture felt condescending, not loving. "We'll have plenty of time together once the children are grown and I'm retired."

Lucy felt panic rising like a wave. She could be a mother in a little over a year if they had a honeymoon baby. And then what? Would she have to quit her job and be a stay-at-home mom like Charles wanted? Would she then be expected to get pregnant again so they could manage to have ten kids before her ovaries permanently shut down?

"I don't think we need a house this big," was all Lucy could manage to say.

Charles took a step closer to her and planted a kiss on her forehead. "You're probably right. I'll ask the real estate agent if she has anything else to show us today."

Lucy closed her eyes and listened to the echo of his dress shoes as he left her. She couldn't help but think this shouldn't feel so hard.

* * *

On his way home from the airport, Emerson went out of his way to drive by his father's house. Like the homes in Sugar House, the houses in the Avenues were old and novel, with pitched roofs and sloping front lawns. His father's house was made of bricks painted lime green. The front porch sagged, and the lawn was overgrown with weeds. Emerson parked his car across the street and sat, his eyes fixed on the familiar front window. No lights were on, but there was still plenty of afternoon daylight. His courage faltered with each beat of his heart.

When Emerson had first stopped drinking, he'd attended AA meetings for support. The eighth step in recovery was making amends with anyone who had been wronged. His father was at the top of the list. After the divorce, when Emerson had lived with his mom full-time, he'd spent his summers in Salt Lake. And he'd been a little punk about it, sneaking out and disregarding his father's rules. Church became a huge point of contention, so his father had stopped making him go.

Emerson had blamed his parents' divorce on his father because it had been easier that way—Emerson hadn't seen him every day. But really, no one was to blame. When his father had been offered his dream job working for the *Salt Lake Tribune*, his mother had refused to give up her tenured position at the university to move with him. So they'd split, each loving their work more than each other.

Emerson's relationship with his father had grown even more tenuous once he'd joined the military. His father hadn't been supportive of the decision, and whenever they'd spoken, he had reminded Emerson of his disapproval. The Air Force Academy had been difficult, as Emerson had expected it would be, and he hadn't needed any outside stresses, so he'd cut off all communication with his dad.

But then Emerson had needed money. He had bought a condo in Madison at the height of the housing bubble, and when the bubble had popped, he'd been upside-down twice on the property. He couldn't justify keeping it when he got deployed, so he sold the condo and lost a lot of money. His dad had stepped in and paid off the debt. Emerson had gone to Afghanistan and hadn't sent as much as a thank-you card.

Shame like an acid grew inside Emerson as he thought of how he'd treated his father. The man had deserved better than Emerson had given. Way better. And he needed to make it right somehow. He hadn't seen his father since the funeral over a year ago. And he hadn't been able to bring himself to call him since he'd come into town. There was so much bad blood between them, he preferred not having a subtext-filled phone conversation. If he saw his father face-to-face, maybe he'd be able to say all the things he wanted to say.

Movement in the house's window startled Emerson, his heart racing in a sudden panic. What if his father had seen him? Without a second thought, Emerson turned on his car and drove away.

Not today. He wasn't ready.

* * *

After being home all of ten minutes, Emerson's doorbell rang. He felt like he was being stalked. He answered the door, expecting another young woman with a plate of cookies. Instead, he found Freddy Kappal looking like he'd rather not be there.

"Hi . . . Emerson." Freddy said his name like he wasn't sure he'd get it right. "I'm Freddy. I live down the hall."

Emerson smelled Church in this meeting. "I know who you are," he replied.

Freddy laughed. "Right. Of course. Listen, I'm here on official business, but I sense you aren't really into fake friendliness."

"You guessed right."

"So I'll just be straight with you," Freddy continued. "I'm the ward mission leader, and the bishop has asked me to fellowship you."

"Okay." Emerson was used to being a project by now. He was Mindy's project and Ellie's project and numerous other people's projects from his ward in Atlanta. The hand-holding had been nice at first; it had provided a good support system, but once he hadn't needed help anymore, a lot of those hands had vanished. He hoped he'd have a different experience here.

"But I don't want to fellowship you," Freddy continued, totally catching Emerson off guard. "I don't think pretending to be your friend will work for either of us."

"Then what are you doing here? Because you're beginning to sound rude."

Freddy laughed again. "Let's just try to be friends for real. And I'll introduce you to more people in the ward and get you feeling at home."

Emerson studied him for a moment. Freddy and Lucy hardly looked alike. Freddy had dark hair and olive skin while everything about Lucy was fair. There was something similar in their mannerisms, and they shared the same keen gray eyes. Freddy clearly didn't mince words, and he didn't seem to want to play by all the unwritten rules of the Church; that had been clear when he'd backed Emerson up in elders quorum. Freddy was being genuine. He wanted to either be Emerson's friend or help him find friends. "Sure," Emerson said. "Let's be friends."

"Cool. You busy right now?" Freddy rocked back on his heels with his hands in his pockets.

Emerson was still in his work clothes. He wanted to change, shower, and eat food he had cooked himself. "Maybe. What were you thinking?"

"My sister is out for the afternoon—house shopping with her Fiasco." Emerson smirked at the nickname. So Freddy wasn't a fan of Charles. Interesting. "It's the perfect time for video games," Freddy continued. "No women folk around to complain about how we're wasting our time."

Emerson had to stop himself from being calculating. Freddy was here without ulterior motives, so Emerson needed to stop the next thought in his head from fully forming. If he became friends with Freddy . . . No. Lucy was off the market. No amount of time spent with her brother would woo her back. It wasn't fate that had brought Emerson to Windy Corner Apartments; it was Charles and a coincidence. This was not a divine design to bring Lucy back into his life.

"Can you give me an hour?" Emerson asked. "I just got back from a three-day flight schedule."

Freddy appeared to take note of his clothes. "Oh, yeah, sure. Whatever you need. I'll just be at my place, saving the universe. Come over whenever." He offered a wave before moving down the hall and disappearing into his apartment.

Emerson took his time showering and eating, grateful to be back on the ground with unrecycled air and enough room to stretch out. As he walked down the hall to Lucy's apartment, he couldn't help but relish in the possibility buzzing through his body. Maybe he would see her again.

Chapter 23

"You really didn't like any of the houses?" Charles asked.

Lucy stared out the car window, admiring the cute old houses on Thirteenth East as they drove back to Windy Corner. "No, not really," she answered, glancing briefly at Charles before returning her gaze to the street. "I know it makes sense to move farther south since you work at BYU, but . . ." She sighed. "Everything we looked at was so generic. I grew up in a place like that. I know how boring it can be."

"Is that really what it is?" Charles asked, pulling into the driveway of his house. "You don't want to live in the same area where you grew up?" He put the car in park but kept it idling as though he wasn't committed to the idea of her staying for dinner as planned. Even without those clues, Lucy knew Charles was mad at her. They'd spent the morning trying to finalize more wedding details, but Lucy had been ambivalent. And now she wouldn't commit to putting down an offer on a house. Charles had every right to be angry. Lucy wasn't acting like a woman who wanted to get married.

"I really love Sugar House," Lucy said. "I love the novelty and history of each home. I love all the local shops and that so much is within walking distance."

"I'm sure we can find a neighborhood with rundown old houses somewhere in Utah County."

"Are you sure?"

"Lucy, I want you to be happy. I don't care where I live as long as it's with you."

She felt the corners of her mouth tug upward.

"Let's go in," he said, turning off the car. "My parents are expecting us on Skype soon." Charles got out of the car, walked over to her side, and opened the door. He held out his hand for her, and Lucy slipped her hand in his. His skin was smooth and his fingers long and thin, so unlike the hands of another she thought of more often.

They entered the house, and the smell of roasting chicken greeted them. Charles turned on the lights as Lucy went to the oven to check their dinner. She retrieved a hot mitt and a fork from a nearby drawer and carefully removed the lid on the roaster. Lemon-scented steam touched her face. Moving a lemon slice aside, she stabbed the chicken and pulled the meat back. It was tender and white. Perfect.

Over her shoulder, she saw Charles fiddling with the laptop, trying to bring up Skype. She closed the oven door, turned off the heat, and joined Charles at the computer. The face of his mom appeared on the screen.

"Oh, Lucy, I am so glad to see you again!" his mother exclaimed.

"Hi, Sister Buffington," Lucy replied with a little wave. She'd met Charles's parents only via Skype and still wasn't sure what to make of them.

"Where's Father?" Charles asked.

His mom looked behind her, then waved a hand. "Somewhere. I'm sure he'll come in soon," she said.

"So, how are you?" Charles asked. "How's the work?"

Lucy took this opportunity to excuse herself to finish getting dinner ready. She pulled the asparagus from the crisper drawer. She was too hungry to do anything fancy with it, so she chopped off the ends and threw it in a pot to steam. She hoped Charles wouldn't mind dinner being a little simple tonight. She usually loved cooking elaborate meals, and Charles was an excellent sous-chef. On one of their first dates, they'd made a beautiful meal of marmalade pork medallions with sage risotto, roasted garlic brussels sprouts, and a fig-and-raspberry tart. It had taken hours, but Lucy had felt so comfortable with Charles and they'd seemed so in sync. Their dance around the kitchen had been so perfect that Lucy had been sure she would want to make dinner with him every night for the rest of her life.

"Lucy," Charles called from the next room over. She hadn't even heard him leave. "Mother wants you to play her something." Lucy moved into the living room, where Charles had set the laptop on the piano.

"I'd love if you would," Sister Buffington said. "You play so beautifully."

"Sure," Lucy said and positioned herself at the piano.

"Play some Beethoven," Charles suggested. "You play him so well."

Lucy offered a polite smile, set her fingers on the keys, and did not play Beethoven. She saved him for herself. Instead, she played Schumann. Her fingers pressed the cool keys, and she fell into the memorized rhythm.

Playing the piano could carry her to a new setting. Perhaps that was why she loved to play, the experience was transportive.

The rising and falling notes reminded her of a walk through the woods. An image formed in her mind. She saw a bronze boy posed on one leg, playing a flute. The second vignette formed into a grove of trees. She stood there with a man. In the third vignette, Lucy became lost in the sound of blue cornflowers, her eyes pressed closed and her body moving with the music. The fourth vignette brought the dangerous touch of another's lips against hers. The sensation expanded through her in a slow, constricting ache and stayed there in the music. She ended the piece at the fifth vignette, finding it redemptive, her fears and worries flooding out through her fingers. She could do this. She could put the memory of Emerson to rest. She could marry Charles.

The sound of clapping broke her spell, and she opened her eyes to see Sister Buffington on the screen, tears streaming down her cheeks. "That was so lovely!" she exclaimed.

Lucy felt a touch on her shoulder and turned to see Charles, his face nearly ashen. "I've never heard you play like that," he said. "Lucy, you are truly a work of art."

Suddenly, a small feeling of embarrassment crept through her. To think she'd shared such a personal experience with two other people in the room. "I should check on dinner." She stood and went to the kitchen. Behind her, she heard Charles say, "And to think I wanted her to play Beethoven! Schumann was perfect for the evening, and Lucy knew it!"

"She's becoming one of us," Sister Buffington said. "Just keep working on her, Charles, and soon she'll fit in perfectly."

The powerful resolve Lucy had felt while playing began to fade. Keep working on her? Was she really so lacking? Lucy felt betrayed; she didn't hear Charles defending her. Could she really marry him in January? Would she actually be happy with him?

She checked the chicken in the oven and took it out. She turned the heat off the asparagus and removed the lid.

"Just steamed asparagus?" Charles asked, joining her in the kitchen. "I was hoping for something a little more flavorful."

* * *

Later, through the closed door of her apartment, Lucy could hear the cranked-up volume of the TV and the voices of two males shouting insults at each other. She stepped inside, and the door clicked softly behind her. She intended to sneak off to her room before being seen, but she found herself frozen. Emerson stood on the couch, doing some sort of victory dance, as Freddy shouted pseudo-curse words at him. Emerson looked carefree and surprisingly young, not at all like the morose man she'd met in London.

"Lucy, hello!" he shouted before hopping off the couch.

Lucy felt color coming to her cheeks. She felt like she'd peeked in on something she shouldn't have seen. But Emerson didn't seem embarrassed at all. Exhilarated, maybe—probably from the video game win—but not at all embarrassed. Lucy couldn't take her eyes off him as he grinned like a little boy. His eyes stayed on her too. She felt warm and dizzy and . . .

"Hey, Luce," Freddy said, bringing her back to reality. He turned down the volume on the TV. "How was house shopping?"

Lucy swallowed and touched her forehead, willing the heat the leave. "It was fine." She noticed Emerson had returned to sitting on the couch and Freddy was gearing up the game for another round.

"Did you pick one out?" Freddy asked.

Lucy took a few steps away from the door. "No." She didn't say anything else. Laser fire punctuated the silence.

Freddy glanced back at her.

"You've met Emerson, right?" he asked.

Emerson watched her, and she felt an incredible amount of pressure pushing on her chest. "Yeah, we've met." How could he have such an effect on her, even from across the room, even when she was engaged to someone else?

She remembered the music, the blue cornflowers, and the kiss. Like a warm liquid melting through her veins, a heaviness dripped into her limbs. Their eyes stayed on each other, even as breathing became difficult and the pressure became unbearable. *I was never supposed to see him again*, she thought. Willing up the strength to blink away the eye contact, Lucy gracelessly excused herself. In her room, at the side of her bed, she wanted to pray for direction but couldn't.

I was never supposed to see him again.

* * *

At church the next day, Lucy sat beside Charles, his arm draped around her shoulder, his legs crossed, and his posture rigid. Freddy sat next to Charles against the wall and away from the couple. Lucy thought it strange that Charles had sat between her and Freddy, but much of what Charles did baffled her.

As the bishop opened the meeting, Lucy composed a list in her head. "Things to talk to Charles about: 1. The realistic number of children they planned on having and when. 2. Her desire to continue working, even if it was part-time, after said children were born. 3. The awful comment his mother had made about her."

The organist began to play the introduction of the opening hymn. Lucy grabbed a hymnbook from the back of the pew in front of her while Charles swiped his finger across his tablet to bring up the words there. For someone who loved books so much, Charles rarely read anything on paper. Lucy peeked over at his tablet to see what language the words were in. She forcefully held back a groan. The words were in Spanish.

The introduction ended, and Charles's booming vibrato sang, "*¿Con fervor orar pensaste al amanecer?*" Lucy glanced over at Freddy so they could share a look, but Freddy was too busy signaling someone over. Probably his friend Ammon, who was supposed to stay with them this week.

With nothing else to do, Lucy joined in the singing, her voice blending pleasantly with Charles's. That was another one of the first things she had noticed about her and Charles: they sang together beautifully if she sang soprano.

Then the air shifted beside her, and she smelled a blue cologne that normally existed only in her memory. Her heart started racing. Emerson smoothed down his tie as he sat beside her. Was he active in the Church now? Lucy offered the hymnal to him because that was the polite thing to do. With a large rough hand, he grasped his end of the book. Lucy pointed to the place they were in the song, and he began singing.

His wasn't a skilled, careful voice like Charles's, but it was smooth and unselfconscious. Lucy relaxed her vocal cords and dropped her voice to an alto, where she'd always felt most comfortable singing, though her voice didn't sound as nice in that range. But sitting next to Emerson, hearing his unpracticed notes vibrate through her, made her not want to try so hard. Made her feel like she *didn't* have to try hard. She could be herself, sing an alto instead of a soprano, and enjoy the way the hymnal felt almost weightless in their shared hands.

Chapter 24

"Like a Band-Aid," Emerson said to himself. He stood on the front porch of the green brick house. The front door was worn and a little warped, with a one-inch gap at the bottom. The doorknob seemed to be original to the house, a heavy dark-brown metal engraved with scrolling patterns. The keyhole probably fit a skeleton key. Emerson had forgotten the details of the doorknob in his time away, but he was surprised the door still hadn't been replaced. The doorknob could stay, Emerson thought, but the door needed updating. A strong kick would do it in, and the inch gap at the bottom couldn't be good in the winter.

He knocked on the door and took a step back, then clenched and unclenched his fists, trying to give the adrenaline some place to go. Taking slow, steady breaths, he tried to find courage in the fact that this was the right thing to do.

A man in his midsixties opened the door. Every time Emerson saw his father, he was surprised by his appearance. He looked ancient and youthful at the same time. He stood a few inches shorter than Emerson, with messy, thick, graying brown hair, lines that indicated years of smiling, and blue eyes that shone with the same kind of idealism found in a child's. His father blinked and squinted at the sight of him. "Emerson," he said, seeming knocked back. He steadied himself against the doorframe. "What are you doing here?"

Emerson gulped and tried to hide his nerves with a smile. "Hi, Dad. I, ah, moved to Salt Lake. Thought I would stop by and say hi."

His father stared for a moment, his mouth slack. Perhaps Emerson shouldn't have pretended they weren't estranged.

"I suppose you'd better come in," his father said, stepping back and motioning for Emerson to follow.

Emerson stepped into the old house, the door creaking shut behind him. The front room was still messy, like it had been years ago, and held the musty scent of decaying paper. Sunlight streamed in through a dirty window, lighting the room with a dusty haze. Boxes, books, and stacks of newspaper occupied all the available space in the room, covering a couch, two chairs, and an old piano. A thin path led them through the room to the kitchen, which was spotless.

The contrast between the disaster in the front room and the cleanliness of the kitchen still unsettled Emerson, reminding him that he had never understood his father and his eccentricities. That same feeling of embarrassment of his dad crept back in. He felt fifteen again, shipped off to Utah to spend the summer in this drafty, old house.

"How have you been?" Emerson asked.

His father moved around the kitchen, acting like Emerson wasn't there. He looked up at Emerson, blinked as if surprised to see him, and resumed his search through the cabinets. "I'm fine, son," he replied. He ducked down and disappeared behind the counter for a moment, then popped back up, a boyish smile on his face. He'd put his glasses on, and his eyes became twice their usual size. "You remember this?" His father held a green handmade mug in his hands. "You gave it to me on Father's Day when you were nine."

What even made his father think of this? Shouldn't they be talking about Emerson now living in Salt Lake? Or the fact that they hadn't spoken in over a year and now Emerson had randomly shown up on his doorstep?

"Yeah, Dad," Emerson said, taking the mug from his outstretched hands. "I made it in that pottery class Mom made me take."

His father chuckled, took the mug from him, and returned it to its place in the cabinet. "You said you're living here now?" he asked.

"Yes."

"Strange that you decided to stop by to see me." He laughed, but it sounded more like a hiccup.

The comment stung like the snap of a rubber band. But Emerson deserved far worse.

"Are you doing okay?" his father continued, his hands roving over his face, through his hair, touching the pens bulging in the front pocket of his shirt. "I know you were close to your mother."

"I'm doing better; thanks for asking."

There was a long pause, and a cuckoo clock went off somewhere in the house. Emerson shifted his weight, and his father tapped his fingers on the kitchen counter.

"Do you need money?" his father asked.

Ouch. But Emerson deserved that too. "No," he replied, trying to keep the edge out of his voice.

"I guess I don't understand what you're doing here."

Emerson sighed, his nerves growing. "I've come back to the Church." His father blinked. "And I'm trying to make things right," Emerson continued. His father blinked again. Emerson couldn't tell if the blinks were skeptical blinks or blinks of disbelief. The rest of the words came fast, Emerson cringing as he said them. "So I had this stupid idea that I would show you how sorry I am about the way I've treated you by serving you."

More blinking. More tapping. More shifting of weight.

Emerson had most likely offended him.

"Like, I could fix your front door. Or help you organize the front room."

His father cleared his throat. The kitchen seemed to grow smaller, or maybe it was the changing light from the setting sun. His father's all-too-bright eyes stared at something on the wall behind him. "I'll take your olive branch," his father finally said. "Do whatever you think this house needs." He circled around the counter to stand closer to Emerson and wagged a finger. "Just don't throw anything away."

Relief broke through Emerson. It had almost been too easy, and he was acutely aware that he also didn't deserve it.

Chapter 25

"Lucy, did you hear?" Her mother stood at the stove, stirring a large pot of minestrone. "Mary and Harold's basement flooded."

"Really, how did that happen?" Lucy joined her mother. Charles was taking a Sunday nap on the couch. Freddy and his friend Ammon were in the backyard playing Frisbee. This was Lucy's ideal way to spend a Sunday.

"Their sprinkler line broke in the middle of the night, and they awoke to a swamp leaking through the windows."

"What a disaster," Lucy said.

"They've decided to go to Hawaii while the repairs are made," her mother continued. "And they wanted to know if you could do them a favor."

"Really?" Lucy knew where this was going.

"Charlotte doesn't feel safe being home alone with the repairmen. And she can't go to Hawaii with her parents because school's already started for her. Would she be able to stay at your place until her parents get home?"

Charles entered the kitchen and joined them by the stove, his white dress shirt wrinkled from sleep. He set a hand on Lucy's shoulder, and she had to make herself not shrug it off. "What's happened?" he asked.

"Nothing," Lucy said. She knew he wouldn't take her side.

"Charlotte needs a place to live for the next few weeks," her mother said. "And I'm asking Lucy if she'll take her in."

"Oh, I would love to have Charlotte around more," Charles said.

She shot Charles a glare. Did he forget that things were still awkward between Charlotte and her? Plus, Emerson was around, and Charlotte was bound to have opinions about that. Lucy didn't want to go digging up those skeletons.

"Mom, the apartment is pretty crowded," Lucy said. "Ammon is staying with us right now, remember? Where would Charlotte sleep?"

"Could she sleep in your room?" her mom asked.

"Yes, your room," Charles agreed. "It will be like a sleepover."

Lucy sighed in resignation. She didn't have it in her to fight. "Can we talk about this later?" *Preferably without Charles.*

Freddy and Ammon came bounding into the house, and everyone settled down to dinner around the big oak table. Charles ladled soup into the bowls, and soon the sound of spoons clicking against porcelain filled the room.

"Lucy," Freddy said. "What kind of guy is Emerson?"

She nearly choked on her soup and brought a napkin to her mouth to cover up her reaction. "Ask Charles," she replied. "Emerson is his friend."

"I hardly know him," Charles said. "I merely brought him to Windy Corner."

"Who's Emerson?" Lucy's mother asked.

"He's our new neighbor," Freddy said. "Lucy met him in London."

Lucy could feel her mother's eyes on her. She stole a glance in her mom's direction—raised eyebrows, mouth forming a silent "Oh." Her mother knew all about the man in London. It was clear she found this revelation more than a little interesting.

"I can't really get a read on him," Freddy continued. "Is he a friendly guy, or is he kind of guarded? Because sometimes he seems really nice, but other times he seems distracted or bored."

"He's definitely bored," Charles said, soupspoon poised in the air above his bowl. "Emerson is like me; he needs a certain type of intellectual stimulation. Some people are unable to keep us entertained for long. When you've read as many books as we have, you've seen and heard everything." He punctuated his declaration with a delicate slurp of his soup.

The wide-eyed silence that followed enveloped the room like a black hole.

There were so many things wrong with Charles's statement that Lucy hardly knew where to start. First, Emerson was nothing like Charles. Second, Charles just said he hardly knew him. Third, Charles had insulted Freddy's intelligence. She ground her teeth together. Her gaze wandered over to Ammon to see how he was reacting to this exchange. She already knew without having to check that Freddy was politely seething. Ammon stared into his soup bowl, and the stare even convinced Lucy that what he found there was preferable to this conversation.

"I'd like to have Lucy tell me about Emerson," Freddy said to Charles, "so you don't have to bore yourself."

Go, Freddy!

Charles sat up a little straighter. His foot knocked Lucy's shin under the table as he crossed one leg over the other. He made his posture even more rigid as he brought his spoon slowly down into his soup.

"Emerson is guarded," Lucy said. "Like Charles, he's a thinker." There, that should do it. It was a sort of honest appraisal of Emerson, and it didn't sound like she was taking anyone's side.

"That's what I thought," Freddy said and returned to his soup.

After a long beat of silence, Lucy's mother spoke. "Interesting that you never mentioned Emerson was your new neighbor."

* * *

Lucy submerged a soup bowl in sudsy water and scrubbed the inside with a brush. Being elbow deep in warm water, with the soft touch of her mother's arm against hers, felt soothing in a way nothing else had recently. She passed the bowl to her mother, who rinsed it and set it in the dish rack to dry. Charles had gotten a ride back to Salt Lake with Ammon and Freddy. Her mother's constant throat clearing let Lucy know she was working up the courage to say something. Emerson. Charles. Lucy could only guess what she wanted to talk about.

Lucy sighed. "Just say it."

"Why does Charles have to be rude like that?"

Charles it was. Which Lucy actually preferred, because if she had to talk about Emerson for one more minute, she'd start looking at plane tickets.

"I don't know," Lucy replied.

Charles had been in rare form at dinner. His rudeness had extended beyond the conversation about Emerson. After Lucy's mom had shared some ward gossip, Charles had said, "I once heard this saying: 'Great minds discuss ideas. Average minds discuss events. Small minds discuss people.' Let's try to be great minds, shall we?"

"Charles has specific aesthetics," Lucy continued, handing her mother another bowl. "Like he said, he gets bored easily."

"And that's an excuse to be hurtful?"

Lucy stared down into the dishwater, fingers gliding through the bubbles and floating grease. She felt chastised, like a little girl who'd broken her mother's favorite vase. "What do you want me to do? Slap him on the wrist and tell him to behave?"

"You could have stood up for us. We might not be as refined as the Buffingtons, but that doesn't make us Neanderthals." Her mother placed a bowl in the rack and turned to Lucy. "I'm worried about how different you are with him."

Lucy felt herself shrinking beneath her mother's gaze. *She's becoming one of us . . .*

"London was good for you, wasn't it?" her mother asked. There was that pointed expression again. Lucy picked up a bowl and watched the water slosh inside. London *had* been good for her, but it had also been a fantasy. She was never supposed to see him again. *He* hadn't wanted to see her again. And now that she had seen him, everything was getting muddled.

When she didn't say anything, her mother continued. "My biggest concern about you and Charles is that you don't seem to communicate with him. You should be able to talk to him about anything." Lucy handed over the bowl. "I've never known you to not speak your mind. Where did my confident daughter go?"

Lucy gulped.

She's becoming one of us.

Being a Buffington would mean good seats at general conference because their grandfather was a General Authority. It would mean destination family reunions to exotic locations because his father was a millionaire. Being a Buffington would also mean living under the microscope of Charles and his family's creation. Lucy knew without it being explicitly told to her that Buffingtons lived by a higher law in terms of righteousness. Not only was she expected to enthusiastically live the gospel of Jesus Christ, but she also had to make sure everyone around her knew she did. Her visible devotion and faith were to be a missionary tool, and she was to be a standard bearer. Anything less than external perfection would be a problem.

Charles knew Lucy wasn't like them, but he still loved her. So, couldn't his love be enough? Or was he already changing her in ways she hadn't recognized. It was what his mother wanted, for him to keep working on her. Was she really becoming one of them? The last thought made her shiver.

As Lucy and her mother finished the dishes in silence, Lucy considered the possibility of hurting Charles again and spending the rest of her life alone.

* * *

But Charles did it again. She arrived home to her apartment to find him pensive, waiting in her room, distress etched deeply into his usually smooth forehead. "My behavior at dinner was abhorrent," he said as he stood to meet her in the center of the room. She wondered if someone had put him up to this.

Charles took her hands and looked at her earnestly. His eyes were an impossible shade of blue, and her heartbeat picked up a little. "I don't know what came over me today," he said. "I think I must be overly stressed with the wedding plans and the house shopping and school starting and my manuscript. But I shouldn't take it out on the people you love the most. I'm sorry I behaved so badly."

And instead of saying the easy thing, Lucy said what she wanted to say. "You have to treat my family better, Charles." She could feel herself start to shake a little.

"You are absolutely right," he agreed.

"And I don't think I can marry you until we talk about some things."

He blinked in surprise and swallowed. She felt his grip on her hands tighten. "We can talk about anything you like."

He pulled her down to sit on the floor with him. "I think yesterday really upset me," Lucy began, her chest growing heavy and her throat thick.

"Yesterday?" he asked. "I thought yesterday was lovely."

Lucy tried not to scowl, but she could feel her face tighten. Had he forgotten that they'd fought?

"I'm sorry," he continued, adjusting his glasses. "That wasn't very validating. Tell me what upset you."

Lucy swallowed the rock forming in her throat. "It was upsetting when you suggested that we could have ten kids."

"I was only joking," Charles replied.

"I don't think I can joke about that," Lucy said.

He patted her hand. "Okay, no joking about having a dozen kids."

"I think I only want two kids."

It was Charles's turn to scowl. "Only two?"

Lucy nodded, a pulsing starting in her ears. Was this a deal breaker? Is there where it ended?

"Let's have two, then," Charles said. "And maybe we'll want more, but we will decide that later."

"And I want to keep working after I have children," Lucy added, the pulsing almost drowning out all sound.

Charles gaped.

"What?" Lucy asked.

"I'm shocked, that's all," Charles said. "I mean, I just assumed you'd want to stay home. Why *wouldn't* you want to stay home with the kids?"

"Then you stay home with the kids," Lucy said. The pulsing turned to rushing.

"I value my work far too much to be a stay-at-home dad."

"And maybe I feel the same way about my work."

He paused, then said, "Ah, I see. Then work you shall."

Lucy let out a long breath. "I think we're putting too much pressure on ourselves house shopping."

He gripped her hand again. "I was thinking the same thing. Let's just find an apartment somewhere—it could even be in Salt Lake—and house shop next summer."

The pulsing stopped, and warmth bubbled up in her chest. Charles wasn't so bad.

But there was still one more thing.

She cleared her throat and tried to hold on to the warm bubbles. "I heard what your mother said about me," she said, her voice small.

Charles furrowed his brow. "I'm not sure what you're talking about."

"At dinner last night. She said, 'Keep working on her.' It hurt, like I'm not good enough as I am now."

He shook his head. "You must have misheard her," he said. "Or misunderstood what she meant. My mom adores you, I'm sure of it."

Every last bubble popped inside her, leaving a strange weight hovering above her chest.

Lucy walked Charles to the door and kissed him good night. Again, everything appeared to be perfect. She had this feeling that her inability to communicate with Charles was her own fault. He seemed reasonable when they talked. He hadn't been belligerent and opinionated like she had expected. Charles loved her and wanted to make her happy. She just needed to tell him what she wanted.

She closed the front door behind him, locked the dead bolt, and took a deep breath. No more keeping things from him. It was okay to fight with him and advocate for herself. She loved Charles, and she was going to marry him, even if the weight hovering above her chest made it hard to breath.

Chapter 26

EMERSON STOOD IN THE MIDDLE of his father's front room. He'd made some good progress the last week, sorting through stacks of newspapers, trying to order them by date. His father had kept a paper copy of each edition of the *Salt Lake Tribune* that his articles and columns had appeared in. In addition to the book, movie, and event reviews he'd written over the last fifteen years, he had also written a weekly humor column, often discussing Mormon culture and talking about local issues. Emerson had recently started reading his father's column and found himself feeling even more regretful that he hadn't maintained a better relationship with him. They thought the same way.

Emerson went to the piano, a baby grand with peeling varnish and chipped keys. He pressed down on a key in the middle of the piano marked with a large C in black Sharpie. The note sounded twangy and dull. He needed to ask his father what the plan was for the piano since he didn't play and it looked in need of repairs.

Before Emerson started down the dark path of thinking how the piano was a symbol for his father's life, he grabbed a banker's box from the piano bench and sat on the floor in a space he'd cleared. Moths didn't fly out when he took the lid off, but it looked like they should. He leafed through the first few pages, trying to determine where to catalog the contents. These papers were from his time at the *Wisconsin State Journal*. His father hadn't kept nearly as many of those editions as he had the *Tribune*.

Halfway through the box, Emerson hit a brown photo album. He recognized the worn edges and faded gold scrawl on the cover. He pulled it from the box. This album had sat on the living room coffee table when his parents had still been married.

Something heavy shifted inside him, and that same hurt he'd carried after his parents' separation returned. He had always assumed his mother had destroyed the wedding album because he'd never seen it after his father had left. He had internalized his mother's supposed act of hatred, and he'd hated his father too. But all along, their album had been here.

Carefully, Emerson opened the cover, which felt loose at the binding. The first page held a large picture he knew well and had looked at a hundred times. It was a little faded now, the vibrancy of the colors having disappeared with time. His mother wore a brown skirt suit with large shoulder pads, her eighties hair teased. In her hands, she held a bundle of white daisies. His father stood beside her in a tan tweed suit, a big grin on his face. They had been married at the courthouse on a Thursday afternoon, exactly three weeks after meeting. It was the kind of impulsive thing he never imagined his practical mother doing. But she had.

Emerson ran his finger over his mother's young face. She had been beautiful in her youth and had grown handsome as she'd aged, her face gathering dignified wrinkles in all the right places. Then he touched his father's grin, one he often still wore. In terms of behavior and mannerisms, his father still very much reminded Emerson of a boy. He must have sparked something remarkable in his mother to convince her to marry him. But what had compelled his devout Mormon father to marry an agnostic woman? He had been older when he'd married—at least by Mormon standards—somewhere around thirty-two—and maybe that was why. Or maybe because his father had grown up in Milwaukee where members were few and far between, he'd always assumed he'd have to marry outside of his faith if he stayed there. Whatever the reason, it didn't seem to matter now. Their marriage had ended, and his mother was dead.

Emerson closed the album, a musty scent swirling through the air. This was his closure: myriad unanswered questions and stacks and stacks of his father's life to sort through.

Chapter 27

CHARLOTTE MOVED IN ON MONDAY night. She had one large suitcase and a backpack. She kept apologizing for burdening Lucy but also claimed there was no other place she could stay. They didn't talk much more than that since it was late and Charlotte had to be at school early the next morning.

Tuesday night, Lucy arrived home hours later than usual. She had been busy at work and had used it as an excuse to stay away. Through the front door, she could hear talking and laughter. Lately, when she came home to her apartment, the turn of the key felt too much like Russian roulette. Who would be on the other side of the door? And by "who," she really meant "Emerson." The door wasn't locked this time, so with a skipping heart, she went in.

Freddy, Ammon, Charlotte, Ellie, and Emerson sat around the coffee table, Cards Against Humanity in hand. Their energy nearly knocked Lucy backward.

"That is so inappropriate!" Charlotte shouted. She tossed some cards at Freddy's head.

He didn't even try to shield himself as he shook with laughter. The rest of the group watched the exchange and chuckled. Lucy tried not to look in Emerson's direction or pick out his laugh. She couldn't remember what it sounded like. Had they even laughed together in London?

"You told me this game was like Apples to Apples!" Charlotte continued to yell. "I didn't know the cards would have suggestive material on them. You've exposed me to impurity, Freddy!" She threw her remaining cards down and stalked out of the room.

Oh, sweet, naive, self-righteous Charlotte.

"That was weird," Ammon said. He knew Charlotte the least of anyone in the room.

"Someone should go after her," Ellie suggested, her eyes on Freddy. But Freddy was still in a fit of giggles. Ellie's eyes flickered to Lucy standing by the door. "Oh, hey, Lucy."

Lucy tried not to shiver as all the eyes in the room turned to her. And by "all," she meant "Emerson's." Her mouth and throat became deserts, and she licked her lips with a sandy tongue. Keeping her eyes trained on Ellie, Lucy rasped, "Hi." Sheesh, she should be able to stand in the same room with him without turning into dust.

Like he was some sort of magnet, her gaze slid to Emerson. His eyes darted from hers to the scarf tied to her purse. His mother's scarf. That Lucy now took everywhere. She let out a slow breath, her heart ping-ponging in her chest.

"Would you mind checking on Charlotte?" Ellie asked. "She's angry with us."

"Sure." Lucy couldn't have asked for a better escape and scooted out of the room, relief nearly deflating her.

Charlotte sat on the edge of Lucy's bed, examining her hands. She may have even been crying a little, but Lucy didn't want to notice.

Charlotte looked up when the door clicked behind Lucy.

"Everything okay?" Lucy asked.

Charlotte's sigh rattled her shoulders.

"There's nothing wrong with being sensitive," Lucy said carefully.

The look Charlotte gave Lucy could have crumbled a daisy. "Does Charles know about *him*?"

"Yes, he does." But then Lucy bit her tongue. She should have pretended not to know who "him" was. She shouldn't have answered so quickly. Plus, why was Charlotte bringing this up?

"And he's okay with Emerson being in your apartment?"

"Emerson is Freddy's friend," Lucy replied. "I can't ask him to leave."

"Well, I think you should stay away from him." The self-righteousness in Charlotte's voice was almost enough to make Lucy rush into the other room and lay a big one on Emerson's lips.

"Are you done?" Lucy folded her arms over her chest. Really, she should take the passive route she'd become so good at taking and let this go since she was going to have to live with Charlotte *in her room* for the next two weeks, but maybe this was what they needed. To get it all out there. It seemed to work for Charles and her. So why not Charlotte?

"I don't want to see you hurt Charles again," Charlotte said. "I know how you feel about Emerson."

"*Felt*," Lucy corrected, more anger than she expected seeping through. "How I *felt* about Emerson. He left London and didn't want to talk to me again. Which was fine. I understand why he did that. But apparently talking to Ellie was okay. And Emerson chose Ellie over me when I didn't even know we were in competition. But that's fine too, because I have Charles. So I am over it, okay, Charlotte?"

Yikes! Where did that come from? Lucy had broken out in a hot sweat. Anger and jealousy she hadn't even known she'd felt coursed through her. Ellie! Emerson! She didn't want to confront any of this.

Charlotte's eyes glowed electric. "You don't sound like someone who's over it. If there's even a chance you still harbor feelings for Emerson, you need to figure it out before you hurt Charles."

Lucy scoffed. "Figure it out? You just said I need to stay away from him. Which is it?"

Charlotte stood and headed to the door. "Are you sure Charles understands exactly what happened between you and Emerson in London?"

Lucy went from hot to cold in less than a second. No, he didn't. All he knew was Lucy had kissed a man while in London. He didn't know she'd fallen absolutely in love with that man. And the reason Lucy hadn't gone right back to Charles after she'd come home was because she'd needed time to get over Emerson. She had been waiting for him to change his mind and contact her. But then he never had and her heart had needed the hole filled. And Charles had been there, like he always had been. He was her constant, and she didn't have to be alone.

The weight that had been hovering just above Lucy's chest slammed down against her heart. For a moment, she couldn't breathe or move. Lucy wished Charlotte wouldn't judge her so harshly so she could tell her the whole truth, so she wouldn't have to navigate this river of changing emotions alone. "I don't want to hurt Charles again," Lucy said, the quiver in her voice unmistakable.

"Then stay away from Emerson," Charlotte said and left the room.

With the click of the door, Lucy sank to her bed. *Okay, okay, okay.* Her stupid heart wouldn't stop trying to bounce out of her throat. Taking a slow, deep breath, she closed her eyes. Her fingers found their way to the scarf Emerson had given her, the silk cooling her skin. She needed to figure this out. If she married Charles now, a part of her would always wonder about Emerson and that was not how she wanted to spend the rest of her life.

London was a fantasy, she reminded herself. She just needed to shatter the illusion so she could move on. But how?

Chapter 28

LUCY SCRATCHED SOME NOTES ONTO the legal pad on her lab table, then put another spoonful of ice cream in her mouth. The sweet, creamy mixture slowly melted across her tongue, filling her mouth with hints of butter and brown sugar. She swallowed, opened her mouth, and, on an inhale, tasted the distinct flavor of artificiality. Something plasticky and almost chemical.

This was the ninth caramel flavoring she'd tried for the New Jersey *dulce de leche* ice cream she was attempting to replicate, and it wasn't going to work. The original recipe from the small ice-cream shop called for homemade brown-butter caramel, which was mixed into the ice cream base and ribboned through it. She'd found a delicious caramel sauce to ribbon through the ice cream, but adding that sauce to the base was causing too many texture problems. So the next solution was to find an artificial caramel flavor to add to it. If that didn't work—and it was likely that would be the case—she would have to reformulate the ice-cream base to work with the caramel sauce. And that would be much harder and make the ice cream more expensive.

She moved over to her laptop and opened her web browser. There were still a few more suppliers she could get caramel flavor samples from. She began to compose an email to one of them when she heard the door to the lab open. She looked up, expecting it to be her boss, but found herself locking eyes with Emerson.

Her heart took off at its usual erratic pace whenever he was around, but she fought to keep herself visibly unaffected. She held one finger up to let him know she needed a minute and then finished her email, her fingers clumsy as they typed. She hadn't seen him in over a week, not since the Cards Against Humanity debacle. She'd heard from Freddy that Emerson was away on flights. Not that she had asked or anything.

Steadying her breath, she hit send, then looked back up at him. She hoped her smile looked friendly but not too friendly. "What are you doing here?" Did that sound too accusing? Or did she sound genuinely curious.

"I hope this is okay. I haven't been able to catch you at home, so Freddy told me where you work," he replied, taking a few slow steps into the lab. He looked Photoshopped against the silver surfaces of the lab. Lucy didn't want to look at him, so she went to her bowls of ice cream, dipped in a clean spoon, and offered it to Emerson. "Here, try this."

He took the sample from her and appeared to not find the request out of place. She watched as he turned the spoon over and put the ice cream directly on his tongue like she had shown him in London. *Why does he remember that but Charles doesn't?* She tried not to stare at his mouth longer than necessary—was it necessary to look at his mouth at all?—before asking him, "How does it taste?"

"Delicious," he said. "Really rich and buttery."

"Inhale through your mouth," she instructed.

He did and grimaced.

She shrugged. Yup. Back to the drawing board on that flavor. "I still don't know what you're doing here," she said, feeling herself relaxing a bit. Ice cream was her element. Emerson was on her turf. She could handle this. And not read too much into his visit.

"My dad has this old piano," Emerson said. She scooped out a spoonful of the original-recipe ice cream and handed it to him. Their fingers didn't brush when he took it, but she could feel the electricity in the air around them. "I wanted your opinion." He stuck the spoon in his mouth, and Lucy watched his face for a reaction. His eyes rolled back ever so slightly as they closed. "Wow." He sighed, and Lucy shivered for a reason she didn't want to think about.

"Good, huh?" she said, feeling more empowered by the moment. If she kept feeding him ice cream, this would be like a tasting and not some random drop-in from a former love interest. "Tell me about this piano."

"It's ancient," he began. "And ugly. Keys are missing, and the finish is cracked. Do you think you could take a look at it and tell me if it's salvageable?"

Lucy handed him another spoonful of ice cream. She noticed her heart had stopped its crazy pounding. And she didn't feel very nervous to be around him. Could that be right? Had she just needed to spend more than a few minutes with him to get over seeing him and then she could interact with him like a normal person? Had this been only physical attraction all along? Was this the shattering of the illusion that was London? "Yeah, I can take a look," she said. "When did you want to go?"

He raised his eyebrows and took the spoon out of his mouth. "When are you off?"

Oh, did she just get goose bumps? Pretty sure that question wasn't supposed to sound alluring.

"Soon," she replied, checking the clock on the wall. "Let me make sure it's okay with Charles first. Not sure how he'll feel about us hanging out because of . . ." She couldn't finish and didn't have to.

"Of course," Emerson said. "Do what you need to. Mind if I look around?"

"Go ahead. There are samples in the freezer. Help yourself."

Lucy typed out a text message to Charles: *Emerson needs an opinion on an old piano. Mind if I go with him?* While she waited for a response, she cleaned up the lab. She wiped down the tabletops with sanitizer, loaded the dishwasher, and shut off her laptop.

Her phone buzzed with a message from Charles. *Sure, love.*

"I'm ready," Lucy said, meeting Emerson over at the samples freezer.

He held a brown-and-purple striped pint-sized container in his hand. He spun it around, reading the label: Lavender Love. Lucy's heart started its wild pounding again. Emerson peeled the lid off and found a spoon. The spoon sank into the chocolate-swirled vanilla ice cream, and Lucy could smell the hints of lavender. She was transported in time, she and Emerson standing by a table with lavender chocolate between them, their breath sweet and heavy.

Emerson placed the ice cream on his tongue, and Lucy held her breath. "It tastes like London," he said.

Lucy took a deep breath. London was so not over.

Chapter 29

As a teenager, Emerson had been ashamed to bring friends home to his father's house. The dust and the boxes so clearly pointed to his father's weirdness that he had always made excuses to meet at other places. He'd spent only eight weeks a year in Utah as part of the custody agreement, and he hadn't wanted to jeopardize any friendships by having them see how he lived. Or rather, how his father lived. Some of that same trepidation weaved its way through Emerson as Lucy followed him up the walk to the front porch.

When they reached the door—newly replaced—Emerson put his hand on the antique doorknob and turned to Lucy. She stood close to him, and he could smell the faint scent of vanilla on her skin. "The house is a mess," he said. "Well, some of it."

"I think I can handle it," she said.

Emerson took a deep breath and opened the door. He stepped into the musty house, Lucy close behind him. He tried to see the front room through her eyes—the piles and piles of newspapers, the old furniture, the cobwebs streaming from the ceiling and the dust-covered drapes. He saw nothing but a giddy glint in her eyes. "Can I look around?" she asked, taking a step farther into the room.

"Sure, go ahead," he said.

Lucy went to a stack of papers and lifted the top sheet. She skimmed over the page, then fingered the pile, seeing what was there. She went to the next pile and fanned through the pages again. "This is kind of incredible," she said. "What are all the newspapers for?"

"My dad writes for the *Trib*," he said. "He likes to keep a paper copy of each edition he's published in."

Lucy continued her exploration of the room. "What does he write?"

"Mostly reviews, but he also has a weekly humor column."

"I grew up with the *Tribune* in my house. I wonder if I've ever read any of his articles. What's his name?"

Emerson hesitated. Lucy would probably know who his dad was. He was sort of a Mormon cultural icon, at least for the people who read the *Tribune* on a regular basis. But he also knew his father's column was controversial, especially among conservative Mormon circles. He wasn't sure if Lucy's reaction would be a good one.

"My dad is George Emerson." He cringed as he admitted it.

"Really?" A huge smile spread across her face. "I read his column every Thursday."

Emerson chuckled, surprised and relieved.

"So your first name is actually your dad's last name?" she asked.

Emerson nodded. "My mom was a feminist and wanted me to have her last name. I guess my dad didn't want to be left out."

"It was a good compromise," Lucy said, stopping at one of the paintings on the wall, admiring it a moment before touching another stack of papers. She gestured around the room. "This is a really impressive collection."

An unexpected ache moved through his chest. She didn't see a mess like he did. She saw something important or special.

Lucy circled through the room, touching each stack of newspaper. Her fingers brushed over a sign on the wall that read Mistrust All Enterprises That Require New Clothes. She ended her tour at the piano. Emerson watched as she moved aside some papers and gingerly opened the cover on the keys. With a thin, long finger, she hit the key marked with a *C*. The twangy note echoed against itself.

She carefully moved a stack of papers from the piano bench and settled in front of the keys. She ran her fingers over the keys without pressing down. Then, methodically, she pressed each key down, starting with the highest note and working her way down. Some notes made no sound, others a soft thud rather than their usual reverberation. Emerson broke out into goose bumps as the notes grew lower and lower.

Her posture relaxed further as she appeared to sink into her element. The familiarity of the keys and the sounds of the notes seemed to slowly unwind her. Or maybe it was Emerson falling into the sound. How had he let this woman get away from him?

"How are you doing, Emerson?" she asked. Her gray eyes met his for a brief moment before returning to the keys. She began to play a haunting melody made even stranger by the tin-roof sound of the notes.

"I'm okay," he replied. "Better."

She nodded her head, and her fingers continued their slow dance across the keys. Emerson's knees grew weak. He leaned against the side of the piano.

"I've seen you at church at few times," she said. "Did you figure out what you needed to?"

"Yes," he replied, feeling like he was in an interview with his bishop. "Enough to keep coming, at least."

"What finally made it enough?" There was another short glance in his direction, one that stripped him bare and made his bones hurt.

You, he wanted to say. *Meeting you made it seem like enough.*

He took a slow, deep breath. "Your testimony of the Atonement in London changed how I viewed things." He looked down at his hand resting on the piano. "And once I allowed the Atonement to work in my life, I didn't want to live without it. I didn't want to give up the feeling of daily redemption." He peered up at her to gauge her reaction.

She closed her eyes and seemed to disappear inside herself. She continued playing, the notes deep and progressively more unsettling. He wanted to know what she thought of him. Her opinion seemed so important.

"Why did you stay in touch with Ellie?" she asked, turning her head toward Emerson and opening her eyes. There was no break in the music. It seemed almost disconnected from her, becoming a dark soundtrack.

"I . . ." he started. Her eyes returned to the keys and her moving fingers. He felt less imprisoned. "Ellie reached out to me." He shook his head. "She's not what everyone thinks she is."

The briefest smirk appeared on Lucy's lips. She didn't like that answer.

"Lucy," he tried again. "I thought by cutting you out of my life, I'd keep my intentions with the Church pure. I owed that much to myself and God." A heaviness settled in his legs. "For the most part, it worked." He sank to his knees, the weight becoming too much. "But I couldn't forget you or London no matter how hard I tried."

Her fingers stilled on the keys, the notes leaving behind the faintest hum. She didn't look at him, her gaze fixed on a spot of peeling varnish.

"You, or at least the thought of you, became my reason for everything," he said, the words tumbling out of him now. What was he doing? Lucy was engaged to someone else. She had moved on. But now that this confessional had started, he couldn't stop himself. Emerson was selfish, plain and simple, and he wanted her to know, even if she didn't reciprocate. "I wanted to become the kind of person you wouldn't be afraid to love."

Lucy met his eyes, and the air around them pulsed. She looked frightened and beautiful. He didn't dare touch her, although his fingers ached to. His voice broke. "I wish I weren't too late." An impossible, searing pain coursed through him.

"Oh, Emerson," she whispered.

He couldn't breathe. He couldn't move. He wanted to live in the breath of her saying his name.

The front door slammed.

Emerson jerked away and stood, feeling like he'd been caught stealing. Lucy's eyes were trained on the man standing at the front door. She looked like she'd been broadsided, her face pale and eyes watery. And she had. Emerson's confession was out of line.

"Why'd the music stop?" the man standing at the front door said. "It was such a pleasant stroll up the front walk, listening to Beethoven's 'Moonlight Sonata.' I thought I was in a dream."

Emerson cleared his throat and turned to the man. "Hi, Dad," he said.

"Hi, Emerson." His father took a step farther into the room "Who's this?" he asked, gesturing at Lucy.

Lucy's lips rose into a smile, her face suddenly unshaken.

"This is my friend Lucy," Emerson said. "She came by to look at the piano."

His father approached her, his steps short and hurried. Emerson felt like he was in high school again, mortification heating his face like an oven. His father grabbed one of Lucy's hands between his two. "Your playing is lovely."

"Thank you," Lucy replied softly.

He released her hand. "Are you going to stay for dinner?" he asked.

Emerson shook his head. He didn't want to spend any more time with her. Not with his confession out there. Not when she was engaged to another man. He wanted her to leave so he could stop feeling so tortured. She glanced at him and saw the expression on his face. Her brow furrowed. "I should be going," Lucy replied, standing from the piano bench.

"No, no, no," Emerson's dad said. "You must stay. It's the least I can do after your playing such a beautiful recital."

"Dad, I don't think—"

"Lucy, you don't need to be polite," he interrupted Emerson. "Please stay for dinner."

She shrugged. "Okay, thank you, Mr. Emerson."

"Call me George," he said. "Come with me to the kitchen."

Emerson trailed behind his dad and Lucy as they headed for the kitchen. Every molecule in his body felt out of whack. If he could go back in time fifteen minutes, he'd never tell Lucy how he felt. He shouldn't have thought for even a moment it was possible to be around the woman of his dreams without doing something stupid.

Emerson's dad pulled a bar stool out for Lucy and motioned for her to sit. She surveyed the spotless kitchen as she took her seat, her eyebrows up and her mouth hiding a tiny smile. Emerson settled onto the stool next to her. His arm brushed against hers for a brief moment, and the accidental touch sent his stomach into a spiral. He felt so uncomfortable in his own skin that he couldn't bring himself to return her polite smile and acknowledge that, yes, he'd touched her arm, but, hey, it was okay. It was an accident. Things like that happened. Instead, he focused on his father.

He moved around the kitchen like he wasn't used to being in one, opening and closing cabinets without retrieving anything until he finally found a large pot.

"Can I help with anything?" Lucy asked.

"No, you just enjoy yourself." Emerson's father filled the pot with water at the sink. "So, how do you know my son?"

Emerson gulped and moved to answer, but Lucy spoke before him.

"We met in London in March," she said, her eyes sliding in his direction. "He was the pilot on my flight over, and then I ran into him at my hotel."

"And now you are here together in Utah." His dad shook the box of macaroni and cheese in his hand. "That's fate if I've ever heard of it," he declared.

Heat crept up Emerson's neck. His father had pronounced aloud the thought Emerson had never allowed himself to fully think. And the statement sounded just as stupid and implausible as Emerson had imagined it would.

"Lucy has a fiancé," Emerson said, his jaw tight. "I don't think it's fate."

"Of course it's fate," his dad replied. He poured the macaroni into the pot of water before it reached a full boil. "If you hadn't met Lucy in London, you probably never would have thought to move to Utah." He waved a plastic slotted spoon around as he spoke. Emerson felt the heat deepening in his cheeks. "And if you hadn't moved to Utah, we'd still be on the out and out. It's fate, Emerson. The cosmic force doesn't always have to have romantic intentions."

"The circumstances were strange," Lucy said quietly, the phrase causing a chill to run down Emerson's back. He had said that in the letter to her. Did she think his moving to Salt Lake was fate? Did she think they belonged together too?

His dad went to the refrigerator and pulled out a package of hot dogs. "Emerson, will you slice these for us?"

Hot dogs. Nothing like toddler food to impress a girl. Emerson stood and retrieved a cutting board and knife from a drawer, feeling Lucy's eyes on him. Tension pinched the spot between his shoulder blades. Did his dad not feel the awkwardness, thick as fog, hanging in the air? Emerson could barely breathe. When he returned to his seat, he was careful not to bump into Lucy again. But still, he could sense the vibration between them.

Emerson carefully sliced the hot dogs.

"I haven't had mac and cheese from a box since grad school," Lucy said.

"Grad school?" his father asked as he searched through the cabinets again. "Who's your alma mater?"

"UW Madison," Lucy answered.

His head popped up. "UW Madison!" He disappeared below the counter. "Emerson, are you sure you don't think this is fate?"

Emerson kept his focus on the hot dogs and worked his jaw. Best to act like he hadn't heard. The fate conversation was unproductive. "The hot dogs are sliced," he said, pushing the cutting board across the countertop to his dad.

"I'm sure Emerson told you he grew up in Madison," his father said, taking the hot dogs and throwing them in with the macaroni. He continued his search through the cabinets.

"Check the dishwasher," Emerson said.

His dad opened the dishwasher. "Ah ha!" he exclaimed. "Great suggestion, my boy." He pulled out a metal colander, the edges of the holes rusty, and set it by the stove. "Just a few more minutes." He stirred the noodles and looked back at Lucy. "What did you study?"

She kept her eyes on his dad, so Emerson felt it was safe to look at her. She sat on the edge of the stool, her back staying straight as an arrow. "Food science."

"And do you have job in that field now?"

"I work for an ice-cream company."

"Very good," he replied. "And what did you think of your time in Madison?"

"I loved it," she said.

Emerson watched her talk, her face expressive as she told his father about her time in Madison. And when he served up the bowls of macaroni, Lucy ate with gusto, not at all put off by the choice of food. A feeling Emerson could describe only as cozy settled around him. His father, eyes alight, fumbling around the kitchen, a beautiful woman happily engaged in conversation with him, and Emerson sitting in the warm kitchen, a welcome observer. He could do this and be here with them every night for the rest of his life and simply be happy.

His gaze drifted to Lucy as she laughed, her eyes meeting his for a moment. The look crushed his heart like a tin can. None of this was an option for him. And to do himself a favor, he'd need to stay away from Lucy Kappal. It would be easier on everyone.

Chapter 30

As LUCY LEFT THE OLD house, she couldn't help but think the macaroni and cheese George Emerson had made was the best meal she'd ever eaten. Sure, the noodles had been on the crunchy side and the sauce had needed a lot more milk, but she loved that he was the type of person who would serve mac and cheese with hot dog pieces to a stranger for dinner and not once apologize for what it was or seem self-conscious about it. Charles would die if someone served him boxed macaroni. He'd flat-out refuse to eat it. He'd comment on the amount of preservatives and how the dye used to color the cheese powder was banned in Europe. He'd share all the gritty details involved in the production of hot dogs—things everyone sort of knows but never wants to think about. Lucy shivered at the thought of how this meal would have played out had Charles been there. But he hadn't been, and she'd eaten the mac and cheese and even put ketchup on her hot dog slices and felt perfectly at home in that kitchen, perched beside Emerson on a wobbly bar stool.

Behind her, Emerson exited the house and shouted a good night to his father, then followed her down the front path. The night was cool and smelled of jasmine. His steps behind her were slow, and she felt his presence like a warm energy. Her heart rattled as she thought of his words earlier tonight. *I wish I weren't too late.*

Without the buffer of his father, the delicious tension that seemed to brew between them grew with each step away from the house. She wanted to live in his energy, wrap herself up in it like a blanket until the heat reached her marrow, and maybe then she'd feel satisfied. Emerson began to hum Beethoven's "Moonlight Sonata," the vibrating notes reaching the deepest part of her. She wanted to stop walking and turn to face him to see what would happen, meet his eyes to see how long it would take before their breathing synchronized.

Then the guilt rushed in.

Charles.

Her fiancé.

She shook her head and walked on, feeling electric and heavy, the hair on her arms standing on end. Emerson stopped beside her when she reached her car. She turned to face him, his expression pensive and guarded. The ache that lived beneath the surface of her heart pushed through, and she almost gasped from the pain. She'd lost him again. The pressure in the air changed around her as Emerson took a small step closer. The pain in her chest cavity grew and expanded beyond her rib cage. She would be consumed, for sure.

Lucy thought of their moment at the piano. How dreamlike it had been. How perfectly scripted the words had been. How his posture had mirrored that of a marriage proposal. How elated she'd felt. And it hadn't been a dream. It had been her reality. Emerson had really said those words, and she felt the same way. She couldn't forget London, no matter how hard she tried. She stared down at her engagement ring. But it was too late.

"Lucy," he breathed out her name like a sigh, and it drew her closer. "I . . ." A breeze blew past, and the words died in the space between them. His eyes searched hers, and she felt something precious slipping away. Again. "I'll be gone for the next few days," he said. "And when I get back, I'll try to keep my distance."

Why? she wanted to ask, but her desperation must have shown.

"It's harder than I thought it would be to be around you," he said. "And I don't want to complicate things with you and Charles. You were right to move on, Lucy. And I need to figure out how to do that too."

She reached out and grabbed his hand, trying to grasp what was disappearing. Her hand felt like it belonged in his. He pulled her ever so slightly closer, her stomach dipping and flipping. Their gazes remained steady on each other, searching as if the answer lay somewhere in the other's eyes. His fingers slid across her palm, the touch causing goose bumps to break out on her arms. She held her breath and felt her eyes closing in a partial escape. This couldn't happen, but, oh, how she wanted it to. His exploration of her hand was slow and careful, ending at her engagement ring. He held it between his fingers, pressing the large gemstone into the pad of his thumb. Then he let go and stepped away. "Good night, Lucy."

* * *

When Lucy arrived back at her apartment, she found the lights in the front room dimmed and flute music playing. Charles sat on the couch, and Charlotte stood behind him, her hands on his shoulder and her face near his ear.

"What's going on?" Lucy's voice sounded rough, like she'd been crying.

"Oh, Lucy," Charles said, reaching for his glasses from off the coffee table and turning around to see her. "Charlotte was practicing some of the relaxation techniques she's learning in midwifery school."

Lucy found Charlotte looking rather flushed, her hands tucked behind her back, her eyes everywhere but on Lucy. Charles stood from the couch, placing his glasses on his face. "You know how stressed I've been lately with work and my manuscript," he said. "And add the poetry workshop I'm teaching in two weeks . . ." He shook his head. "I've taken on too much."

Lucy's throat hurt too much to speak.

"Do you feel better?" Charlotte asked quietly. "Was I a help to you, Charles?"

The corner of his mouth turned up, and his eyes softened with affection. He never looked at Lucy like that anymore. "Of course, Charlotte."

Charlotte's cheeks flamed, and Lucy tried hard to feel upset or jealous by what she was seeing, but she couldn't muster the energy. All her electricity existed with Emerson. What right did she have to call out her fiancé for accepting a shoulder rub from her cousin when she'd been aching to kiss someone else just moments ago?

Charles skirted around the couch and met Lucy by the door. Gripping both her arms, he kissed her on the cheek. His breath smelled of sweet cloves and cinnamon, and she fought the impulse to recoil.

"Have you eaten dinner yet?" he asked.

"Yes," Lucy replied. Her vision seemed to grow fuzzy, like she was in a dream or fun house. "Emerson's father had me stay for dinner."

"Ah," Charles replied, his thin, delicate fingers lacing into hers. "Do you mind if I eat?"

Lucy shook her head and moved with him into her kitchen. She felt so disconnected she didn't even bother asking why he didn't go home to eat his own food.

"How is George?" Charles asked.

"George?" Lucy said. "How do you know Emerson's dad?"

Charles clicked his tongue impatiently, and the censure stung. "He teaches a journalism class at BYU every once in a while. I've mentioned it to you before."

He hadn't, but Lucy was no match for Charles's infallible memory.

The soft sound of a throat clearing drew Lucy's attention to the living room. Charlotte was still there. "Do you mind if I join you for dinner?"

"Of course not," Charles said. He resumed his search through the refrigerator. His ability to craft a five-star meal out of the contents of her refrigerator was admirable.

She placed a hand on his shoulder, and he turned to face her. His eyes looked especially luminous in the bright light of the kitchen. "Charles, if you don't mind, I think I'll just head to bed."

"It's only seven thirty," he said, glancing at the clock on the wall behind her.

She gave him a half smile and shrugged. "It's been kind of a weird day," she said. "I think I need some quiet time to decompress."

He let the refrigerator door close. A gentle hand pushed hair from her face. "Of course, darling," he said. Lucy leaned into him, pressing her lips against his, willing the kiss to reach her toes and send her stomach into a free fall. Neither of those things happened. Instead, the kiss felt familiar and sweet. *There is nothing wrong with that*, she told herself.

"Good night," she said to Charles. "See you tomorrow?"

"Yes, love," he said.

As Lucy left, Charlotte stepped into the kitchen, taking her place.

* * *

The week moved forward, and as promised, Emerson was away on flights and she didn't see him. Instead of going straight home after work, Lucy stopped by George's house on three different nights. She sorted through stacks of newspapers, arranged for someone to come repair and tune the piano, and ate dinners of Hamburger Helper, ramen noodles, and SpaghettiOs. Lucy never ate food like that anymore. Compared to made-from-scratch dinners, she found the food oversalted and the flavors one dimensional. But she loved spending time with George and enjoyed the meals he so generously prepared. As they ate, he told her stories about Emerson growing up, and Lucy talked to him about work and her family. Charles didn't even seem to notice she'd been missing all week since he was too busy working on his manuscript.

On Friday night, Lucy and George sat on stools at the bar in the kitchen with bowls of homemade ice cream in front of them. The living room looked cleaner, with a little less than half of the stacks of newspaper sorted and filed way.

An easiness had developed between Lucy and George. The man was eccentric but extremely intelligent and kind. He thought carefully about everything, his words measured and meaningful.

"Tell me about your fiancé," George said. "He must be quite the fella to have caught you."

Lucy stared down into her bowl of strawberry ice cream. She had made it with a puree because chunks of fruit didn't belong in ice cream.

What could she say about Charles? Thinking back to the list she had made months ago on the flight to London, she found herself still wondering if she should marry Charles Buffington. Were these doubts because Emerson had shown up again? Or were she and Charles really a bad match? A coldness that she attributed to the ice cream snaked its way through her limbs.

"Well," she began. "He's very smart. And ambitious," she added after a moment. "He's president of the elders quorum." She shrugged. "What do you want to know?"

George studied her for a moment, his eyes moving over each feature of her face—her perpetually wrinkled forehead that she couldn't get to relax, her clenched jaw that seemed to be sewn tight by stress, her weary eyes from not sleeping.

"That's not the glowing appraisal I'd expect to hear from a bride-to-be," he said. "You smile when you talk about Emerson but not your fiancé?"

She felt effectively chastened, like a child sitting with a dunce cap on. How could she marry Charles if she couldn't list more than three nice things about him? Why did she keep thinking about Emerson and smiling when she talked about him? Was it really that obvious that she still had feelings for him? Did Charles notice?

Her ice cream had turned into a pink puddle, and she swirled it around a few times before answering. "It's complicated," Lucy muttered.

"It shouldn't be, my dear," George said. "It shouldn't be."

When she returned to her apartment, she found Charles and Charlotte sitting on the couch, Charles reading poetry from his manuscript. Lucy had come home to this all week, and his time with Charlotte was always under the guise that he was waiting for Lucy. And tonight, Lucy did what she had been doing all week: she made up an excuse to retire to her room early. Charles stayed anyway, as usual, treating Charlotte with the adoration he seemed to lack for Lucy.

Late into the night, Lucy lay in bed and wondered what was happening. She stared at her engagement ring in the dim light coming through her window. The stone was too large for her taste, the cut too clean and angular. She would have preferred something smaller and colored. Something that didn't draw attention but meant something precious to her.

Charlotte crept into Lucy's room after saying good night to Charles, and Lucy pretended to be asleep so she wouldn't have to talk to her.

And everything remained quietly tense and distant with Charlotte and Charles.

Chapter 31

FEW THINGS IN THE WORLD could be more difficult than nine o'clock church. But Emerson had made a commitment to attend every meeting possible since he often worked Sundays. So that meant even if he returned home at three o'clock Sunday morning from a five-day flight schedule, he'd be to sacrament meeting on time.

Most Sundays, his goal was to find one thing he could think about through the week. But this Sunday was different. This Sunday his goal was to avoid Lucy. He sat in the back of the chapel, took note of where Lucy was sitting, and made sure not to look in her direction again.

Usually, he went to Gospel Principles for Sunday School, but Freddy often taught that class and Lucy would be there. Instead, he went to temple prep. The bishop said he could go to the temple as soon as January if he wanted, so maybe he should start thinking about that more seriously. It was October.

Then came elders quorum.

Emerson took the empty seat beside Freddy. Charles led the group through the opening exercises, and everything about the guy made Emerson angry. His stick-straight posture, the way he sang the hymn in Spanish, the tightness of his pants. Could he get any more pretentious? What did Lucy see in him?

As Emerson quietly seethed, Charles began the lesson on true conversion. Emerson had thought about this topic a lot and had already read the general conference talks Charles kept referencing. The lesson progressed in the way elders quorum lessons usually did. Charles would read a quote, offer some thoughts, ask a question to the class, and then have a discussion, usually wrought with clichés or Sunday School answers, until it was time for another quote. It was all fine and dandy until Charles began to pontificate.

"On my mission," he said, crossing a leg over his knee. Emerson noticed the ugly pattern of his sock and how it matched his tie. "I taught a young woman, an American living in Spain. She had multiple colorful, muralistic tattoos. We worked with her for a few months. She had to give up drinking and smoking and move out of her boyfriend's place, and eventually she was ready to be baptized. I had the opportunity to baptize her." Charles held up his tablet to show a photo of himself standing beside the tattooed woman in their baptismal clothes. Emerson and Freddy shared a look. "We stayed in touch after I left that area, and I later learned that she was preparing to go through the temple. She wrote me a letter about her temple preparation and told me she was getting her tattoos removed. She wanted her outward appearance to match her inward appearance."

Emerson felt himself bristle.

Charles turned his eyes on him as he finished his story. "She said she felt unclean to enter the temple with her body marked in the way it was. I found this so inspiring and such evidence of true conversion to the gospel." Charles steepled his hands together in front of his lips. "What are some things we can do to show God we are truly converted?"

Emerson shifted in his seat. He felt Freddy's eyes on him now. Emerson had figured out his first Sunday in this ward that going against Charles was counterproductive. But someone had to say something. And the guy with the tattoos had to be the one.

He raised his hand, and Charles gave a long blink before indicating with the point of his finger that Emerson could speak. "I think acts that demonstrate true conversion depend on the person," Emerson started, hoping he sounded diplomatic. "Your friend felt removing her tattoos was an important step for *her* in preparing to attend the temple. But I don't think that same action applies across the board or that it should be suggested that tattoos make someone unclean."

Charles took a deep breath before speaking. "Years ago, the prophet announced that girls should not have more than one piercing per ear, and *every* girl I knew with multiple piercings removed her extra ones. When do we start following the prophet, Emerson? Just going forward? Or do we try to right our past wrongs?"

Emerson felt his blood pressure going up. He imagined his face turning beet red as he tried to contain himself. The eyes of every person in the room were on him, and the tension felt like a taut rubber band. "Tattoos are a little bit different than an extra ear piercing."

Charles held up a hand to stop him. "If you had a lip ring, would you remove it?"

"Probably. But like I was trying to explain—"

"I see no difference," Charles said.

"The difference is that for many people, tattoos have emotional or symbolic meaning." Emerson sounded remarkably calm, although he wanted to rage. If he weren't so determined to stay in the Church, conversations like this would send him running to the nearest bar. "I have a tattoo that represents my fallen brothers in war. And another to commemorate my dead mother. You look me straight in the eyes and tell me those tattoos are the same as a lip ring."

Charles met his eyes. The coolness Emerson found there was disturbing. "Just because something has emotional significance doesn't mean it needs to be kept. There are other ways to remember or commemorate the dead. We are talking about temples! Are our bodies not temples? They don't also need to be shrines to the deceased. To be truly converted, we must forsake everything from our past lives."

Emerson ground his jaw, and the desire to punch Charles in the face grew in his fists. He kept his voice as even as possible when he spoke next. "Even the Son of God chose to leave marks on His body from His past life."

Charles did another slow blink, his cheeks turning ruddy. Emerson did his best to keep any smugness off his face. "It appears we've gotten off topic," Charles said. "Let's continue reading from the conference talk, shall we?"

Emerson stole a glance at Freddy, who dropped an imaginary microphone, delight shining in his eyes. For the rest of the lesson, Emerson stayed quiet, avoided eye contact with Charles, and left as soon as "amen" was uttered. In his flight from the meetinghouse, he saw Lucy sitting on a sofa in the lobby, Charlotte next to her. A new anger flared inside him. A kind, reasonable, nonjudgmental person could not possibly be in a relationship with Charles. Either Lucy had been a complete phony with him in London or she was going to marry Charles and be absolutely miserable. Emerson disliked both of those conclusions and, by extension, wanted to dislike Lucy.

If only he could dislike her. That would make all of this so much easier.

Emerson got in his car and drove straight to his father's house.

When he walked in, he found his dad standing in the living room. "Lucy's moved everything around," he said to Emerson, scratching his head. "And I can't find my Oxford English Dictionaries."

"Lucy?" Emerson asked, wondering if he'd ever be able to truly escape her.

"Yes, she came by while you were gone and helped with the clean up." He gestured around the room. Emerson noticed that the room was less cluttered and the air didn't taste as dusty. He moved over to the piano and pressed one of the keys. The note had lost its tinny sound and now had a smooth reverberation. Lucy had done all this? Why?

"Interesting friend you have," his father said. "Really sharp. Kind. And a good conversationalist."

Emerson nodded, his stomach rolling.

His father shuffled off into the kitchen, and Emerson followed. He grabbed a pan from the cupboard, put it on the stove, and added butter. Most of his dad's meals began with butter and boiling water. Emerson took a seat on one of the stools. His father didn't have church until one and spent most of his Sunday loafing around the house, preparing his Sunday School lesson. If he wasn't working, Emerson joined him for lunch.

"Did Lucy say why she came by to help?" Emerson asked, staring at his hands resting on the countertop.

His dad tapped a spoon on the side of the pot. "She must like me."

Emerson laughed but quickly grew weary. The fact that Lucy liked his weird dad was a testament to her kindness.

Emerson's dad added a box of Rice-A-Roni to the melted butter in the pan. "Did something happen between you two in London?" he asked. The question felt like a static shock, and Emerson almost jumped in his seat. So much had happened in London.

He wasn't sure if he should answer honestly or tell his father to mind his own business, as the old Emerson would have done. His dad stirred the pan of rice, waiting for Emerson to speak. When he stayed silent, he added the water, covered the pan, and joined Emerson across the counter. Emerson's palms grew damp as his dad assessed him. His father never shied away from sharing his thoughts, even if he shouldn't. "Sometimes it takes courage to love the right person," his dad said. "Emerson, my boy, what are you going to do to show Lucy she can be brave?"

Emerson felt like he'd been kicked in the stomach, the air rushing out in a swift breath, leaving him aching and empty. He met his father's eyes, his gaze sharp. Was he suggesting Lucy loved Emerson and Emerson should break up her engagement? "It's not my business who Lucy marries," Emerson replied.

"Nonsense!" his dad exclaimed. "You love her, and you must try, even if you shouldn't."

Emerson shook his head and took a deep breath. His father was crazy. It wasn't his place to interfere, even though it was obvious Charles wasn't right for Lucy. *She* needed to realize that herself and call the wedding off because she didn't want to be with Charles, not because she wanted to be with Emerson more.

Besides, she hadn't made any indication that she wanted to be with Emerson. Since London, she'd been friendly and polite; it was Emerson who kept pushing the boundaries of what was appropriate. Hadn't he already tried last week when she'd come to look at the piano? And nothing had changed. She was still with Charles.

"Dad." Emerson said. He slumped on his stool. "Can we talk about something else?"

His dad clicked his tongue and, after a pause, said, "Tell me what happened at church today."

As Emerson told him about what had occurred in elders quorum, he couldn't help but think he needed to try again even though he shouldn't. Charles was awful for Lucy, and she could be brave. In fact, Emerson needed her to be, for her own sake.

Chapter 32

CHARLES REFUSED TO PLAY, LEAVING the sand volleyball teams uneven. Lucy glanced over at him sitting beneath a tree with a stack of papers before she served the ball. Freddy returned the serve, and Charlotte gave the ball a hearty whack, sending it over Freddy's head and landing just inside the out line.

Freddy narrowed his eyes at Charlotte and Lucy. "The game is still young," he said. "Maybe I'm letting you win."

Today was not the best day for his competitive streak to show since Lucy was on edge. She'd had Sunday lunch with Charles's siblings, and the Buffingtons had been in their usual form, giving unwarranted opinions and advice on the wedding plans. And now Charles was being... well, Charles. Lucy let out a frustrated sigh. Maybe they should let Freddy win since it seemed so important to him. "Where's Ammon?" Lucy asked. He had found his own place up by the U last week, so he lived close by. Freddy shook his head. "He's on rounds today."

"What about Ellie?" Charlotte asked, wiggling her eyebrows at Freddy.

"Ellie only comes around when she wants to," Freddy said, his voice too even and cool, giving him away.

Lucy didn't want to know what was going on there. She picked up the ball at Charlotte's feet and tucked it under her arm. She put the other hand on her hip. "Charles! We need you to play."

He looked up from his papers, adjusted his glasses, and shook his head. "You know how awful I am at sports."

"You don't need to be good," Freddy said. "I just need a warm body to occupy the back court."

"You can play on my team," Lucy offered. "And Charlotte will move to Freddy's."

"Sorry, love," he replied, his eyes returning to whatever he was reading. "I must get these poems read and responded to before my big poetry workshop."

Lucy held in a growl and tossed the ball to Charlotte. If she pointed out he was working on Sunday, he'd probably do something to guilt them into not playing volleyball on Sunday. Charlotte moved to serve when Freddy held his hand up for her to stop. "Hey, Emerson!" he yelled. A shiver moved through Lucy's body. "We need another guy."

She pivoted around to see Emerson in the courtyard on his way to his apartment. He twirled his car keys on his finger, his eyes trained on Lucy—the look causing her heart rate to accelerate—then shrugged his shoulders and moved toward them. "Sure, I can play for a while."

She knew logically that he wasn't trying to be especially attractive as he walked over to the volleyball court. He was walking like anyone else would walk, and he put his keys in his pocket like anyone else would, and the collar of his button-up shirt blew slightly open in the breeze like anyone else's would. But Lucy felt like her head had become a balloon floating above her body. When he began untying his shoes, Lucy had to look away.

Ah! What was her problem? So what if Emerson was ridiculously good-looking? That didn't mean she needed to forget she had a fiancé. She didn't need to do anything about her attraction to Emerson. He might as well be Brad Pitt because that was how off-limits he was.

He joined Freddy's side of the court, and Freddy said something to him in a low voice that Lucy couldn't make out. The two men shared a conspiratorial look, and Charlotte served the ball.

One minute into the game, it became clear this was more than a friendly Sunday afternoon sand volleyball game. Freddy and Emerson were out for blood, diving for the ball, sending powerful spikes down on Lucy and Charlotte, celebrating with obnoxious chest bumps and shouts with every point scored. And it was during this that Charles decided it was time to read them bad poetry, strolling around the court on his long, lanky legs.

"Listen to this, Lucy," he shouted out as he walked past her. Lucy served the ball and glanced in his direction. "'Your eyes are like buttons on an old rag doll/the only thing left solid and not ragged at all.'" Charles shook his head and chuckled to himself.

The teams volleyed back and forth, Lucy and Charlotte matching their opponents' intensity with each hit of the ball. "Oh, it gets worse!" Charles shouted. "'You are not the person I once knew/just like the wind that by my face blew.'"

As she tried her best to both listen to Charles and pay attention to the game, Charles won out and the ball landed by her feet.

"Lucy!" Charlotte shouted.

Freddy and Emerson exchanged a high five. What was with Emerson? He was supposed to be avoiding her, yet here he was, winning a game of sand volleyball and rubbing it in her face.

The game continued, Charles kept reading poetry, and Lucy's irritation grew. She did her best to block out his voice and concentrate on the game. After a long rally, Charlotte and Lucy finally scored a point. Lucy jumped in the air, squealing, and flung her arms around Charlotte in a tight hug. Caught up in the excitement of the moment, Lucy had forgotten that she and Charlotte weren't the type of friends who hugged.

"Fine, I'll stop," Charles pouted from the sideline. "Apparently, no one else finds this amusing."

Lucy let go of Charlotte and tried to catch her breath to reassure him, but Charlotte beat her to it.

"I'm listening," Charlotte said. "I think it's funny."

"Yes, Charles," Lucy said. "Keep reading aloud if it makes you happy."

Freddy came up to the net. "Let's take a break. I think you ladies need it."

Lucy swatted at him, but he dodged her. Charles approached and took her hand, pulling her to the tree he'd been sitting under. She sat next to him, trying to feel comfortable at his side. Charlotte sat on the other side, touching her knee to Charles's leg in a gesture that appeared both innocent and territorial. Freddy sat across from Lucy, leaving Emerson to sit on her other side. At his nearness, her heart contracted painfully, wanting to both race and stop in his presence. It had felt so easy to be with him in London, and she longed for that easiness to return. But anything she felt for Emerson was forbidden, so she scooted closer to Charles.

"There is one poem that is quite good," Charles said.

"Any crazy passenger stories?" Freddy asked Emerson, ignoring Charles.

"No," Emerson said, picking at the grass, the tattoo on his forearm rippling over the tendons. "It was a pretty boring flight plan, actually."

Lucy noticed the tightness in his shoulders and looked away when his eyes met hers.

"Oh, before I forget," Lucy said, trying to appear like she wasn't totally derailed by Emerson, "Freddy and Charlotte, my boss texted me this morning. I'm leaving Tuesday for Minneapolis, so I won't be around this week."

Freddy cocked an eyebrow and shared a look with Charlotte. He motioned for her to come closer, and they began whispering. Charles leaned in too. Lucy laughed, and for the smallest moment, she felt that this was right.

But then she felt an electrical tap on her knee, and her eyes darted to Emerson. "Hey, thanks for checking in on my dad while I was gone." His voice was low, and the conversation felt private. Freddy and Charlotte's voices disappeared, and Lucy slipped her hand from Charles's. She felt herself being pulled in like Emerson was an undertow.

"It was nothing," she replied, feeling her cheeks heating. "He's a wonderful person to spend time with."

He studied her for a moment, and if he stared much longer, she would become lost in his caramel eyes. "It took me thirty years to realize that, but it only took you one hour," he mused. "I'm glad you like him."

Lucy nodded, her balloon head floating higher and higher into the air. Emerson was such a kind person. In London, he had shown his kindness in a dozen small ways—offering to switch rooms and then paying the difference when he left, helping her the day she was mugged, giving her his mother's scarf. And it was clear he wasn't trying to be nice either; it was just the way he was. He was thoughtful, genuine, and didn't care if he impressed people. Pretty much, he was the exact opposite of—

Charles cleared his throat. "Like I was saying"—his voice was gritty—"I have a poem that is actually quite good. Mind if I favor you with a reading?"

Freddy sat up straighter and pretended to adjust a tie. "Yes, please, Charles. And, Charlotte, pass the Grey Poupon."

Lucy held in a laugh and nudged Charles in a way that she hoped he interpreted as encouraging. "Go on," she said. "Read the poem. We need something good after the word salad you read us earlier."

Charles beamed at Lucy and adjusted his glasses. "It's a prose poem," he explained and began to read.

"Two driftwood souls converged on a plane from New York to London. He believed in flight, and she was engaged to another man. Their polite conversation was almost poetic as elbows bumped on a shared armrest.

"Two azure souls found each other in the tea room of the same hotel. They sat on opposite sides of the table and looked away when the other smiled. Ice clicked in glasses between sips.

"Two threadbare souls shared a basket of chips at a pub across the street. Her ring sparkled in the dimming light, and his hand brushed her wrist. The imprint of his touch hummed through her as she promised it would never happen again.

"Two stained-glass souls walked along green paths of flowers and rock, weeds, and grass. The sun was out that day, and ash blew by in a slow-moving breeze. Blue cornflowers gripped them in a stolen kiss in Kensington."

Lucy sat unmoving, her heart galloping. The poem couldn't be about London—how could the author know?—but she had been transported back and she felt again like she did that day in Kensington. The sky had been infinite, and Emerson had been real and tender. He had cherished her in that tiny moment in a way that had not yet been replicated, even in her many kisses and soft moments with Charles. With Emerson, she had felt both loved and infinite.

Her gaze drifted to him, whose eyes had turned a burnt caramel. His pinky touched hers in a movement that she could not have invented; she checked, and their small fingers were joined. A horrible heat melted down her chest and legs, leaving her body numb. If only she were brave.

Charlotte laughed, and Lucy turned her attention to the noise. She slipped her hand away from Emerson's, touching her littlest finger, wanting it to not control how the rest of her body felt.

"That's Ellie's poem!" Charlotte said after a snort. "I can't believe she turned that in to your workshop!"

"Ellie writes poetry?" Freddy asked, shocked.

But Lucy didn't hear the rest. She turned again to Emerson, his mouth a grim line. His eyes didn't quite meet hers. The poem *had* been about them. He'd told Ellie all about London and how they'd fallen in love.

Lucy had to get away. She couldn't spend one more moment with him, the feelings too fresh and awful. Nudging Charles, she forced a smile. He wouldn't be able to deduce the poem was about Lucy and Emerson, right? And Charlotte wouldn't mention that, would she? "I need a drink of water," Lucy said through dry lips. "Would you like me to bring anything back?"

Charles shook his head and continued to say whatever he was saying about Ellie and her poetry.

Lucy stood, her legs wobbly, and she gripped the tree while she took a deep breath. *Just make it to the apartment*, she told herself. The instinct to run brewed strong in her limbs. *Tuesday. Minneapolis.* Maybe she would never come back.

She walked back to her building, and as she moved inside, she heard, "Lucy, wait!"

She stopped on the first step, and Emerson caught her by the elbow. In perfectly choreographed steps, he pulled her into his arms. She felt the air slip from her lungs as he caught her mouth with his.

He felt solid and tasted as she remembered. She touched his face, hoping when she opened her eyes, they'd be surrounded by blue cornflowers again and this wouldn't be wrong. The stone on her engagement ring scraped against his cheek, and she remembered her reality. She pulled away and slapped him, her hand stinging with the impact. That restless feeling in her legs released, and she ran up the stairs to the door of her apartment. She shook and couldn't fit the key in the door. He shouldn't be able to make her shake like this. She shouldn't still feel anything for him.

Stop shaking! The key finally fit, and the lock yielded. She went to hide, but Emerson followed her.

She raked her fingers through her hair, feeling like she was trapped on a runaway roller coaster. What was she going to do? What was Charles going to say when she told him Emerson had kissed her? Because she had to tell him. She couldn't marry him and keep a secret like this.

Would he still want to marry her?

Emerson stood pensively by the front door, an unwelcome audience to her breakdown.

She touched her hands to her lips and swallowed her rage. "What are you even doing here?" she choked out. She moved toward him, adrenaline coursing through her like fire. "Everything was perfect until you showed up. I was going to forget about London and marry Charles." She stopped right in front of Emerson. Oh, she wanted to slap him again. Her fingers tingled and needed another sting. "My wedding is supposed to be in three months."

"You're not seriously going to marry him, are you?" Emerson asked, his exasperation like hot air.

"That's none of your business," she replied, although she'd asked herself that exact question more times than she could count.

"Lucy, you can't marry that man," Emerson said. "Charles is awful. There's no way he will make you happy."

"And when did you become an expert on my happiness?" Lucy stepped away from him and willed herself not to turn her back.

"Have you ever talked to Charles and really said what you thought?"

She wanted to be indignant but opened and closed her mouth, feeling like a guppy, the words trapped.

"You haven't," Emerson continued. "It's impossible to really have a conversation with Charles, with all his throat clearing and sighs. He doesn't care what anyone really thinks, unless it confirms what he believes. And he doesn't want anyone to have their own thoughts. He wants to change you,

Lucy, and I can't stand here and let that happen." He pushed his fingers through his hair. Lucy noticed a flush on his cheeks. "It's bad enough to lose you, but to lose you to someone like Charles? If I saw you were happy with him, I wouldn't say anything. But I love you, and I want you to be happy, so I have to say something."

She felt woozy at his admission. He loved her. But Lucy and Charles had gone on for so long and she was in so deep, she couldn't get out now. She crossed her arms over her chest and clung to the last bits of fury flinging through her body. "Is that why you're here? To break up my engagement?"

Emerson opened his hands as if to reach for her, and Lucy stepped back. "I just want you to be happy," he whispered.

She ground her teeth together, so tired of people deciding for her what would make her happy and what wouldn't. "Did you think kissing me would make me happy?" she asked.

Emerson examined her like she was a stranger, like her face held a newness that puzzled him. She felt herself shrinking under his scrutiny. Shame swelled inside her like a looming wave. She would drown. *Please stop looking at me like that*, she wanted to say. "Why did you kiss me?" she asked, her voice revealing her desperation.

He took a small step forward, and her heart jumped to her throat. He touched a lock of her hair between his fingers and tipped her chin up so she was staring right into his eyes. The wave grew larger and larger behind her. "To make you brave," he said.

He stepped back, her hair slipping from his fingers. She blinked, long, and her exhale felt like the wave crashing over her. When she opened her eyes, he was gone.

* * *

On trembling legs, Lucy walked back to the tree beside the volleyball court. The air had turned apple crisp, and the leaves on the trees were yellowing. It wasn't summer anymore. Freddy and Charlotte stood in the sand, hitting the ball back and forth. Lucy sat beside Charles beneath the tree. He took her hand and offered a squeeze. How was she going to tell him?

"Where's Emerson?" Freddy asked.

Lucy cleared her throat. "He had to take care of something."

"But he left his shoes."

That their feet had been bare when they'd kissed and later when they'd argued seemed significant, but Lucy didn't understand why.

Chapter 33

MONDAY NIGHT, LUCY SAT IN Charles's living room, leafing through bridal magazines while he read more poetry manuscripts for his workshop. Her guilt had become a physical thing, a stone pressing on her torso so heavily that she couldn't take a full breath. She imagined her heart had turned purple from the constant racing.

Soon after returning to the volleyball court last night, she had excused herself and left Emerson's shoes on his doorstep. Sleep had eluded her as she'd replayed the kiss and then their argument. *To make you brave.* But as the night and the next day continued, she felt no braver than before. The courage she needed to make whatever decision she was going to make—how could she still not know what she was going to do?—was like a rainbow, big and bright but moving away with every step she took forward.

I have to tell Charles, she repeated to herself as she turned another page in her magazine. *I have to tell him about the kiss.* She wasn't really looking at the pictures, just going through the motions. Standing, she set her magazine down. She went to the kitchen, drank a glass of water, and returned to the living room, her stomach grumbling in protest. Charles looked up as she sat beside him. He removed his glasses and rubbed his eyes. "Something that happened in elders quorum yesterday has been bothering me," he said, replacing his glasses.

Lucy raised her eyebrows. "Hmm?" Freddy hadn't mentioned anything.

"What do you think of Emerson?" Charles asked.

Her heart jolted painfully in her chest. "I don't . . ."

Charles chuckled. "Well, you must have thought *something* about him if you kissed him."

The blood drained from her face. Charles knew. How did he know?

"But then again, people are different when they are on vacation," he said. "So I can forgive you for your poor judgment."

She exhaled and sank deeply into the couch. Maybe if she concentrated hard enough, she would dissolve.

"I don't like what he brings to our discussions," Charles said. "He's too open about his past."

Lucy lifted her head off the back of the couch. She couldn't for the life of her remember what she used to do or say when Charles got like this.

"It's not that he brags about what he's done," Charles said, "but he doesn't shy away from sharing that he's committed significant sins."

"What's wrong with him admitting he's needed to use the Atonement?"

"There's nothing wrong, per se, but you're not supposed to be specific in the ways he is."

Lucy found this discussion tiring. Would she always feel this tired when she talked to Charles?

"He comes across as really unrepentant is all."

Lucy sat up straight as she grew cold.

"I don't want the younger men in my quorum thinking you can ever really come back from such things, but that seems to be Emerson's message."

Oh, this was much more awful than Lucy could have ever imagined. Charles finally looked over at her. Lucy pictured her face white as ash.

Something heavy and fragile shattered inside her. How had she ever stood Charles, even for a minute? A hot flash of energy moved through her. She stood and took two steps away from him. "Charles, I can't marry you." Her voice did not shake, but her hands did.

He uncrossed his legs and put his papers down. "Lucy?"

She shook her head and said it again. "I can't marry you."

His eyes widened in panic.

"You won't make me happy," she continued.

He reached for her. "Is there something I've done?"

Lucy wasn't sure how to answer that. There were too many little things, and she had no interest in repairing this. "We're just too different," she replied. "I don't feel like I can be myself with you. And I don't think I will make you happy in the long run."

"You're just getting cold feet again," Charles answered, his mouth a grim line. "You do this all the time, and you always come back to me. So let's skip the part where you leave and just stay engaged."

"No, Charles." Her voice didn't sound forceful enough. She sat on the coffee table directly in front of him. "I know for a fact I don't want to marry you." She leveled her eyes with his and waited for the words to sink in.

His eyebrows dipped, and a crease appeared above his nose. "You're serious?"

Nodding her head, Lucy tried not to smile, but she felt giddy, a heavy weight lifting off her shoulders.

"This seems rather sudden," he said, adjusting his glasses. She noticed a slight tremble in his fingers, and his cheeks grew ruddy. "Just yesterday, you were talking about the wedding with my sister."

"I—" Lucy didn't want to have to explain herself, but she guessed she owed Charles that much. "I've felt unsure the last month. At first I thought I had cold feet, but the feeling never went away and has kept getting worse. I didn't want to break it off until I was sure, and now I'm sure." She didn't think the words were true enough, but she wanted to spare him. She was hurting Charles *again*, the thing she had been trying to avoid. The least she could do was keep her thoughts to herself about how horrible she found his character.

His blue eyes examined her, and she felt her skin prickle. He reached for her hand, and Lucy let him take it. "I want to make you happy, Lucy." He looked desperate, like a drowning child. "Tell me what I can do better."

Her eyes moved up to his. He couldn't save this. She didn't want him to. "Please, Charles." She pulled her hand away. "I don't want to fight. And I don't want to hurt you any further." She tugged the gaudy engagement ring off her finger and placed it in his palm. His long fingers curled around it. "One day you'll realize we were never a good match."

She fled from his house, afraid if she stopped moving, the reality of what she'd done would send her back inside. In the driveway, she saw Charlotte, who looked like she'd been caught stealing. Charlotte started to babble out an explanation for what she was doing at Charles's house. "Go to him," Lucy said. "Charles could use a friend."

When Lucy got back to her apartment, she finished packing for her business trip and took a sleeping pill. How lucky she was to be leaving town. She wasn't running away; it was simply a perfectly timed business trip. By the time she got back, the grape vine would have done its job, and the news of her breakup would have reached Emerson. Then she'd live happily ever after.

Chapter 34

EMERSON PLACED ANOTHER LOG ON the chopping block and swung his ax down. The thwack of the hit and the crack of the splitting wood broke through the stillness. He flexed his fingers, his hands and forearms vibrating from the force. He tossed the split wood into a pile by the cabin and steadied another log on its end. If he paused too long, he'd remember all the stupid things he'd done.

He swung the ax again.

He'd kissed Lucy and told her to leave Charles. And she'd given no indication that she would. Perhaps he was humiliated. Or maybe just angry. But he couldn't stay at Windy Corner. Monday morning, he moved a good portion of his clothes to his father's house and settled into his old bedroom. That afternoon, he signed over the lease for his apartment to Ellie and told her he would collect the rest of his things later. Tuesday morning, he caught the first flight to Milwaukee and shut off his phone with no intention of turning it back on until his return to Salt Lake. Mindy had joined him Wednesday, and they'd spent the last two days painting and winterizing their grandmother's cabin and *not* talking about what had happened. She was good that way. She knew when to push Emerson and when to leave him alone.

She came out of the cabin with two steaming mugs on a tray. "Let's take a break," she said from the porch.

Emerson split one final log before driving the ax into the chopping block. As he joined her on the porch, he rolled his shoulders and neck, the stiffness like concrete. He sat in a wicker chair beside her and took a mug from the tray. The smell of chocolate reminded him of Lucy. He might have to switch to herbal tea.

He stared out at the woods. They were surrounded by tall deciduous trees, their leaves beginning to turn bright orange and red in the October fall. Now that he'd stopped moving, the chilly air felt sharp against his skin and in his lungs. The scent of decaying leaves and a coming frost hung in the air.

He remembered playing in these woods as a child in the summer. His grandmother would take all ten of her grandchildren for a long weekend every year while the parents went down to Chicago. It wasn't until Emerson was a teenager that he realized his father had been raised by a single mother. She was eighty-four now and lived in a retirement community but held on to the cabin in case any of her children or grandchildren needed it.

"I'm heading home in the morning," Mindy said. Emerson nodded and took another sip of his hot chocolate. "I think you should too."

He didn't answer and chewed on the inside of his cheek.

"You can't hide forever."

His eyes slid in her direction. "I thought I had changed," he said and shook his head. "But I'm still the same selfish idiot I've always been."

Mindy set her mug on a side table. "Does this mean you're ready to talk about it?"

He kept his eyes on the trees. The heavy, oppressive guilt he'd hoped he'd put behind him when he'd returned to the Church hung like a mill-stone around his neck. He'd crossed an awful line when he'd kissed Lucy, letting his impulses get the best of him. It wasn't the right way to make her brave, but it was the perfect way to prove he was a caveman.

Mindy had blue eyes, like his father and their grandmother. Not just the coloring was the same, but they also had the same perceptiveness. Their grandmother was a master at reading people and knew better than the person what they were thinking. When Mindy's eyes narrowed, Emerson knew she'd figured something out, something he probably hadn't.

"Let's pretend for ten seconds that Lucy has broken off her engagement. What would you do?"

"I'd marry her," he replied too quickly.

Mindy frowned, which he hadn't expected. "I know we all want to believe in love at first sight," she said, "but how well do you actually know her?" She leveled her eyes with his.

In reality, he hardly knew Lucy at all. But he felt he knew the right things about her. The important things. Like the kind of person she was, her character. Their interactions in London had been so brief and intense, the emotional stakes high for each of them, that there hadn't been time to hide who they really were from each other. In the ways that mattered, he knew Lucy better than he'd ever known anyone.

"I just worry," Mindy continued. "That you love the idea of Lucy more than you actually love her."

No, Emerson was certain he actually loved Lucy, but it was best to let Mindy finish.

"You two met at a really vulnerable time in your life," she said. "And you knew her so briefly that I think it's really possible you've painted this picture of her in your mind that isn't accurate."

Emerson kept his gaze on the trees and took a sip of his drink.

"Look, there's a good chance you're going to get back to Salt Lake and she'll still be engaged. And if that's true, you need to stay away from her and her brother and maybe even Ellie until after she's married. And then you need get serious about moving on and start dating."

If Lucy actually married Charles, Emerson would get the message loud and clear. He'd have to move on. He wasn't going to pine for a married woman.

"But if she's single when you get back," Mindy said, "then I think you need to take it slow. There's no harm in getting to know her better. If you still feel the same way about her in a few months, marry her. Don't be impulsive about this."

Emerson shot Mindy a scathing look but only because he knew she was right. So he'd take it slow. And once he was temple worthy, he'd propose. This was the best-case scenario. What Emerson really needed to prepare for was the possibility that Lucy was still going to marry Charles.

He finished the last of his cocoa, which had cooled significantly, and set the mug on the side table. "Thanks, Mindy," he said. "You're always there when I need you, and I'm grateful for it."

She squeezed his forearm. "Everything will work out as it should."

Emerson stepped off the porch and returned to the chopping block, his feet crunching the fallen leaves.

Chapter 35

FRIDAY AFTERNOON, LUCY'S PLANE TOUCHED down in Salt Lake City. Her trip had been a success, and Lavender Love would be hitting the shelves in Target stores across the country in two months. It was her biggest distribution area yet, and it added to the happiness that kept swelling up inside her. In less than an hour, she'd be standing face-to-face with Emerson as a free single woman. She wasn't sure what she was going to say to him yet. Perhaps she'd kiss him and see what happened from there.

Freddy picked her up from the airport. "New rule," he said without offering a hello first. "The next time you break up with Charles, you can't leave town."

"Was he awful?" Lucy asked, scrunching up her nose. "Did you bill him for the therapy sessions?"

"Ha ha," Freddy said. "He spent Tuesday evening crying on our couch. Luckily, Charlotte was there."

"Charlotte," Lucy said without an ounce of bitterness.

"His family is going to eat her alive," Freddy said.

"I don't know," Lucy said. "Maybe she's exactly what he's looking for."

Charles would be okay. She shouldn't have strung him along like she had, and she didn't expect Charles to ever forgive her. Her fear of ending up alone and her desire to not hurt Charles again had caused her to hang on to something she didn't really want.

Once she arrived home, Lucy showered and spruced herself up like she was getting ready for a date—cute outfit, tousled hair, makeup, and perfume. But she didn't look like she was trying too hard. Nice but not too nice. She didn't want Emerson to think she was desperate or anything.

Freddy was kind enough not to comment as Lucy left the apartment. She stepped down the hall to Emerson's door, her heart thundering, and took a deep breath. Two knocks. Lucy clenched and unclenched her fists. Her chest started to hurt. Maybe this was a bad idea.

Noise on the other side of the door caused Lucy to tense. Yes, this was a terrible idea.

The door opened, and there stood Ellie.

Of course. Eleanor Lavish.

Lucy's stomach dipped. "Is Emerson home?"

Ellie smiled, but it wasn't her usual Cheshire cat smile; she almost looked friendly. "He moved," Ellie said. "Charlotte and I live here now."

"Moved?" Lucy felt like she was being swallowed up by quicksand. She looked behind Ellie and saw Emerson's bookcases and furniture still there. Why did he leave all his things? "Do you know where he went?"

"Wisconsin or his dad's. I can't remember which. He said he'd be back for his stuff later."

Wisconsin? Why hadn't she called him as soon as she'd broken off her engagement? She felt like she was stepping into an ice bath. "Did he say why he was leaving?"

Ellie frowned. "I don't want to get in the middle of this."

Lucy would have laughed if she hadn't felt so awful. *Now* Ellie didn't want to interfere? If only that had been her position in London.

"When I hear from him, I'll let him know you came looking for him."

Lucy stepped back from her. "Okay, thanks."

Moments later, Lucy was in her car, driving to the Avenues to see if Emerson had moved in with his father. And if he hadn't, she was sure George would be happy to get in the middle of this. As she pulled up outside his house, she didn't see Emerson's car. Her stomach sank. Maybe he really did move to Wisconsin. She parked and ran up the front walk. Even though she'd walked through the door without knocking before, she felt like she couldn't do it now.

She knocked, and as she waited for the door to open, she thought she was going to have a stroke. Her fantasy of falling into Emerson's arms and driving off into the sunset were quickly evaporating. George opened the door. He blinked in surprise but quickly smiled. "Lucy, come in, come in! What a pleasant surprise."

Lucy stepped into the house, the front room now void of newspaper stacks. He motioned for her to have a seat on the now-cleared-off sofa.

"Is Emerson here?" she asked, hoping she sounded nonchalant.

"No, he's taken a trip to Milwaukee to his grandmother's cabin. He should be back Saturday night."

"Oh." Lucy felt a wave of relief. He hadn't moved to another state. "So he lives here now?"

George nodded. "Yes, he's back in his old bedroom."

Okay, she could work with this. She'd be able to see Emerson on Saturday, and *then* they'd live happily ever after. Not the dramatic, spontaneous reunion she'd pictured, but they would still be together soon.

"I broke off my engagement," she said, staring down at her now ringless finger.

"Did you, now?" George asked, sounding surprised. "And how do you feel?"

"Relieved," Lucy admitted. "Charles wasn't right for me."

"And you're here because you suspect Emerson is?"

Warmth expanded through her chest, and tears pricked her eyes. She could hardly look at George as she nodded her head yes. Emerson was it for her. He was who God intended for her all along. It was ridiculously clear now, how their lives had paralleled each other for so long before finally meeting and how he'd found his way to Windy Corner when they were never supposed to see each other again.

"Might I offer you some advice?"

Lucy took a shaky breath.

"Take your time."

There was a jolt inside her.

"Give yourself some time to just be brave."

Lucy nodded, a lump growing in her throat. She had never been good at bravery. Running or avoiding had always seemed easier. But everything was catching up to her now, and it was clear she'd taken the more difficult path. If she hadn't been so afraid of never marrying, she never would have gotten engaged to Charles. She wouldn't have allowed fear to convince her she loved someone who was wrong for her.

"You've taken a big step in the direction of true self-discovery," George said. "What are you going to do with your new-found courage?"

She finally looked at him and swallowed, the lump growing smaller as her heart began to beat just a little faster. The warmth returned. "I'm going to just be me." It was an unremarkable sentiment, but she felt weightless at the idea. She could sing the alto part of hymns or make steamed asparagus or buy an old home in Sugar House. She could eat macaroni and cheese with hot dogs if she felt like it and talk about people instead of ideas. She could have a spring wedding with a knee-length gown. And more importantly, she wouldn't have to run anymore.

Chapter 36

Saturday night, Emerson's plane touched down in Salt Lake. He'd flown standby and sat in a middle seat at the back by the bathrooms. As the plane taxied to the gate, he switched his phone on. His pulse throbbed in his neck as the screen lit up. He couldn't decide which made him more anxious, finding out Lucy was still going to marry Charles or finding out she'd broken up with him.

The phone vibrated as it caught signal. A dozen missed calls, mostly from his father but two from Ellie and one from Freddy. He checked his text messages, opening the one from Ellie first.

His blood rushed loudly in his ears. He felt like he'd been sucked into a vacuum. The noise and commotion of people standing to gather luggage seemed far away from him.

I think you should know Lucy broke up with Charles.

He checked to see when Ellie had sent the message. Tuesday night.

Emerson exhaled, more regret edging in. Maybe he should have left his phone on while he was away. Knowing Lucy had left Charles would have cut down the self-loathing he'd been doing all week.

It was his row's turn to exit, so he gathered his belongings and got off the plane. His heart felt like it was lodged in his throat as he walked through the airport. He kept thinking about what Mindy had said, to take his time with Lucy. To get to know her better. He couldn't mess this up.

Emerson went to his car and started his drive to his father's house. If he gave the events of the last week too much mental energy, he'd realize how impulsive he'd been about moving out of his apartment and start to hate himself. But what was done was done, and he lived with his father again.

The freeway was mostly empty as it was nearing midnight, and the moon shone bright white in the sky. Emerson considered what he would do next. He needed to talk to Lucy. He needed to hear from her own lips that she had ended things with Charles. And then . . .

He gripped the steering wheel tighter. And then what? They fly off on a magic carpet, fireworks bursting in the sky? This was real life, and he needed to be realistic. He probably needed to take Mindy's advice and take it slow . . . if Lucy even wanted to be with him.

He parked his car outside his father's house. Most of the lights were still on inside. His father must be waiting up for him. He exited his car and carried his suitcase up the front walk. "Dad? I'm home," he called as he let himself in.

His father shuffled out of the kitchen. "Good to see you, Emerson." He patted him on the arm. "I'll be off to bed now that you're home."

Emerson tried to smile, but movement behind his father stopped him. A pensive Lucy appeared in the doorway of the kitchen.

Emerson felt like he was standing in the eye of a storm—calm while chaos blew around him. He wanted to go to her but was afraid that if he moved, he'd be swept up. He hadn't expected to see her until tomorrow, but she was here now. Did that mean she loved him?

His father touched Lucy's arm. "Be kind to yourself," he whispered to her, then disappeared up the stairs.

Emerson let go of the handle of his suitcase, the bag hitting the floor with a thump. His heart was back in his throat, and Lucy took a step closer. She had dark circles below her eyes.

"What are you doing here?" he asked, his voice rough.

"Trying to be brave." She wrung her hands. "I'm here to see you."

Emerson's stomach did a backflip. He took a deep breath and told himself to not read into this, to wait for her to explain. But he still hoped.

He cleared his throat. "I heard about you and Charles."

Lucy nodded, her eyes darting away. She shifted her weight from foot to foot. He didn't know what to say next, and the air grew pregnant with their silence.

Lucy broke the quiet, her voice choked. "I'm sorry, Emerson."

His heart clenched. "For what?" he asked. If anyone should apologize for something, it should be him.

She looked back at him, tears rimming her eyes. "I was so scared I was missing my chance at marriage." She shook her head. "I shouldn't have nearly settled. I should have been brave."

Emerson took a few steps closer, entering the storm surrounding them. "But you *are* brave."

"I'm not."

"You are." He came closer and took her hands. Her fingers felt light as feathers against his palms. "You went on a mission to Germany and went to grad school. Those two things take courage. In London, you switched rooms with me, even though you were afraid of me." She bit her lip but didn't look up at him. "You were kind and welcoming to me when I showed up in Salt Lake, and that couldn't have been easy for you." Slowly her eyes met his, and Emerson's pulse ratcheted up. He could hardly breathe. "You broke up with Charles, and now you're standing here. If you aren't brave, I don't know who is."

A tear slipped down her cheek, and Emerson pulled her into his arms. She pressed her face into his chest, and he felt her shoulders shake. She felt so right in his arms. He rubbed her back, touched her hair, and tried not to worry about why she was crying. She soon lifted her head and met his eyes. With the pad of his thumbs, he smoothed away her tears.

"I need time," she said.

Emerson exhaled. "I know."

She touched his face, her hands on his cheeks and her thumbs brushing his lips.

"I'll wait as long as you need," he said. "I'll wait until you realize how brave you are."

"What did your mother used to say are the only two things you need in life?"

Emerson swallowed. "Courage and love."

"Well, we have love," she whispered. "Emerson, I love you so much."

"I love you too," he said, his heart almost bursting from his chest.

Lucy wrapped her hand around the back of his head and pulled him in for a fierce kiss. It was the kind of kiss Emerson had hoped for, one that contained every ounce of Lucy's bravery. He held her close and kissed her until he could no longer taste her tears. Then Lucy settled back into his arms.

"I love you," he whispered into her hair. Saying the words felt as natural as breathing, so he said them again. "I love you."

About the Author

SARAH ALVA LIVES IN SALT Lake City but calls Arizona home. She graduated from the University of Arizona with degrees in creative writing and political science. In college, she once told a creative writing class she wanted to grow up and be a stay-in-bed mom. She is almost living that dream as a mom to two little boys who don't like naps or sleeping in as much as she does. When Sarah's not busy doing mom or wife things, she enjoys reading romance novels in excess, shopping online, and listening to National Public Radio. You can find her on social media at facebook.com/sarah.alva, @writerlysarah, or at sarahalva.com.

Epilogue

Mid-March
London

EXACTLY ONE YEAR AND ONE day after they first met, Lucy and Emerson entered the hotel's lobby, a warm sweep of nostalgia greeting them. A bell-boy took their luggage at the door, and a valet was parking their rental car. Hand in hand, Lucy and Emerson walked to the front desk.

"Reservation for Mr. and Mrs. James," Emerson said to the desk clerk.

Lucy squeezed his hand and grinned. "We were married yesterday," Lucy added.

"Congratulations!" the desk clerk said and then typed away on his computer. "It looks like you have a reservation for a king suite. We'd be happy to upgrade you to the honeymoon suite, our treat."

"Which room is actually better?" Emerson asked.

"The honeymoon suite has a whirlpool and a complimentary champagne gift basket." The desk clerk offered a knowing smile. "However, the king suite has a view of the city."

Emerson looked over at Lucy, their eyes meeting. At the same time, they said, "We'll take the room with a view."